This is for Eunice and Regina.
We see the end of pain & restoration of order. From
your children, their children and their children

"If no one will listen then someone must write it."

ANONYMOUS

PROLOGUE

Somewhere in England...2021

It was two days before Christmas and out of all the days that he could have chosen he chose this day to leave.

The future of two little girls was shattered as daddy would not be coming back home.

Four and three were their ages but their resilient little hearts allowed them to jump up and down on the old springy mattress which was on the floor of the mouldy bedroom.

A woman stood by the window and looked out. She watched as daddy was packing his belongings into the boot of a taxi and probably chanting profanities, in her honour, under his breath.

The belongings were not in suitcase's just black plastic bin bags hurled in a disorderly fashion. That is how he had travelled every time they moved from home to home. They were always in a rush, no time for suitcases because the Landlord wanted their house back *'pronto'*.

But this time he was leaving alone. His lease on their union had expired and it was up to her to raise them.

She could hear their chuckles and saw their little bodies darting up and down in the corner of her eye. She looked tired. Like someone who had lost the fight, because he had succeeded at wearing her out.

She turned and gazed at the Giltwood, over the mantel, mirror. She wanted to see if she really looked as disgraceful as he said she did. But she saw nothing. She saw no one.

She shifted again to look out the window and watched a couple as they strolled down the road. She watched their every move with interest. They were dressed well which was miles away in comparison to her 3 holed, bake bean sauce stained smelly t-shirt.

The man pushed the double buggy through the soft snow whilst the woman held onto him. She watched how he held her. She watched in pain. It was a reminder of what she had never experienced. It seemed to her that he cared for his woman. He took the weight of the buggy and he held her close. Their bond was a picture of what she had never had. She had carried herself and her children and he had never cared.

As the couple went out of view she shut the window to keep out the cold. She wiped the tears from her eyes then jumped on the mattress and joined in with their song, "If you're happy and you know it clap your hands..."

#

Chelsea, London...2016

Summer had come early with a heat wave that was delicious for the London holiday hopefuls. Everyone was out and ready to get their skin sun blushed. This was everyone including Dr. Michael Marshall. He had returned from his sabbatical and was steadily growing his clientele at his Therapy practice.

But on this day he had decided that he was going to relax and remember the good times when he was with her.

He waited outside Sloane Square station for the 137 bus. He looked at his watch. It was delayed. He preferred to wait instead of making the 20 minute walk.

"It shouldn't be too long," someone said.

Michael turned to find an elderly woman perched on the bus stop seat and leaning her weight on her trolley.

"Thanks," he said.

"It's late on occasion," The old lady patted her silver wool hair curls.

Michael was polite so he nodded but was really not in the mood to entertain a chat with a little old lady. He perched on the other end of the seat hoping that the old lady would get the hint that a conversation is neither what he wanted or needed. He fished out the pamphlet in his pocket. He tried to look busy whilst looking at it.

The old woman arched her neck so that she could get a peek at what he was looking at. He felt her stares and tried to turn slightly to block her vision but it didn't work.

"Off to the Flower Show are you?"

He gave in and faced her. "Yes. It's lovely weather for it."

"Lovely weather it is my dear. Is it your first time?"

"No I've been before but that was a few years ago."

"Umm... I used to love the gardens I did. But I haven't been for years either."

Against his original intent to be left in peace he dragged himself into the conversation. "Oh? Why's that?"

"Well you see I haven't been ever since my Arthur died. There's just no point."

He looked at her in painful thought. "I know what you mean. I'm sorry for your loss," he said.

"Just isn't the same." She looked down the road. "Bus still hasn't come."

"I'm thinking of walking down."

"With a little patience you'll see the bus zooming down soon."

"I suppose," he said.

"Is that a South African accent I hear on your tongue?" The old lady showed her shiny front tooth.

"You're close but no, I'm Zimbabwean."

"Oh you're from Mugabe's country."

Michael regretted having telling her as he was tired

of getting into the endless debates about his country and President Mugabe whenever he happened to mention that he was from Zimbabwe. He was tired of giving his opinion about whether Mugabe should or should not go and whether he agreed with the *Land reform* or not. He just wanted to go to the Chelsea Flower show because he had to keep his promise to her.

To his relief bus 137 zoomed down the hill. He stood up.

"Your bus is here," she said.

He pulled out his hand ready to usher her in as the bus pulled up.

"No I'm not going in love."

"You're not?" He was puzzled.

"No I only sit here so I can find someone to talk to. I've been so lonely since Arthur died."

His countenance fell as he felt so bad about not being in the mood to talk to strangers.

"You best get on then. You don't want to miss it after waiting all this time. Safe journeys love," she said.

As he got on the bus he looked back to see her cheerful face turn to sadness. Michael felt bad. He was the kindest, greatest listener there was but this time he had let someone down and he didn't like it.

The RHS Chelsea Flower show was abuzz with people. He walked slowly past the pair of elephants and took in the vibrant colours of their flowers. They helped him to remember why they loved coming to the show when they were together.

When he was beyond the elephants there was a sudden crash. He turned to find a woman on the floor and her leg mangled around his ankle. In alarm he bent down to help the lady who was repeating apologies in a frantic manner. He scooped her up.

"I am so sorry. Are you ok?" he asked.

Her hair bun had fallen out of place. She rushed to pick up her yellow stiletto that had gone flying across the concrete.

Her face looked flush as she noticed a mini audience had begun to gather. She came back and found Michael holding her yellow weave bag out to her. In embarrassment she grabbed it.

"Thank you. Are you hurt?" she asked. She gave him no eye contact.

"No, I'm ok thanks." He could not help but to notice her beauty. It was the soft kind. Her eyes tugged at his inner being. She was the kind of woman that you wanted to sit with at a park bench and talk for hours and hours. And she was the one that you could tell your deepest secrets to and they would be safe. He deciphered all that in just one look. It's either he deciphered it or he hoped that someone this beautiful outside would be just as beautiful inside.

She touched his arm then she lent her weight on him so that she could put her shoe on. He gladly held her.

"I'm glad you are ok Sir. Next time I will look where I'm going."

Before he could say please don't call me Sir, call me Michael and it's a pleasure to meet you', she had shot past the elephants and disappeared into the crowd. There was something about this woman that pulled on his insides and this is something that had not happened to him in a long time.

After he had walked a few miles taking photographs and enjoying the gardens he decided that it was time to call it a day. He saw a few benches and decided to walk towards there, sit down and rest his feet for a brief moment.

He saw her on the edge of the wooden bench under the olive tree. Her yellow bag was by her feet and her yellow stilettos were off and neatly placed next to her bag. He stopped and watched her. She would look down at her hands that were flat on her white tea dress and then straight into the distance. She looked sad and she looked lonely. He wanted to rescue her and tell her that everything would be alright but then everything within him changed gear and came to a screeching halt. Right there and then he decided that he was being foolish and impulsive. He couldn't possibly have fallen for her. She was just some random woman whom he had bumped into and more importantly it was too soon to feel anything for anyone else besides Clara. He doubled back and began to walk away in the other direction.

The faster he walked the more he saw her face, her eyes and her loneliness and wondered whether the tingling in his deepest heart space was love. He had fallen for Clara on the spot so why would it be any different for this woman. He was a love on the spot kind of guy.

A complete turn saw him walking back towards the benches and rehearsing a conversation in the fashion of 'Oh, it's you again', 'I hope I didn't break your leg', 'Please let me buy you a coffee to make up for it.' He rearranged several conversations in his head until he reached the olive tree. But she was gone. He looked around but she was completely gone.

#

Hertfordshire...2018

Michael was in his office waiting for his 11am client. This was a new client that had purchased a block of Psychotherapy sessions. The background story of this client was intriguing and he was eager to get started with an attempt to help.

He had not always been the handsome Psychotherapist. He had come from a modest background that was filled with its own troubles. His real name was Michael *Mandirova*. His surname meant *'you have beaten me'*. This was quite befitting since Tabitha his mother was beaten black and blue every night by her very light skinned husband Tapson. She was beaten into submission and he spared a few slaps and shoves here and there for three year old Michael. He was not Michael's father who had sadly died a year earlier. Instead he was Michael's Uncle who had looked at Tabitha at her husband's funeral and told the clansmen that out of the goodness of his heart he would take her as a wife as she was too young to be sent back home to her parents. But what came out of his heart was not good at all.

Tabitha with the help of a friend escaped with Michael to a woman's shelter after Tapson had almost beaten her to death. From there she found work in a nearby farm working for Mr and Mrs Marshall. But within a year she had died leaving Michael in the caring arms of Mr and Mrs Marshall who, after a terrible custody battle with the evil Tapson, made him their son.

Tapson had fought to keep the child. "He is my late brother's son," he pleaded to the court. The judge explained that they were concerned about the child's welfare, considering the history of domestic abuse. Then in a childish fit Tapson's cool exterior crumbled. "*Mutongi uyo asvikirwa nemuvengi.* (This judge is possessed by the devil)" His Lawyer tried to calm him down but Tapson was furious. "*Makambo zviona kupi kuti mwana wemunhu mutema ano chengetwa nemurungu?* (Where have you seen a black child being raised by a white person? *Saka achagona kutaura Shona sei?* (How will he learn his Shona language?)*Saka makuba mwana wedu nhai*? (So are you stealing our child?)," he said.

Unfortunately the judge had had enough of his rant. He ruled in favour of the Marshalls who had provided ample evidence that it was Tabitha's wish for her son to be taken care of by them.

He thus became Michael Marshall. The surname *Marshall* meant '*careful leader*' which became a befitting name for the very caring man that he had become.

The 11am appointment knocked on his door. "Please

come in. It is open," he said. He stood up and walked to the front of his desk ready to greet his new client. He prepared his award winning smile. He noticed her shoes. He recognised those feet. He travelled up and there was that face. He was dismantled. He froze.

"Are you Dr Marshall?" she asked.

His insides were undone. "Yes. You must be Sofia Blackwell."

"I am," she said. She looked at him for a moment. He knew that she didn't remember him. He took in her hand for a shake. Their eyes interlocked. He let go and ushered her to her seat.

CHAPTER 1

Hertfordshire...2018 continued.

Her eyes shifted from his as she turned her head to look out of the window. It had started to rain and large drops of water streamed down the glass until they landed on the window sill. The wind rushed into the room and swept some papers from his desk to the floor. He stood to pick them up whilst her gaze was still fixed on the window. He blocked her view and rolled the window down. He turned back to look at her. She looked away again then he noticed the tears rolling down her cheeks.

She was beautiful. Not tall, not short but somewhere in between. The delicate features of her face complimented her stunning, sculptured figure. She dressed well. Her hair was in place and her nails were attractive. She was a beauty to behold and he stole the moment to take it all in.

Breaking his gaze he sat down and placed the papers down in a disorganised fashion. He reached for his journal, flicked through to a page and jotted down a few lines in pencil. He breathed in.

She came out of her thoughts and smiled at him.

"Are you ready?" he asked.

She nodded.

He pushed the button on the Dictaphone and it began to

roll. It was an old fashioned type that he had won at the local auction house. He sunk a little further in the armchair and clasped his hands together.

"So why now?"

She frowned.

He noticed that she had not understood. "I mean what made you book a therapy session. Just to be clear, you have already given me part of your background story but why did you feel you needed a therapist?"

She took in a deep breath. "My friend and colleague took me to a Motivational evening with Zane West. I don't know if you've heard of him?"

"Yes I have. He's an incredible speaker."

"That he is and he said things I'd never heard of. Prior to me hearing him I had read tonnes of self-help books but he opened my eyes to an aspect of my life that I had never considered before. He said something that made me cry. He said *'when God made me he didn't make a mistake'*. I hadn't been much of a God-person in my life but the prospect of having someone who cared about me was an attractive thought. Anyway that line alone was a game changer for me because the running commentary in my head up until that point was that I was my parent's mistake." She hesitated. She looked at him and observed the look of care in his eyes and was encouraged to carry on. "Anyway, after a few conferences I signed up to a one on one session with a member of his team. I told her my story and she suggested that therapy might help me to get the intensive input that she felt may be helpful. I agreed because I really wanted someone to talk to. I went for a few counselling sessions that didn't go so well. Then Jacob, my colleague at work, said a friend of his highly recommended you and that's how I got your card."

He nodded. "So you have already started your journey which is a great thing. And I would like to walk alongside you on this journey taking one step at a time." He smiled.

She looked tired. She looked out the window again as if in deep thought.

"We can take a break if you like," he said as he organised the pile of papers next to him.

"No. I have to do this."

"You don't have to do anything."

"But I need to."

"Ok Sofia." He cleared his throat. "Let's talk about how you met and how you felt the first time you realised you had fallen in love with him." He waited for her reaction.

"Do you mean Uche?"

"Yes, your ex-husband."

She wiped the tears that had settled at the bottom of her cheeks and began to talk.

He had listened to many clients and heard many stories but Sofia was different. Somehow she had caused him to let his guard down because to others he was known as Dr Marshall but to her he was Michael.

CHAPTER 2

Ojuelegba Lagos, Nigeria... 2009

"Ewa ra buredi Agege O (come and buy Agege bread)" shouted the stout Agege bread hawker all the way down Ayilara Street.

Her neck ached from the weight of the 50 loaves of bread that were neatly arranged in a circular platform that was balanced upon her head. Again she called out "Ewa ra buredi Agege O."

From behind her she heard the distinct voice of a man "Sister a fe ra buredi (sister I want to buy bread)." She stopped to look at who had called her. The man stood in front of her holding some Naira (Nigerian currency) in his hand. She became nervous. "Good morning Oga." She curtsied, which is what the regal figure commanded.

"Good morning. Is it fresh?" he asked with his eyes piercing hers and establishing a level of intimidation.

"Yes Oga. Fresh buredi Oga. Four corner."

The woman offloaded her heavily laden Agege bread platter from her neck and began to unwind the giant polythene bag that protected the bread from the Ojuelegba dust. As the polythene was unravelled the smell of the sweet fresh bread wafted in the air.

"I hope there is no Potassium Bromate in this bread," said the man.

"I no get Bromate Oga (there is no Bromate Sir)"

"Give me one loaf," he said.

With business haste she wrapped the bread with one rectangular shaped piece of newspaper. The man took the bread and tore it in half.

"Abeg my money Oga (Please my money Sir)."

"But this bread is not fluffy enough," said the man.

"It is sweet. Abeg Oga. My money," the woman pleaded.

A small queue of people had begun to grow as people waited to buy the sweet Agege bread. The woman began to serve them one by one with a growing concern about the man who was eating her bread but had not paid for it. The man took one big bite and began to chew with vigour.

Another man who was in the queue waiting to buy his own loaf called out to the lady. "Madam. Open eye. Lest you lose your money."

He spat like a viper and a mound of bread flew from the corner of his mouth. "Wetin concern you? (Of what concern of yours is it)"

The man in the queue held up his hands. "Abeg no vex. No wahala bros. (Please don't get angry. No problem brother) I'm just concerned about justice."

"Rubbish. Do I look like a common criminal to you? Do you see the way I am dressed? I am a University graduate. Do you know I am going overseas? And you think that a University graduate that is going overseas should pay for substandard food? God forbid."

"Justice Oga," said the man. The other people in the queue began to murmur in approval of the woman being given her money.

The man with the half eaten loaf of bread in his hand exploded and grabbed the shirt of the man in the queue. The people deciphered exactly what was about to happen and moved out of the way. The man in the queue wriggled out of his grasp and shot down Ayilara Street followed by the man with the loaf in his hand. The two men disappeared out of sight.

The woman held up her hands then touched her head. "Chineke(My God). Oga did not pay me. Biko Oga, dem send you? (Sir have you been sent to torture me?)" The woman's cries were useless as the man had disappeared with her bread, half eaten.

Those still paying for their bread engaged in small talk and tried to comfort the woman.

A short boy holding a tyre said, "Mama the water wey dem use take eba can never be recovered back (Mama don't cry over spilt milk)."

Then a girl who had seen everything from across the street walked over and added her words, "Mama no matter how hot your tempa be e no fit boil beans (calm down your temper won't solve the problem)"

Then another "Mama cool down. Just be wise next time. We know this guy from our side. Uche Onyeme is a man of serious hustle. Mama custard na just pap wey hand (looks are deceiving). I went to school with this guy. I know him well well. Leave it lest this guy take revenge and scatter your business. Cool down Mama please."

He took the bread that the woman handed to him. She put her hands on her hips in amazement as she was offered the revelation. "That man be area boy abi? Wayo (That man is a street smart fraud isn't it.)" She looked up and raised her hands towards the sky. "My God, I don do wetin you say make I do (My God I have done what you said I should do). Anyway I learn every day." She bent down and began to dish out the loaves she was selling whilst trying to bite the tears that wanted to flow because of the cruel injustice that had taken place. Uche Onyeme never returned to pay her and the paths of their lives never crossed again.

#

He went by the name of Uche Chidinma Onyeme. Only he knew

if that was his real name or not. He was highly confident and yet insecure.

It was hard to tell how old he was. He fought hard to present himself with the youthful vigour that was carried without effort by the college students he hung around and yet there was this underlying sense that he had aged in a very painful way. At first glance he was handsome; with striking eyes that were alluring and yet intimidating.

He dressed sharp. He detested shabbiness. Every line and silhouette was presented with express precision. Everything was pressed, everything was tucked in and everything was the picture of perfection.

It was hard to tell if he was cruel or whether he was kind. The mystery was whether he was dependable or unreliable. However, what was certain was that Uche was confusing to the point where you wanted to hate and love him all at the same time.

He considered himself as streetwise, having grown up on the streets of Lagos Nigeria. He was the modern man who vowed to never again live like a pig whilst watching the muscular men from the industrial sites come to buy the sour ebba and eghusi soup from his sisters' make shift restaurant on the busiest section of Ojuelegba.

His sister had raised him and sent him to school. Their parents had died and so they only had each other. Their extended family had washed their hands of them because their father had been a hard man who found it easy to make enemies. His excuse was that he was forced to marry the wrong woman; their mother. He became the angry man that gave birth to angry children that were forced to witness the insults and infidelity that eventually drove their mother to the grave and him to the bottle. He was soon found dead in a ditch covered in alcohol and excrement.

They buried him in an unmarked grave because they had lost the will to care. This was Uche's cue to leave Nigeria and get everything that his parents never gave him. His education bought him the lifting power he needed to take him out of the pig pen. Then some hard work coupled with a few streetwise tricks of the trade allowed him to *'top up'* and afford an airplane ticket with a year's tuition at a college overseas. He felt that he had made it. There was no going back. He was going to England.

CHAPTER 3

Somewhere in London 2009...

Sofia and Hortense took the number 8 bus on their way to college. They laughed hard and chatted loud much to the annoyance of the other passengers.

"Have you seen your nails?" asked Hortense.

"What's wrong with them?" asked Sofia as she bent her nails over so that Hortense could not over inspect them.

"Girl a little colour will not kill you. They say any old room can be jazzed up with just a lick o' paint."

"I like nail varnish. I just never seem to think about it. I've got a lot on my mind."

"You stressed Sofia."

"No I am not."

"Any woman that hasn't got time to do their hair and nails is stressed. You need to unlock that chastity belt of yours and live a little. Drink a bit o' rum." Hortense grinned.

"Hortense," said Sofia with a crimson cheek of embarrassment beginning to surface.

"What? If you just let me fix you up with Walter. He will do you up good." Hortense laughed loud.

"No thank you Hortense."

"That church of yours is robbing you."

Sofia shook her head. "I'm not being robbed Hortense. Celibacy is a personal choice."

"What do you mean by celibacy? So, you are the angel and the rest of us are the black sheep? Is it a crime to enjoy a little here and there? You're not normal if you're not doing it."

For a moment Hortense sounded angry but Sofia brushed it off convincing herself that her friend could not have been offended. Sofia laughed. "No Hortense. I'm not an angel. Is it wrong to keep myself for my husband?"

"At your age, which husband? And besides, you don't even date. You look a mess and..."

Sofia didn't hear the last part of what Hortense was saying because she was stuck in the *'you look a mess'* comment. A comment that was very hurtful to her. She brushed it off in spite of her wounds. "God will provide, Hortense. God will provide."

"Well for all our sakes, I hope you are right. Single women of our age should go out and get some. It keeps you young. It's a health risk if you don't." Hortense turned and looked out the window. Sofia chuckled but had the unsettling feeling that she had offended her friend once again.

Hortense was Sofia's vivacious friend whom she had shared a flat with when she first came to London. Hortense had held Sofia's hand and helped to mould her into a bonafide Londoner. Sofia having never gone further than the borders of Dorset was all too grateful to have found a friend in Hortense.

They were both studying for a diploma in business administration. Armed with a Horticultural degree from Bournemouth University, Sofia hoped to start her own business. Hortense was still unsure as to what she wanted to do. However, her concrete plan B was to meet a rich man, marry him and shop for the rest of her life.

Hortense was a Jamaican and had moved to England to live with her Uncle. Her parents had lived in England several years before. They gave birth to Hortense but sadly her father died when she was two years old. Unable to cope with looking after a two year old her mother sent her to live with her grandmother in Jamaica. This was a grandmother who was a strict

Catholic Nun who could not fairly identify the difference between mischief and simple childish fun. So Hortense lived an eternal life of being punished and grinding corn for her porridge in the barn.

Her mother would continuously promise to send for her to come and live in England but each year this never materialised. Her hopes were completely dashed when her mother had returned to live in Jamaica for good.

But several years of punishing her mother with guilt eventually yielded a plane ticket and a promise of accommodation with her mother's old friend in Dorset. That is how Hortense ended up with an Uncle in England.

She furnished Sofia with an elaborate story of how her stay with her Uncle was cut short due to his pervert tendencies that she was no longer willing to entertain. In desperation she moved out to London and landed a flat that she could not afford. Sofia became her Godsend when she had responded to an advert that she had placed for a roommate and the rest was history.

They enjoyed each other's company and their relationship fared well with Hortense's outgoing, bubbly exterior and Sofia's closed, shy persona. They were different. Hortense often taking on the role of chalk and Sofia easily squished into the role of cheese.

Sofia was insecure. She would go as far as to take a shower, brush her teeth and comb her hair but nothing more. In the words of Hortense she was the attractive end of shabby. It was a generous way of acknowledging the pretty face of a very poor dresser.

Getting off the bus they walked through the turnstile at the college entrance. Sofia rushed through causing the handle of her bag to get caught. She tried to walk backwards to loosen it but she couldn't because someone came through just behind her. She turned around to get her bag but standing in front of her was a man holding it.

He stood almost tall with a physique that expertly lined the crisply ironed shirt and trousers. He spoke softly, barely looking at her. "Is this your bag?" he said.

"Yes. Thank you." She grabbed hold of it.

He spoke with an accent that she could not place. "You are welcome," he said. Just then he stared into her eyes. The hazelnut centres piercing hers. She felt uneasy in a position she did not want to be in. His eyes were striking. His scent was addictive. He was beautiful and she was transfixed. But almost as soon as he had captured her attention, he walked off leaving Sofia confused as to what had just happened.

Hortense walked back towards Sofia. "Very nice. Very nice indeed," she said as her gaze followed the man down the hall.

"Really? I didn't notice," said Sofia as she began to walk away.

Hortense shook her head and followed.

CHAPTER 4

"I look too fat in this" she thought.

Sofia stood back from the mirror and adjusted her dress. She should have tried it on the week before as at least she would have realised that the dress was a disaster and would have had time to get a better one.

A quick rummage through her wardrobe revealed the black sequin jacket that she had worn on their first date. "Perfect" she thought. She put it on to tame her fast growing love handles that were bulging out of her sides. It was the camouflage that she needed to help her feel streamlined and beautiful.

From the first time they met at the turnstile they kept bumping into each other mainly in the cafeteria. He would say "excuse me" and brush past her. She wasn't sure whether she should say hello to him or not.

From that first stare she had felt that she knew him but he made her unsure. He would sit at a table where he knew she could see him. He would never look at her. He focused on his lunch and then out the window. This drove her insane.

He seemed so alone. He seemed sad. And this was attractive to her.

Then came the day which was three weeks after the meeting at the turnstile and three weeks after days of "excuse me", brushing past her and allowing Sofia to secretly watch him from a distance. On this day he sat next to her, looking at Hortense. Her heart had skipped a beat and felt uncomfortable. He looked at her. "Hi," he said and then asked if it was ok to join them for lunch. Sofia was speechless.

Hortense was a flirt and was not afraid to play with him. "As long as you are handsome there is space for you."

He too had a flirtatious way about him which Hortense lapped up, making Sofia very jealous. Aside from this slight confusion about the object of his interests it was clear that his target was Sofia.

From this day they spent every lunch together. He would flirt with Hortense and Sofia would feel sick to her stomach. Then he would focus on Sofia and talk about world events that made Hortense extremely bored and Sofia on red alert with affection. It was unsettling but she found herself sinking further and further into an attraction for him.

Then came the day when he took her out of the cafeteria insisting that they should leave Hortense behind. He led her off the campus and proceeded towards the High street Burger King.

Over a Burger King Whopper he opened his heart to her. His name was Uche Chidinma Onyeme from Lagos Nigeria. It seemed that he was comfortable in her presence. He was a Christian and so was she. His parents had passed away and so had hers. He wanted all the good that life had to offer and so did she. He shared with her the horrors of his childhood and the heartache of his last relationship with a woman that didn't appreciate him for who he was. She shared her insecurities and how she had been abused by life. "I felt so alone even though I was with my family," she told him.

"That is exactly how I felt," he told her. "It's worse when your parents are Nigerian. They can be really cold," he said.

Sofia's heart bled for him and was so grateful for how he had chosen to trust her with the most vulnerable part of his life. He wasted no time to tell her that he liked her and that he was comfortable around her. He wanted to see her again. She wanted to see him again. That was officially their first date and many dates followed after that.

CHAPTER 5

Uche and Peter squeezed up behind the crowd of people queued up for the 'Street goes Gospel' concert. They bounced small talk off each other whilst expressing a healthy appreciation for the gorgeous women that were gracing the event.

"I hope you have the tickets," said Peter.

"As if I would forget" said Uche as he adjusted his Rolex watch.

"Chai you get Rolex (wow you have a Rolex watch)? Dat ting de shine o (That thing is shining)" said Peter caressing his goatee that he had paid top dollar to sculpt.

"Yes now Fine quality." Uche grinned as he did a mini bow.

"Is that why Sofia follow you everywhere?" asked Peter.

"What do you think? Of course. She is the envy of every woman. You think this is cheap? I make her look good." He waved his watch.

"Uche be careful. This woman is big o."

"Big in more ways than one." They both laughed.

"Uche I'm serious o. You don't want to put yourself into something you can't get out of." Peter adjusted his crisply ironed cravat.

"Relax I'm the best thing that ever happened to her. Fine boy like this. I'm gold."

Peter shook his head. "My guy dis no be small ting o (My friend this is not a small thing). The girl is marriage material. Too much wahala (problems) and I know you can't handle marriage wahala."

Uche did not respond. Peter punched him on the shoulder to get his attention. Uche was transfixed.

Peter looked towards the entrance and there she was ready to present her ticket. Immediately his eyes travelled from head to toe following every angle of the hour glass figure which was sculptured to perfection as it clung to the red gown, draped in black. She turned and looked in their direction. Uche caught her eye. She looked away disinterested.

"Chai who be red dress? (Wow who is in the red dress?)" She fine o (She is good looking)" Peter asked.

"I don't know but I go conquer tonight. God don butta my bread (God has answered my prayers)," said Uche.

"Abeg (please) bring out ticket. Fine girl like that have man already. You get me?" Peter pushed Uche to present their concert tickets. Red dress disappeared as she passed through the door.

"Peter listen 'well well' (pay attention). Has another guy ever stopped me from getting what I want?"

Abeg this is London and not Lagos. She is not village o," Peter said trying to reason with Uche.

"Neither am I village. Just watch me in action. She is calling me to come chop (come and eat)."

"Comot (get out of here)," said Peter as he pushed Uche along. "So you have now forgotten Sofia the marriage material?" Uche presented their tickets. "Shut up,".
Peter laughed as they disappeared through the door.

#

Uche's number kept going to voicemail. Sofia had left him several messages but no response. She was getting cold. She tugged on her black sequin jacket to try and keep out the cold but the stress had bloated her belly out and the seams of her dress were screaming for freedom. The sequin jacket could not cope.

The concert was over and everyone was in a rush to get home. She had missed half of the concert waiting outside for Uche and when she finally decided to go in she didn't enjoy it because she was worried that something might have happened to him.

She spotted Peter at the bottom of the street. "Peter" She started running towards him. He stopped walking. He looked nervous which Sofia noticed. "Hi Peter."

"How far Sofia (Hi Sofia). How you dey? (How are you doing?)"

"I'm ok. Just looking for Uche. Did he come? I've been calling him for ages and no response."

"Huh he didn't call you?"

"No. Is everything ok?"

"Well maybe he didn't receive your calls."

"Is he here Peter?" Sofia's patience was running thin.

"Ok let me ring him." Peter gave his back to her.
She wanted to cry but the tears refused to surface.
He began to talk. "Abeg. Sofia is here. She vex (she is upset)" He turned to face her. "He's coming. I'm really surprised he didn't call you."

"So he's here." Her heart bled.

"He'll be here soon Sofia." He looked embarrassed; making it easy for her to clock that something was amiss.

She had an urge to leave. He had humiliated her beyond measure but she could not bring herself to walk away. She felt anger well up. An anger in parallel to the one she had felt when she was 5 years old, standing in the middle of the school playground and watching Harry pick someone else to be his play partner. He had called her fatty and she had wanted to thump him with a rock until it hurt but Miss Crystal her favourite teacher was watching. She didn't want to risk being branded a murderer in front of the best person that loved her in her first year of school.

"Sofia I've been calling you."

She turned to see Uche behind her with one hand on his hip, looking surprised.

"Where have you been?" he asked with a nonchalance that annoyed her.

"What do you mean where have I been? I have been calling you all night." Sofia was trying hard not to sound annoyed and trying hard not to look like a five year old with a rock in her hand.

"I called you and your phone was switched off," said Uche.

"Switched off? I've been calling and texting you. My phone was not switched off."

"Maybe it was the reception," said Peter.

Uche looked at Peter, "Yes the reception could be bad."

"Maybe," said Sofia quietly.

"Well since you stood her up you can at least take her home," said Peter.

"I didn't stand her up. I was here man."

"But we were going to sit together," she said.

"I know. I'm sorry. But these things happen. Who would have known that we would find it hard to locate each other? Next time we will arrange a better plan."

"Uche take the lady home," said Peter.

"Hey she is a big girl. I will call her a cab. You will be ok right?"

Sofia's heart sank even further. She could not bring herself to respond.

Uche closed the door to the black cab. "Call me when you get home. Sorry about today," he said. He seemed genuinely sorry. There was a subtle softness in his eyes that she appreciated. 'Maybe he did care after all' she thought. This seemed to appease her and get her to put her rocks down.

Uche knew he had pacified her. "Let's go," he said to Peter.

Peter had a big apology sign plastered on his forehead. "Safe journey Sofia," he said walking off behind Uche.

The taxi driver drove off and took a left to circle around the building to get to the high street. He stopped briefly at the traffic lights. Just as the lights turned green and the driver was pulling away she spotted them. Uche was hand in hand with a woman. He led her into a taxi cab, he got in behind her and the taxi sped away. A wave of rejection overwhelmed her as her mind was flooded with the image of the woman's very attractive red dress.

CHAPTER 6

Sofia had turned to look out the window again. She seemed lost in her thoughts.

Michael put his pen down. "Maybe we should stop here," he said.

She looked at him. "I didn't realise how strong I have become."

"You've come a long way."

She nodded. "Being treated badly used to feel normal. It's almost like I was being conditioned to accept that I was nothing and would one day cease to exist."

"Do you think you were being controlled?"

"Yes I was. I was addicted to everything about him and I couldn't see how life could exist without him there in it. That's why I made myself immune to his insults and disrespect. The more I became immune the worse it got."

"How did that make you feel?"

"It was weird because I felt caged. I knew he was not right for me but I was terrified of leaving. Somehow I got hold of the notion that if I couldn't make it with him then there would be no one else and I would be alone. That scared me. Does that make sense?"

He nodded. "It makes perfect sense."

"You're so easy to talk to," said Sofia.

"Well I am a Therapist. I guess it goes with the territory."

"You're not the first Therapist I've had but you're top of the list of those I want to talk to." She smiled.

He desperately hoped that he was not blushing. "Thank you I appreciate it."

"It's just refreshing to talk to someone who is not giving you sceptical eyes."

"Well my aim is to provide you with a safe environment where you are sure you are being heard without judgement."

"I'm glad someone is hearing my story."

"Well, I'm glad that you have trusted me with it." He looked at the clock on the wall. "Now, I'm aware of the time and I think we should stop here."

"Oh I'm so sorry. I get lost when talking about this past of mine." She grabbed her bag from the floor.

"No don't be sorry. I'm just interested in making sure that you don't overstress yourself. Bringing the past back can be quite unsettling and I want you to take a break."

"Thank you. I'm looking forward to our next session."

"I'm glad you brought that up. Our next session will be at Tranquil. It's a Sanctuary Restaurant on East Lane."

"I know where it is. But I'm not sure I can talk about my life within earshot of other people. The thought of that stresses me out."

"Of course that's understandable but we have a private sanctuary that our clinic uses for Therapy sessions."

"So why do we need a different setting?"

"A change of scenery can work for some but not all. I believe the environment at Tranquil is conducive for the stage we are at in your therapy."

"Ok I trust you."

"I believe it will help. We're set for Thursday at 10am. Just ask for me at Reservations."

Thursday came. She walked up to the Reservations desk dressed in all white linen.

Tranquil was an oasis. Everyone sat at their tables with the sound of crystal clear rushing water in the background. Greenery lined the periphery and the delicate scent of essential oils laced the air. The centre feature presented a white marble unicorn water fountain spurting out spirals of water and ultra-marine-blue pearls that gorgeously refracted the light. Walking past it the attendant led Sofia to the *Lavender Suite*.

A leather lounger lined the wall in the alcove of the *Lavender Suite*. A floor to ceiling diffuser in the corner puffed a hint of calming Wild Orange and Roman Chamomile. This was a familiar scent that Sofia had been accustomed to in all her sessions with Michael.

"Please help yourself to the complimentary drinks madam," said the steward.

"Thank you." Sofia poured herself a glass of sparkling elderflower water and went to sit down on the leather lounger. She placed her glass on a coaster set on top of an oval oak coffee table. On it she noticed Michael's journal and some papers. It was a distinct journal with black leather and neat orange dividers. She had been accustomed to watching him flick through and vigorously jot notes.

Michael had been watching her from behind concertina doors that led to the conference room adjoining the suite. He slowly watched the flow of her white linen and surveyed the silhouette of her face. It was then that he noticed the sadness in her eyes. He wanted to save her. But all he could be was her Therapist.

"Hello," he said as he quickly walked towards her.

"You're here Michael."

"Yes I was in the back doing a few things."

"It's very beautiful here. Peaceful."

"I'm glad you approve." He sat down on the leather armchair that was set at the foot of the lounger.

"I do," she said.

He opened up his journal. "Would you like anything more to drink?"

"My water is fine but some lemon tea when we finish would be lovely.

He nodded. "Are you ready?"

"Yes thank you."

He crossed his legs. "Good. Maybe today we could start with what life was like when you were together."

"Gosh where do I start?"

"Start wherever you feel comfortable."

She paused for a moment then remembered. "He would say it was all in my head. His infidelities were all in my head. My complaints landed me the title of 'Drama Queen'." She shifted in her seat and looked away. She could never directly face anyone when talking about him. "I was never allowed not to trust him. He would go into a rage. How dare I not trust him was his attitude. He felt entitled to it. He didn't have to earn it. And that hurt."

"Why did that hurt?"

"It made me feel insignificant. My opinion didn't matter and my feelings meant nothing. It is so humiliating when someone deliberately ignores you." Tears rolled down her cheeks.

"Am I right in saying that he failed to acknowledge you and your feelings?"

"Yes that's the best way to explain it. But I felt guilty about it."

"What were you guilty about?"

"At the time I felt my expectations were unrealistic. I kept telling myself that I was being too demanding. One minute I felt degraded and the next minute I was making excuses for him. I told myself that he didn't owe me anything. It's probably because he worked so hard to drum that into my head."

"In a romantic relationship it's not unreasonable to expect mutual giving and receiving of love. Neither is it unreasonable to expect your partner to acknowledge your existence and your feelings. When that acknowledgement is absent it's a breach of trust and one might start to question whether the 'love' you share is real. So you were not wrong to feel that way." He saw her discomfort. "Are you ok?"

She nodded. "I feel angry with myself because I was so stupid to have allowed this to happen. I was just so desperate to be with someone."

"There is nothing stupid about falling in love."

"But that wasn't love."

"You gave love. But I don't think you received it. And that is not your fault."

Sofia nodded, "Do you think we could have that tea now?"

"Of course," he said.

CHAPTER 7

"Next time you want to come with me you need to dress better than that." Uche snarled as he pointed his index finger at her. "You need to know who you are with. If I dress well and you are with me, then you need to measure up." He looked out the window, shuffled back to increase the distance between them. He looked embarrassed.

Sofia was stunned. She said goodbye and got off at the next bus stop without looking back. Walking down East Lane she surveyed her jacket. She wanted to cry but tears refused to flow. She felt so embarrassed. She could not understand why he had to be so rude. She was always the first to admit that she would never be the best dresser but if he said that he loved her why did he have to talk to her that way. The walk down East Lane seemed longer than usual as she figured out how she would end it with Uche.

A week later Uche called her mobile phone. She was reluctant but answered.

"Hi I miss you. Why haven't you called?" he asked.

"Why do I have to be the one to call?"

"Well don't you understand what is going on here?"

"What I understand is that you were extremely rude to me."

"When was I rude?"

"You insulted me when we were on the bus."

He chuckled. "Insulted you?"

"It's not funny. You hurt my feelings."

"I don't understand."

"If you don't understand then no need to continue this conversation."

"What do you mean?"

"You insult me, you insult the clothing that I paid for. You hurt my feelings but it means nothing to you."

"This is just exaggeration. I want the best for you and if I see something to correct I correct it."

She came clean. "Listen I don't think this is going to work."

"Come on. What do you mean?"

"This is not working."

"Meet me at McDonalds."

"I'm doing some work," she said.

"Look I need to talk to you. Come on I will be there in 5 minutes."

She hung up the phone.

For the next 20 minutes he rang her number. He sent text message after text message. *'Please I am deeply sorry'* and then *'Meet me am @McDonalds'*. She went through ping after ping then ring after ring until her head was spinning. She answered the next call just to make it stop.

"Why haven't you been picking my calls?" he snapped.

"What do you want Uche?"

"Please come to McDonalds. Ten minutes only. Let's spend time together. I'm deeply sorry..." Whilst he was still talking she hung up the phone.

Two minutes later Uche, looking troubled, heard a ping on his phone. It was a text from Sofia. It read *'I'm on my way'*. He grinned.

It took her 10 minutes to get to McDonalds. Uche had been sitting at the back of the restaurant staring out the window trying to spot her. She emerged wearing a long black dress and the coat he had insulted because she didn't have anything else. She walked over to him.

"You look good," he said. She ignored him. "Let's go and get something to eat," he said.

They stood in the queue briefly. They decided on what they wanted to order but when it got to their turn to pay Uche left. "I'll be back," he said.

She took in a deep breath and exhaled. She had become accustomed to queuing up in cheap restaurants, getting to the till and Uche disappearing. He would reappear after she had paid the bill and had found a table for them to sit. He would offer excuses and then they would sit down to have their meal. He would subsequently offer up conversation after conversation that would break down her defences causing her to forget the inconsideration. But this time she decided that she had had enough of the merry go round and was going to end it.

Uche reappeared whilst Sofia was slowly sipping on her tea. He sat down. She didn't look up. She stopped sipping her tea and began to bite her burger.

He started popping fries into his mouth. "Are you not going to look at me?" he asked, still chewing.

She was silent. She looked up and away and took another bite of her burger.

"Sofia," he said. "Come on look at me." He tried to touch her face but she blocked his hand. She continued eating her meal. Then to her surprise she heard some sniffing and sobbing. She looked up and Uche, who was still chewing on his fries, had big drops of tears slowly making their way down his cheeks.

"Why are you crying?" she asked.

He was silent but continued eating.

"Why are you crying?" she asked again.

He used a napkin to wipe his cheeks. His eyes were still full of water. These were little pools that began to pull on her heart. "No reason," he said. "I just want us to start again on the same page."

She breathed heavily before she spoke. "Uche I can't start on the same page as someone who thinks it's ok to insult me."

He looked down at his burger and paused whilst deep in

thought. He covered his mouth with the napkin and began to nod his head. He pulled a little smile. "Let me tell you a story."

Sofia frowned. Here she was, ready to end their relationship but he was ready to tell a story. She sipped on her tea.

"My dad was the Chief purchaser for one of Nigeria's largest fashion houses."

"Oh? Which one?"

"The House of Lanre owned by Lanre Oshoko and family. It was big then but now their designs are not as popular as they used to be."

She nodded.

"I remember when we were kids my dad used to bring home these beautiful fabrics from all over the world. And he would show my sister and me how they were going to be used by House of Lanre. The designer was always at our house eating pounded yam and eghusi whilst they planned the next line of clothing. Celebrities would don those garments and I would spend hours looking for those fabrics, which my father would have brought home, in the magazines."

Sofia was hooked. She enjoyed listening to him and watching him talk. But she was wondering how the conversation had shifted from dealing with his insults to talking about the House of Lanre.

CHAPTER 8

U che's face was suddenly filled with pain.

"I remember one day when my dad called me to our front garden. My uncles had travelled from the village to come and roast meat. They did this every year. They would kill one of my grandfather's cattle and just roast and eat. It was a family special occasion so I was wearing a *Mark and Spencer* shirt, crisply ironed collar with starch. No crease just flat. I was king in that shirt with girls drooling. You know when you feel so confident."

She nodded and thought on whether to correct the fact that it was *Marks and Spencer* and not *Mark and Spencer*. She detested the dropping of the 's' but considered that it was not a good time to be petty.

"He called me to come forward and said 'everyone look at my son'. I was so happy because I thought he was going to show off with me. I had studied the House of Lanre fashion magazines for months and I knew that I had the style down packed. All of my friends were in awe." He chewed on more chips whilst another large tear drop flooded his eye, managing to pull on Sofia's heart strings.

She was angry with herself because she was supposed to be angry with him but now she was being sent into a whirlpool of sympathy.

"Then just like that my dad said IDIOT"

Sofia jumped as he bellowed the word. Fear gripped her coupled with embarrassment as the whole of the McDonalds restaurant heads turned in their direction.

Was he out of his mind? She thought. "What are you doing? Lower your voice."

"That's exactly how loud it was. Can you imagine? That man told me I looked like a fool and that I should dress appropriately as his eldest son. My dad's younger brother tried to reason with him by saying 'brother don't be hard on the boy' but it did not work. It made him even angrier. It did not matter what I did. That man would not appreciate."

Sofia was getting confused as she was being dragged into being shocked by his father's response. "Why did he say that?"

"I don't know. My father and I never understood each other. But I will always remember that day. I was humiliated and I wished that the ground would have swallowed me up."

"So he humiliated you?"

"That was his speciality."

"Well I know how that feels," she said trying to pull the conversation back to its original intent. But her exterior had begun to soften.

"I want you to have the best and be the best so that you don't have to go through what I went through."

She was touched. "When you put it that way I understand why now." Right there and then she cancelled all her plans. The House of Lanre had sealed the deal. She was in love with him and was highly unlikely to end it. He was hungry so she paid for another Big Mac meal.

They spent many dates in cheap restaurants. She enjoyed his company and he enjoyed hers. She hung on his every word as he told her stories about Lagos, the numerous women who had broken his heart and about the father who had broken his spirit. He was an amazing storyteller and that made her feel like she had come home.

#

Six months into their whirlwind romance Uche called her and invited her to spend time with him at the shopping centre in Shepherds Bush. She was excited and nervous. The mixed emotions making her wonder whether he was making a move to the next step in their relationship.

Hortense was sure that he was going to pop the question. "I'm telling you he is putting a ring on that finger...maybe now you'll consider a manicure."

"I don't think so Hortense." Although this is exactly what she hoped but refused to make it known.

"Well it's about time. You guys are getting fat on McDonalds." Hortense chuckled.

"How do I look?"

"The same?"

"Hortense please I need to look the part. I don't want to cause an argument."

"Listen fashion is not your strong point. Just slap on some lippy and you'll be fine."

"You are no help." She rushed to get her coat.

"Please forgive me if I'm not a miracle worker."
Sofia looked worried.
Hortense felt sorry for her. "Listen you're beautiful and if he has any sense that should be enough."

"Thanks Hortense."
After Sofia had left the flat and shut the door, Hortense shook her head and said "You're such a fool."

As usual they were munching on two large Chicken nugget meals bought and paid for by Sofia. He didn't have to disappear anymore at the till. Like clockwork she produced her bank card. It was her genuine pleasure to do so and he never made any effort to dissuade her.

She couldn't bear the suspense any longer. "So what is the surprise?"
He grinned. "Let's finish eating."

"Come on. I can't wait." She sounded playful.

"Ok." He reached into his over the shoulder bag. "I just wanted to say..." He hesitated.

Her heart began to pound. This was the moment that would prove that he loved her and that he had forsaken all others. "Just say it," she urged.

"My student visa has been extended." Tears began to well up in the corner of his eyes. He pulled out the documents and opened his passport for her to see. She grabbed a hold of the passport whilst she tried to hide how embarrassed she felt.

"I'm happy for you."

"Thanks. Now I can relax." He took the passport from her and looked at it. He shook his head, as if in disbelief. "I need to call my sister. She put me through school. Without her none of this would be possible.

"Your sister is a special person."

"Yes she is and nothing will ever come in between me and taking care of her. I owe her my life."

Sofia nodded.

The next hour was spent watching him jump, shout and yell down the phone whilst he spoke to his sister in English, Yoruba and Igbo and every now and again calling her 'baby'. He could not contain his joy. He also could not bring himself to remember that Sofia was sat in front of him, waiting to finish their conversation.

After 45 minutes she knew she was not going to compete with the news that his sister's makeshift restaurant had been displaced by government police to make way for Nigeria's new craze for fine dining in Ojuelegba.

She raised her hand as she stood up to signal her departure. He lifted up his head, nodded and then went back to concentrating on his sister. "Yes, she's gone. Anyway, tell me more."

She heard what he said. This broke her heart but she carried on walking without looking back.

#

Two weeks later Sofia was waiting in Starbucks for Skye. Sofia and Skye had been friends for most of their lives. They did not see each other often but that did not break their strong bond of friendship. No matter the lapse of time they just picked up from where they had left off. They had been through so much together. They had both experienced losing their parents and they had weathered the storms of life together. If there was anyone who loved Sofia it was Skye. And she had committed to never be economical with the truth.

Skye walked through the Starbucks doors and scanned the room until she found Sofia with her head down and almost dipping her hair in the cappuccino that was in front of her. Skye almost drifted through the coffee shop in her bohemian wrap dress and papyrus sandals.

"Why such a long face?"

Sofia looked up and smiled. "You're a sight for sore eyes."

"Sore eyes? Why have you got sore eyes?" Skye pulled up a chair and sat down. She placed her banana leaf over-the-shoulder bag on the empty chair.

"Come here you," said Sofia as she pulled Skye towards her. They embraced for a little bit of eternity before Skye broke away and said, "Ok so what's he done now?"

Sofia flinched as Skye had launched straight into the reason for the thorn in her flesh. Taking cover Sofia created a slight diversion.

"Let's talk about you first. How have things been with you two?"

"There's not enough room in the world for both our problems so let's focus on yours. Besides, you look worse than I do." She fished out her pack of cigarettes.

"You can't smoke here."

"Oh shoot I forgot. My nerves were calling so I responded without thinking." Skye returned them to her bag.

"What would you like to eat and drink?"

"I'm so hungry. Can I have the usual please?"

"Ok roasted vegetable Panini and a Green tea coming up." Sofia stood up to order.

"You know you won't be able to avoid me."

"I know," Sofia said.

"Good. So when you come back you'll tell me all about it. Here; pay for it and anything else you want." Skye's 15 arm bangles jangled as she shoved £20 into Sofia's hand. "On second thoughts add two hot chocolates with double whipped cream. I have a feeling we're going to need it."

Sofia ditched the Panini and green tea and brought two tall glasses of hot chocolate with a mountain of double whipped cream, toasted mini marshmallows and chocolate sprinkles. Then on the side were two enormous slices of moist carrot cake smothered in cream cheese frosting and a few candied carrots.

"So how is it in paradise?" asked Skye as she wasted no time in digging her fork into the cake.
Sofia took a large velvety gulp of the chocolate and swallowed. Her face seemed to mellow as the thick, sweet liquid made its way down her throat.

"Doesn't feel like paradise."
Skye's face dropped. "I knew it."
Sofia felt guilty. "But deep down, he is a good man."

"A good man? You look miserable Sofia. You sound miserable every time we speak."

"We have our moments but somehow we always manage to bring things back together."

"You mean he winds you around his little finger trying to convince you to put up with all his crap." Skye stopped talking as she noticed that Sofia had put her head down. She knew that when Sofia put her head down she was hurting.

"Listen I'm sorry. Did anything happen?" asked Skye.

"I've been such a fool. I thought….I thought that…."

"What happened Sofia?"

"He got me all excited. Invited me to dinner and said that he had something to tell me. I thought that this was it and that he was finally going to let me know that it was me that he wanted." A tear streaked down her cheek.

"What did he say?" Skye was worried.

"All he wanted to show me was his visa."

"His visa? What for?"

"His big news was that his visa had been extended."

Skye dug into more cake. "That's a red flag right there."

Sofia recoiled. "I was so disappointed but later on, after giving myself time to think about it, I thought maybe it was his way of telling me that he has more time to stay with me."

"There you go again back tracking on reality."

"I'm just trying to be fair Skye. He does not owe me anything."

"He owes you the time of your life that he has wasted. He has your emotions all over the place and my guess is that this whole visa thing was a game to make you go crazy."

"If love means crazy then I'm crazy."

Skye breathed deeply. "Sofia you are my oldest friend and I would never lie to you. I really don't think that Uche loves you back."

"He does. He just…"

"You make way too many excuses for this guy."

"Skye I just want to feel…" Tears welled up in Sofia's eyes. "I just want you to support me. I just want to feel…" She looked at Skye.

Skye could not hold back her tears. She scooped her chair closer to Sofia, cleaned off the blob of cream that was on her nose and hugged her. "I know," she said. "I know."

CHAPTER 9

"**M**y guy, are you serious?" asked Peter.

Uche picked up the bottle of complexion definer cream and began to massage his cheeks vigorously. "What do you mean by serious?"

Peter chuckled. "You 'wan marry' (You want to marry)? Abeg (please) tell me another joke."

"Which joke? When you marry was it a joke?" Uche's cheeks were turning into a deep purple but he continued to rub.

"Hey my wife was pregnant."

"Ehe (yes) so you marry the mountain for cover up." Uche laughed.

"What cover up? I love my wife. And she's not a mountain."

"Jokes aside but Ngozi is fat. Let's not lie here. She's my sister in Christ but that girl is big. I wonder how you manage." Uche chuckled some more.

"Hey worry about your own mountain. We both know it's bigger than mine. They laughed a deep belly laugh until the tears surfaced."

"Hey stop. I'm serious now. What are you doing? Do you love this girl?" asked Peter.

Uche began to rub his cheeks faster.

"Hey you go blow up your skin. You 'de craze' (Are you crazy)?" Peter stared at Uche's face.

"You 'massage am' (massage it) to get the impurities out."

Uche looked very serious and seemed to focus with intent on his almost bloody cheeks.

"But I think you have done too much. My guy, stop this nonsense."

"To get this physique takes pain," said Uche.

"You 'de craze' (You are crazy)," said Peter. "You de craze." Peter walked out of the bathroom shaking his head.

Uche stared intently into the mirror, transfixed by his own image.

#

Several weeks later Sofia found Uche pacing up and down her kitchen. "Are you ok?" she asked.

"Why do you ask?"

"I asked because you are pacing back and forth."

"I was looking for 'pepe' (Pepper) sauce."

"It's over there." Sofia pointed at the bottle of Tabasco on the kitchen counter. Uche took it and walked past her into the living room. Sofia frowned and watched him sit on the settee. She put her bag on the kitchen counter and poured herself a glass of water.

"How did you get in?" She asked then heard him squeeze the word 'Hortense' under some breathing and very distinct chewing.

"Oh she came back?"

"Obviously."

"I thought she went to work." Sofia came and sat next to him on the settee. He shifted to create a distance. That pinched her to the point of feeling unwanted.

"She came back and went out again." The monotone syllables reluctantly escaped from his mouth. He drowned his burger in Tabasco.

Sofia looked through the take away bags. "Nothing for me?"

"You need to lose weight."

That comment pinched her but she gracefully shrugged it off

with a chuckle. "Why didn't you tell me you were coming? I could have made sure there was something for you to eat."

"Must I announce my arrival every time?

"Of course not."

"Then why ask me why I didn't tell you? So you want to make sure you know when I'm coming?

"Well no I..."

"Is there some other guy you are seeing that you don't want me to meet?

"Of course not. I simply wanted to be able to cook for you."

"Listen if you are playing me then we should end this relationship right now."

"Why are you overreacting? All I said was..."

"I have been cheated on before and I can smell when something is amiss."

"What are you talking about?"

"You see you women these days you don't know when you have it good." He began to raise his voice.

"What has gotten into you? This is getting ridiculous."

"You are calling me ridiculous? You are very stupid."

"Don't talk to me like that."

"Ok let's end this right now." His hand crashed down on the table making the burger jump out of the plate. Sofia froze. He shot up and hurled his burger and cola at the wall. The bubbles of the fizz erupted on the cream wall paper. The ketchup and mustard created haphazard dots of yellow and red.

"It's over. I won't be played by a woman. I'm not an idiot. I am an Igbo man who will not be made a fool of." He went to grab his jacket. Sofia shot up and went to grab his arm. "Uche wait. Don't do this."

"Don't touch me," he said and pushed her away. She tripped on the carpet and lost her footing. Her round frame crashed to the ground. Her twisted ankle and mounting embarrassment were met by the angriest face that she had ever seen him show.

"Uche, why are you doing this?" Tears began to well up

in her eyes. Her ankle throbbed, her heart was burning and her mind was confused.

"Don't try to call me. This relationship is over." He stepped over her, walked out and slammed the front door without a single care that his girlfriend had fallen and hurt her ankle.

CHAPTER 10

Michael stood up from the desk where he had been writing the notes from the session he had had with Sofia at Tranquil. A craving for sweet, creamy cafe mocha led him to walk over to the coffee machine.

The day at Tranquil swirled in his mind with thoughts on Sofia and how he would get her to the place where she would know that she was worthy of love.

His attention was taken by the green marble water fountain, the centre piece of his garden. It was not quite the centre. He had misread Clara's instructions when she had tried to direct him to the point with co-ordinates that were calculated using the unique formula she had found in the Culture Magazine.

She had told him *'left'* and he had interpreted that as *'right'* and therefore landed nowhere near the target.

He dangerously lifted the marble from the trolley instead of using a machine which he didn't want to bother renting. After falling in a heap and Clara falling on top of him in a wave of giggles they decided to cement it down in the not quite the centre spot because it was just too heavy for him to lift again. He remembered touching her hands as they sculpted and shaped the cement. She had beautiful eyes that he always adored looking at and of course he loved touching her delicate belly that was growing with each day. The memories made him smile as he turned on the coffee machine.

Clara was the love of his life. She was not only beautiful but she was compatible to everything that he had hoped a woman would be. They had met at a Psychology seminar. She was the stunning woman at the counter trying to pay for a Starbucks Chai Latte and he was the handsome man who offered to pay for her drink when she realised that she had left her credit card in her hotel room.

They struck up a conversation. She was easy on the eyes. He was polite and funny. They ended up spending the whole seminar sitting together and later exchanged numbers because they didn't want the Psychology seminar to be the last place that they would ever see each other again.

It was a year of him travelling down to her and her travelling up to him for dinner and theatre dates. The attraction was strong but more than anything was their bond of friendship. It was not a whirlwind romance. Instead it was two colleagues who became friends with an underlying strong attraction and desire to be with each other at every event. When their long planned holiday to Cairo came Michael got down on one knee in the sweltering heat in front of the tomb of Tutankhamun. He could not hold his emotions as he asked his best friend to marry him. It was a no brainer for her. They had the most stunning wedding in the spring of that year.

They worked together in Michaels Therapy Practice, nurtured a herb garden at home and enjoyed romantic holidays whilst sampling the finest of wines. Life was almost perfect until the unimaginable happened. A diagnosis of cancer was followed by three rounds of gruelling chemo. But sadly she lost the fight.

Michael lost the battle with her. He could not return to the Therapy Practice that they had had such great plans for. He could not face the memories of when she would rush her hand through his hair and smile. That smile is what would carry him through the day and without it he didn't know how he would carry on. So he took a sabbatical to heal his broken heart.

However, after a period he returned and reopened the practice because he resolved that this is what Clara would have wanted him to do. Business was slow with a small list of clientele. He went through the motions but it was clear that he had lost that fiery passion for his work. This went on for a while until Sofia walked into his office. When Sofia became one of his clients everything changed.

#

Halfway across town Sofia walked into the Garden centre. "Hi Stan can I have a couple of pots of White Rosemary please?"

"That's not like you. Not planting from scratch anymore?" Stan asked.

Sofia chuckled. "I need some for my kitchen window. I just don't have the time right now for seedlings. Give me some of that Thyme too."

"It's flowering," said Stan.

Sofia reached beyond him and grabbed the pair of scissors that was on the counter. She delicately caressed the small lilac blossom. She smiled and thought for a little then in one swift move she snipped off the young beauty. "Not flowering anymore."

Stan shook his head.

"I see. So you don't have time for seedlings. Is someone taking up your time huh? Bout time too anyway." Stan grinned.

"No nothing like that... I'm going through counselling." She waited for his reaction.

He turned to pick up the Rosemary pots. "Well there is nothing wrong with getting a good head and heart check up. We all need one I tell you." He faced her and put the pots on the counter next to the Thyme. "Is the Therapist any good?"

"He's amazing Stan. He listens you know. I mean he really listens. He takes an interest in you and you can feel it. He is the kindest of people and he has this smile that just lights up his eyes..."

"Are we still talking about your Therapist or is this someone else?"

"Yes it's my Therapist." Sarah saw the stare in Stan's eyes

and knew what it meant. Her cheeks went crimson. "How much do I owe you?" She asked.

Stan laughed. "I'm happy for you Sofia."

"He's just my Therapist."

"Ok Sofia," said Stan.

As she shifted her gaze towards the pretty Blue Sails. Stan laughed again.

CHAPTER 11

Michael heard his mobile phone ringing in the living room. He placed his coffee on the counter and rushed to pick the call.

"I'm really sorry for calling you but I didn't know who else to call. He contacted me."

"Sofia?"

"I'm really sorry but I just don't know how he got my number."

"Sofia who are you talking about?"

"He told me what I was wearing. I mean how did he know what I was wearing? He must have been watching me. Michael I can't have him back in my life..." She was breathing heavily.

"Sofia calm down. Tell me who you are talking about."
She began to cry.

"Stay with me Sofia. I can help you."

"I can't go through this again."
Sofia who are you talking about?"

"Uche. I'm talking about Uche."

"He rang your mobile?" asked Michael.

"Yes. I'm sorry for laying this on you but I didn't know who else to turn to. I'm really scared."

"Where are you now?" he asked.

"I'm outside the Garden Centre in town."

"Ok stay there. I'm coming to get you."

"I can't impose on you like that. In fact I shouldn't have

called you."

"You shouldn't be alone. It's no trouble for me to come."

"I will feel better if I come to you."

"Are you sure?" he asked.

"Yes I would really appreciate someone to talk to. I will pay extra."

"We'll talk about that later. I'm at home."

"Oh. I can't impose. I thought you were at the practice. Look we can do this some other time."

He insisted. "I don't think you should be alone Sofia."

"But it's your home."

"If you don't come then I am on my way to you."

"Ok, ok. Can you please text me your address."

Half an hour later Michael opened the door to a red eyed, blue dressed stunning woman. She had been crying a lot and looked quite shaken.

"Come in," he said.

"Thank you."

Her sandal touched the highly polished mahogany floor. Immediately her breath was taken away by the reds, browns, oranges and beige. She smiled at Michael. "You have a beautiful home."

"Thank you. Please, take a seat. I'll take your coat." He reached for her coat. As his hand touch hers a bolt of electricity shot through. She felt it and he felt it. They were both uneasy because their hands had told the truth about the feelings that their mouths were not yet willing to admit. He was a Therapist and had taken an oath to never cross that line.

She took two steps down into the spacious area. Instantly she was hit with the calming scent of wild orange. A seven seat velvet lounger divided the room. At one end was the log fire and the other a drinks bar. The wall with the log fire was built with medieval stone work. To the right were three very high double French doors that allowed the natural light to radiate into the room. Above were three balcony banisters.

Just before the drinks bar was an attractive alcove that housed several books and antique style ornaments.

The rug was a very thick and fluffy white Lion's mane, like a tame polar bear that Sofia longed to fall into and sleep. She took off her sandals as she did not want to ruin the luxuriousness of it.

She sat down and melted into the brown velvet seven-seat lounger. It was warm and soft. She paused to take in the comfort. Tears began to well in her eyes because it was a healing comfort. It was nothing like she had felt before. This felt like home. She felt welcome. Of course she had lived in many houses but she had always felt like an outsider, like she didn't belong.

Michael's home was different to what she had been used to. He had photos, paintings and ornaments on the walls. He had colours, patterns and designs. Someone had taken the time to create a unique space. Someone had carefully thought out and organised things.

She on the other hand had always lived in chaos with papers everywhere in neat little piles where she had tried to organise things but had given up. There was nothing in her home. Her mind which was often preoccupied with one challenge after the next had no time to consider creating beauty around her. Yes there were chairs, a table, a television and a bed and yet it was empty. Photos on the wall would have made her remember the sad times.

She had plants mainly herbs and vegetables. She also had her beloved apple trees, two of them of different variety. And her bonsai grape vine. They were all in pots and never planted in the ground because from her past experiences she had trained herself to be ready to move at any given notice.

Despite all of this greenery this horticulturist never planted flowers. She knew how to grow them from scratch and nurture them until they reached the height of their bloom but never in her home. The blooms represented love and they represented happiness. In her home no one had brought in colours, or paintings or designs. It was just a roof to tide her over until she was no longer welcome. At least this is what was in her head.

The chaos in her life had never allowed her to live and

discover the things that she wanted out of life. She wasn't quite sure what her favourite meal was or her favourite dessert because she had never stopped long enough to listen to her own thoughts. It was the thoughts of others that always drowned her head. It was their opinions, their wants never hers.

Michael came back in. "Can I offer you some tea?"

"Oh yes please. Thank you."

"Lemon tea?" He looked back at her as he walked towards the drinks bar.

She smiled. "Yes that's lovely." She grabbed the opportunity. "Your house tells me that Therapy is big business."

A slight pink appeared in his caramel cheeks. He chuckled whilst he poured the hot water over the lemon. "Yes it's very good actually."

She admired his shyness for a moment. "I really appreciate what you have done for me."

"It's my job."

"But today you're going out of your way."

He nodded. "You needed help so I decided to give it."

"Thank you."

He handed her the tea.

"This is delicious. I can taste a hint of ginger in there."

"Yes I took the liberty of dropping in some essential oil. It just picks it up a little bit."

"Well I'm converted."

"I'm glad you like it." There was a brief period of silence as they both struggled with how the direction of their conversation should go. Michael decided that as he was the 'professional' he ought to be the one to take the lead.   "How are you feeling now?"

"I'm better. Thank you."

"Do you want to talk about it?"

She nodded. She sat forward on the lounger. "I was at the garden centre buying some herbs when I got a call from a private number. At first I ignored it thinking it might be a bogus call. But the caller kept on ringing. I answered it just to stop my phone from buzzing. But I should have known. When I heard his voice my insides must have dropped to the ground."

"What did he say to you?"

"He just said in that awful cocky voice of his- Do you miss me. I was in complete shock. I asked him how he got my number. He asked how I could expect him not to know his wife's number. I felt sick to my stomach. I am not his wife." She began to breathe heavily.

"Take it easy Sofia. If you feel uncomfortable in any way you can stop talking about it if you wish," said Michael who was trying to manage a possible nervous breakdown.

"What's even worse is that he made a comment about the colour of my clothes? That freaked me out. It's either that was an incredibly accurate wild guess or he was watching me."

"Yes that is concerning. When was the last time you spoke to him?"

"I have had one complete year of no contact. And this has been the best year of my life. I've made so much progress and I can't have him coming back to ruin all of that."

"Well it's quite concerning that he managed to get your number. But it's quite possible that he may have studied all your companies Social Media. With all the work that you're doing with the strawberries it's not too difficult to get hold of information about you."

"I can't see who could have given him my personal number though. It's nowhere on my Social Media."

"That's true. So it could be anyone that you both know. Is there anyone you can think of?"

"I can see him smooth talking his way into swindling my number off of someone. But I can't think of who it could be because the people who could have easily given him my number don't have this one. It's new."

Michael nodded. "Umm that's a mystery. Anyway, so what do you want to see happen?"

"I'm changing my number for a start."

"That's a good idea. Do you feel he could harm you?"

"I don't think he would hurt me physically. He never did that sort of thing. All he ever wanted to do was to get inside my mind and drive me crazy. This is all a game to him."

"And he's looking for someone to play. You have to find a way to let him know that you're not going to get caught up in the confusion from your past. Remember, any drama between the two of you is his fuel. He was probably running low on supply which explains the lengths that he went to get back in touch with you. All he needed was your reaction. You got scared and he fed on that. It was just like old times for him, where the two of you would play the dance. He would light the match and you would catch fire."

"So what do I do Michael?"

"What you have been doing all along. You stopped contact. You avoided all temptation to find out how he was. And now you're planning to change your number. All of this drenches you in water so you can't catch fire."

"I don't think I'm strong enough. Just the sound of his voice set me off today."

"You've come a long way Sofia. Keep conversation to a minimum. You don't want to be pulled into circular arguments that set you off and at all costs don't let him get you on the defensive. Remember the role play we did?"
Sofia nodded. "Yes I do. I've been watching the video."

"Good. He may say things to push your buttons. But don't react. If possible walk away."

"What if I mess up?"

"If you mess up, well there is always another day. The next day has the opportunity for you to win and be in control of your life and not him."

"Yes, walk away.... I'm tired Michael."

"I know. We should stop and have something to eat."

"I won't take up any more of your time. You have been incredibly generous." She looked around for her sandals.

"No I insist. Let me do this one thing. I will make a sandwich, and some hot chocolate. It will help you feel better.

Cheese?"

"I love it."

"Great"

She relaxed a little more. His smile brought her a sense of calm. "Thank you."

"Make yourself feel at home." He handed her the remote control. "I will be right back." He disappeared behind a swinging door that was right next to the alcove.

After a period Michael pushed through the swinging door with a tray laden with two tall glasses of hot chocolate and whipped cream and a plate with piping hot grilled cheese sandwiches for two.

He got closer to the lounger and found that Sofia was no longer there. Surprised, he looked around then he noticed her sandals to the side of the lounger. He walked to the centre of the room and placed the tray on the solid oak, oval coffee table. He thought that she may have made her way to the toilet but when he had turned around he saw her. He smiled an affectionate smile as he gently surveyed her. She was definitely a sight to behold as she breathed lightly and turned her body to face the back of the lounger. She had fallen asleep.

Michael went to the hallway and tugged on a floor to ceiling mirror. From the closet he pulled out a luxurious throw. He walked back to the lounger, knelt down on one knee and gently covered her with the throw. Sofia settled into a gentle snore.

CHAPTER 12

He stood up from where he had been kneeling and paced backwards and forwards, seeming a little confused. He knelt down again where she had been sleeping and stared at her for an extended period. It was a cold and disturbing look. He stood up again and walked away but his foot hooked on the blanket that was covering her. She stirred as the cold air brushed her skin.

"Hey. When did you get here?" Sofia asked. She sat up and rubbed her eyes.

"Hortense let me in."

"But she left ages ago. Have I been sleeping that long?"

"She's gone."

"Thanks for stopping by to see me." She stood up and pulled in for a hug. He shot to the ground on one knee. She assumed he had rejected her but chose to act like what had happened was not as bad as it felt.

He remained kneeling and searching for what words to say. He looked overwhelmed with beads of sweat collecting on his forehead.

"Why are you kneeling down?" she asked.

"Oh Sofia, I love you."

The awkwardness of those words filled the room. They were awkward because on some days she felt that he really loved her but then on others she just wasn't sure.

Whenever he said them, which was not often, it was a

walking on eggshells experience - unsteady and ready to crack. It made her cringe but she was always compelled to respond with, "I love you too."

To defuse the tension she began walking towards the kitchen. "I'm making tea. Want some Uche?"

"Will you marry me?" he said. It was not a question. It was a statement, a well rehearsed one.

She stopped and began breathing heavily. She turned around.

"Will you marry me?" he said again.

She smiled. She didn't know whether it was right to hug him or not. She did not want to risk another rejection.

This was exactly what she had wanted but she was not quite sure whether this was how she had envisioned it in her 'little girls dream'.

Then why on earth was she with this man? Why on earth was she torturing herself with the uncertainty of 'whether he loves me or whether he does not?' Why was she placing all her bets on the 'what if?'

"Wow," she said trying to sound enthusiastic.

"Is that a yes?" he asked and sounding a bit like the guy in the movie they had watched the week before.

Her response was an underwhelming tone. "I guess it is. Yes." She was getting married but the news was contributing nothing to what she actually needed.

Tears began to well up in his eyes in a genuine kind of way. It surprised her and touched her heart thus swinging the pendulum towards the 'maybe' he did actually love her after all and placing a winning bet on her 'what if'?

He walked towards her and gave her a hug. She was still unsure as to whether she should reciprocate. God forbid if she upset him. So they stood there, his arms fully around her and hers in a confused V-shape. This was their picture of 'love'.

Three months later Sofia was a buzz organising a wedding with a peach and cream colour scheme and strictly no flowers. She was not into flowers. She knew how to make them bloom but refused to have their beauty interfering with the colour of her life. Flowers meant happy. She was getting married but subconsciously that did not necessarily translate into the word happy, so there was no need for flowers.

She did all her busy bee preparing in the midst of criticisms from Hortense whose absenteeism occurred especially when her presence counted the most.

Uche appeared and disappeared throughout the entire process, frustrating and antagonising Sofia to the hilt. When he appeared it was to put Sofia down, put her in her place then yell at her in front of anyone who was within earshot. When he disappeared he escaped the choice of the cake, the choice of the venue, the invitation of guests and the access to his wallet which he had padlocked until further notice. Yet in spite of the confusion that Uche caused she was still determined to go ahead with marriage.

She was on autopilot organising a wedding but had lost focus of the fact that her husband to be was behaving like nothing of the latter, flirting with the bridesmaids and going on 'no making sense shopping' trips with Hortense.

However, in true Uche fashion after bringing her down he had the way of bringing her up. He surprised her. He bought her the most stunning dress and took her to a fancy, for their standards, restaurant. He was a gentleman. He commented on how stunning she looked, held the door open for her and pulled out her chair. They talked all evening. He made her laugh and told her more stories about his life in Nigeria. He talked about what was needed in the last minute preparations for the wedding and offered to take everything out of her hands. He paid for their meal. Everything about the evening was very passionate. She felt so secure. She felt like she had come home as he dispelled all her doubts.

#

Sofia had lived her life walking around with a gaping wound

in her heart. Constantly seeking the approval others and holding a deep desperation to be loved. For years there had been no hope of a relationship and no offers of undying love. She did not lack in beauty but lacked a sense of self value which ultimately dimmed her light. The way she spoke, dressed and walked clearly indicated that when she looked into the mirror she saw no one there.

So when Uche showed up it was a miracle. He was the confirmation that all her beliefs that she would never be with anyone were a lie. This marriage was her hope and she was not prepared to let hope die.

Her life was enriched by pain from a series of tragic circumstances that happened to her and around her. Many of which began in the Blackwell family.

Sofia's mother was Nouara Russo. She was born in Paris but had visited many countries in Europe whilst travelling with her parents. It was 1969 when she first met Sofia's father in Dover. She was a sixteen year old beauty with rich light brown sugar skin, a full buxom body and a head with luscious long locks of thick, brown hair. Her skin tone was a beautiful mix of her mother and father's love. Her father was a white Italian and her mother a mixed race Zimbabwean.

They met outside the Dover Stage Coach Hotel. She was the girl in the white and blue polka dot mini. She had bubble sleeves hanging out of her dark blue poncho that was draped with striking love beads. She was out with a group of friends, being normal teenagers, giggling and making their way home from the pictures.

She was striking yet unassuming and she instantly commanded his attention. He wasted no time and ignored the advice from his friend to stay away. His friend Max had told him she was a child and that he should stay away to avoid death threats from angry parents. He ignored because he was transfixed.

They struck up a conversation. She was attracted to his looks and his charm and she loved the attention that he paid her. She broke away from her group. He left Max behind and they walked off together. They talked for hours, looking into each other's eyes. He was telling her sweet nothings, being kind and gently touching her hands at any given moment. He took her to a drinking joint and she drank alcohol for the very first time. He was kind enough to stop her from drinking more but it was useless because one drink was more than enough to loosen her inhibitions. Then the unthinkable happened with a man she had just met in the back seat of an abandoned, burnt, Vauxhall 10HP. He had wanted to stop but she had begged him not to. And that was it. He walked her home and they made an arrangement to meet the next day outside Mr Patel's corner shop.

She would leave the house telling her mother that she was going to buy the milk and yet in reality she was off to meet her fancy man.

The pattern of their dates consisted much of doing more and more of the same thing that they did the first day they met. And that was the beginning of her addiction with a man twice her age and of whom she knew nothing about.

His name was Kingston Blackwell, a rich-dark chocolate man who was intelligent with a high sense of self image. Everything he wore had to be perfect. He was everything that she had dreamed of. He played the guitar, showered her with gifts and gave her the attention that she craved. An attention that had been missing throughout her childhood because the focus of her theatrical parents had always been about the next place they were travelling to and never on Nouara, their only child.

"You are my sugar," he would say and then commence to singing her a song which whizzed her mind around in circles.

She began smoking because of him. He lit up a stick of Madison, took a deep puff and blew it in her face.

"Why do you smoke?" she asked him.

"It relaxes me I guess. Go on try it."

"Oh I don't know."

"Well you won't know till you try it sugar."

She coughed wildly after the first puff. He patted her back

and rushed to get her some water to drink. Her face went a deep purple. He apologised and told her to never smoke again or her parents would come for him with a machete. She paid no heed as the next day she snatched the cigarette out of his hand and began puffing like a pro.

So that was their life, meeting at some old shack to play music whilst she sat on his lap and shared his cigarette. Then they would drink alcohol, share intimate relations and then she would go home.

Kingston and his friend Max had moved to Dover to take up jobs as hotel porters and escape the chaos of the London housing riots that were reportedly fuelled by racism.

They came to England in the 1950s as teenagers in search of a better life but were disappointed to find out that they were not welcome. Kingston then looked to plan B which was to work hard, save enough money and go back home to Jamaica and buy his land upon which he would build his home. He was 7 years in but had not saved much. So he drowned his sorrows in amusements.

Nouara loved her parents but she didn't want the traveller life anymore. She wanted to settle down and become a nurse. Kingston promised her that he would help her do it.

"Sugar I love you," he would say. "And you know I will be behind you." This made her commitment to him more solid as it made her do whatever he said whenever he wanted it.

Her parents were against their relationship largely because he was 13 years her senior and less apparently because he was a black man from the Caribbean who didn't even bother to ask for their permission to date their daughter.

However, with Nouara spending too much intoxicating time with Kingston the inevitable happened. She fell pregnant and had to break the news of her impending new arrival. Her mother was heartbroken and her father was furious.

Nouara was defiant claiming her undying love for Kingston. She hurled her parents with insults telling them that he had loved her more than they ever did.

"But you barely know him," her mother pleaded.

"I love him and that should be enough."

"But does he love you Nouara?" Her mother had asked her this question several times and it was always met by silence. "Well, Nouara?" her mother would always ask again.

Kingston's words would always ring in Nouara's mind, "I love you Sugar," but then these words would be blurred by the time that he slapped her for asking why he had been flirting with the girls at the drinks joint without a care that she was watching him. He slapped her after they had had a round of drinks and intimate relations in their regular shack. She hadn't seen it coming because he had made no indication that he was annoyed by her questioning at the drinks joint.

Her crying would set him off into tears and apologising for the hurt he had caused. She would then threaten to leave because she felt she had the right to be jealous. He would then pacify her with intimate relations and she would be back in his arms again ready to go through the same cycles.

It was not just the slapping. He would tell her she was a worthless kid and that he was tired of her and ready to leave her. In terror she would beg him not to and when he was tired of torturing her he would let her know that he had decided to stay in the relationship. He would then control her by giving her what she craved the most.

All of this left Nouara confused about what love was. However, she was certain she could not be without Kingston.

Following death threats from Nouara's father's 'Organized' friends Kingston found himself on a train travelling in a direction away from Dover. Nouara who insisted on following him got on the train and never saw her parents again.

Kingston found work in Dorset managing the cleaning staff on the production floor of a small textile company. Nouara gave birth to their first child and they named him Langton.

Nouara never became a nurse. Kingston didn't keep his promise. Instead he told her that she was stupid to think that she could be anything important after having kids.

By the time that Sofia was born their family was together and yet painfully fragmented. As a child Sofia was left alone a lot. Langton was distant. He never wanted to play. This was partly due to him being five years her senior and partly because he always had this look on his face that made Sofia feel as if she had taken something special away from him.

Nouara was always angry, always shouting and barely ever said a word to Sofia except 'come and eat' and 'get yourself ready for school'. Her father was rarely home. He worked long hours. When he returned all he did was argue with her mother. However, he did take the time to ask Sofia how she was doing at school and she would brighten up and tell her dad how her day was.

"How was your day Princess?" were the words she cherished and remembered the most. They filled the void for attention that was steadily growing inside her.

To receive more of it Sofia buried herself in her studies. Her life's mission became 'to do well and please Kingston'. He would be proud of her.

"Don't spend your time with boys Sofia. They are up to no good. Do your studies Princess." Her notion was that if she excelled he would love her even more.

And excel is what she did. However every effort was chopped down by the criticisms of her brother. According to Langton she would never achieve as much as her friend Skye who was prettier and more intelligent. "I mean why you even bother, I don't know?" was Langton's mantra.

Every day he would tear down the castles she was building. Her mother would never come to her defence, causing her bitterness to fester. Instead Nouara would protect her golden Langton who by the day was spiralling into a dead end life of spliff after spliff.

Langton was often the subject of Nouara and Kingston's midnight vigil fights. He would beat Langston with his fists and yell the question "Why was he not like Sofia?" causing Langton's bitterness to fester.

The fragmentation of their family turned up a notch the day that Kingston lost it and kicked Langton out of the house. It was 1993, Sofia's birthday, and Langton decided to be generous with his opinion that Sofia was 21 but lacking a boyfriend because she was too fat. He told her that turning her nose up to the spliff had poured havoc on her behind and a total turn off for the guys who were not willing to put up with that mess. This he said even though he had not conquered his own fat demons.

Nouara was heartbroken and would not be consoled, not because of the insult on Sofia but because her golden boy had been put out of the house. She took to her bed in a heap of depression.

Even though her brother had mocked her ability to get a man, unbeknownst to him she had had a secret boyfriend or two. They were only secret because they were the lowest of the low of the town and too embarrassing to introduce to relatives. They were the only ones who paid any attention. But Sofia knew that their attention was based on the assumption that no one else of substance was interested.

At most times they were demeaning and cruel however they were useful in that they made her look not quite so handicapped in front of Skye and her circle of friends. She in turn was useful to them because of her uncanny skill at growing and harvesting A grade cannabis in a part of the shed that her father would never ever find out about.

She never sold it though. This was her strict policy. It was a supply for her mother and her brother whose intake she monitored like a hawk. She too had lived on spliffs for a while because it seemed to help her to drown the chaos from her parents out of her mind. But then she stopped because she wanted to be sane enough to complete her horticulturist degree. That is when she jumped from spliffs to donuts which contributed to the embarrassing behind that Langton mocked her for.

She only grew the cannabis firstly because she was very good at it and secondly because she hoped that it would make her mother and her brother like her. But it turned out that they were just using her too.

The secret boyfriends were only allowed a few leaves as long as they promised to swear that they would tell no one else that she had a supply. If only Langton had known he would not have made that careless comment that put him out of the house.

After Langton left, Sofia and her mother's relationship was fragmented even further when one evening Sofia brought the regular bowl of sweet corn soup into the bedroom for her mother's dinner. Sofia had an odd way of looking down and yet walking forward which inevitably caused many *bumps-into* mishaps. On this occasion she bumped into the corner of the dressing table and the bowl went flying. It landed on her mother's Arabian blanket and splattered on the back of her mother's hand. It burnt her. Nouara winced in pain.

Shaking, Sofia ran to get a wet cloth to soothe the area but that's when Nouara brushed her hand aside.

"Go away," she said. "If it were not for you we would not be in all this mess."

Sofia was crushed "Mama?" A lump in her throat appeared.

"Go away," she said.

Sofia's heart was shattered into pieces. It was the moment that Sofia believed that she understood why she had felt all alone, why no one was ever there for her and why Langton hated her so much. It was because her birth had ruined everything.

Her parents had not shared a bed since she was 10 years old. Nouara had begged and pleaded but Kingston had said that he had finally had enough of her. He moved his things into the small room that they used to dump anything out of the way. Kingston moved all those dumped things into the shed and cleared the room to create his mini freedom.

Nouara was ruined, turning to sleeping pills, anti-anxiety pills and more cigarettes. When Kingston was not home she enjoyed the occasional spliff because he detested the habit. But their home was in chaos on the day she lit a spliff on the unfortunate irregularity that he returned home early. When he entered the house and smelt the familiar stench he was furious.

Immediately he clocked Nouara sitting on the sofa. Sofia was at the dining table finishing her assignment before she was shocked into seeing her father lunge at her mother, drag her by the hair into the bedroom and lock it, leaving Sofia to snuff out the spliff that Nouara had dropped.

It sounded like he was beating her black and blue. The noise was alarming but the neighbourhood they lived in came laced with a poverty that gave the guarantee that no one would call the police, so they yelled with freedom. Sofia ran into her room, jumped on her bed and covered her head with her pillow. She bit her nails hoping for the miracle that would ensure that her mother would not tell the truth about the cannabis patch that his aspiring horticulturist daughter had grown at the very bottom of their garden. Still worried she cried herself to sleep.

The next morning Sofia saw her father leave her mother's room. Her mother was at the door in a loosely tied dressing gown with half of her face purpled and swollen and a very telling black eye. Yet she was begging him to come back. He ignored her and went into his small room. Nouara shut her door and was heard crying for hours.

Nouara was never seen smoking a spliff again. Or at least Kingston never caught her neither did she smoke it in front of Sofia. She stuck to her pills, her alcohol and endless crying in her bedroom.

Kingston was hardly ever at home, spending the night with different women and returning in the late hours of the morning. His infidelities were apparent to Sofia although she seemed to brush it aside in a sense of denial.

She caught a woman come out of his small room, in the early hours of the morning, followed by Kingston. Sofia was getting an early morning cup of hot chocolate. The woman was startled by her. Her father was embarrassed.

"What you doing Sofia? I'm just taking Aunty here to the station. Pearl this is my daughter, Sofia."

"Hello dear," said the beautiful, half his age, woman.

Sofia couldn't say a word. She just looked towards her mother's bedroom. Kingston then rushed Pearl out the house.

"Don't wake your mother Princess."

He was the only parent who had even remotely shown an interest in her, so to please him and keep his affection she buried her revelations at the back of her mind. She didn't want her mother to lose it and then risk her father leaving their home. If he left there would be no one who would acknowledge her with kindness.

A few months later Kingston was taken seriously ill. Nouara forsook her depression bed and began to look after him. It was a difficult time for them all but it seemed to bring the tender side of Nouara back. They began to speak to each other with civility. There was never again an argument in that house.

She moved him back into her room. She was now in control and after 12 years of abandonment what she had lost had been restored. They would share a cigarette whilst she sat on his lap, they would drink alcohol then they would share what she craved the most.

But the disease took his ability to walk and then finally took his ability to see. In spite of the challenges he managed to pick up a smile and a chuckle whenever Sofia returned home from her part time job at the garden centre. Even Nouara made an effort by sitting with her daughter at the dinner table and asking her how her day at work had faired. But just when Sofia thought that her family was on the mend they found Kingston's wheelchair turned over at the back of the garden near their chicken coup. They found him face down in the chicken muck. He had suffered a heart attack and was dead. His dream to return to Jamaica was gone.

The funeral soon followed. There was not a dry eye in sight. It was peaceful apart from the time when a very beautiful, smartly dressed woman entered the church and walked straight down the aisle with a bouquet of roses which she laid on the casket. Sofia's mother exploded "Get that woman out of here."

The ruby red lipped woman turned briskly and spoke to

Nouara "Are you going to be insecure even at his death? We were just friends. I loved him too." As they stood face to face Sofia noticed how painfully shabby her mother was compared to this woman.

"I swear I will…" Sofia watched as Uncle Max pulled Nouara away.

"I can't believe this. Max?" said the woman.

"Just leave Hortense. Please," Max said.

Hortense looked around at everyone who was watching and then left.

In the midst of the argument Langton emerged. He walked straight down the aisle slowly. He had changed. He had lost weight. His hair was coiled into locks and he wore spectacles. He walked towards the casket. His eyes caught Sofia's. She lifted her countenance expecting that he would come to her for an embrace. Instead he looked down and walked past her. She was deflated but when she heard her mother cry out "Langton" and saw him running in her direction she deduced that he had not seen her and had rushed at the sound of their mother calling him.

Langton ran into his mother's arms and cried for hours like a wounded animal. This was the most emotion that Sofia had seen him show in all her years of knowing him. As he cried for hours Sofia felt alone. She was not welcome in the embrace that they shared.

A long while later Langton got up and just walked out. He never spoke to anyone. No one knew where he had gone. That was the last time for Sofia to see her brother.

Nouara lasted three years and gave in to her depression. She spent most of her days in her bedroom.

Sofia had the rest of the house to herself. She studied most days for her degree in horticulture. Her spare time was spent working on her horticultural experiments. There were plants everywhere including the cannabis patch that she was growing for her mother.

Nouara would come out for the toilet when she needed it

and once a week for a shower. Sofia was allowed in to the room to bring her meals, a spliff and for a brief clean. It was also Nouara's chance to unleash anger on her daughter. Sofia was told how useless she was. She couldn't cook and 'when would she ever get married and lift the shame from the family'? And the most regular insult was that Sofia's high and mighty behind was the reason why her son was missing.

After enduring several shouting sessions and some beatings that took Sofia by surprise she lost her mother to a stroke. It is when her mother died that she remembered the day when she was 6 years old and in the garden with her father on a lovely summer day. She saw an array of pretty flowers that had grown wildly in the grass. They were stunning shades of blue, pink and purple.

"Daddy, do you like flowers?" She remembered asking him.

"Yes sweet heart. I do."

She remembered picking the small rich violet one. "Why daddy?"

He thought for a moment. "Well, flowers are beautiful and they make you happy," he said.

She picked more flowers until she had a little bunch and ran around in circles, waving her flowers in the air and singing, "If you're happy and you know it clap your hands."

It was the year 2000 and once again she was alone but this time there was no one else in the room.

CHAPTER 13

S ofia's past was definitely a portfolio of pain but the day of her wedding quickly took first place because Uche, in spite of his promises, never showed up.

Completely stung she packed up her £85 diamante wedding dress from China in the box it came in and changed into her day clothes. Whilst trying to hold her heavy head up high, she walked through the church and into the reception room and began helping to stack up chairs. Everybody stopped to look at her but no one dared to say a word.

For months Sofia felt numb. Each day flowed into the next and she did not know whether she was coming or going.

Hortense had not been the best shoulder to cry on as she suggested that Uche was likely to have jilted her because of her sense of fashion which was difficult to understand. Hortense took it upon herself to pinpoint every fashion mistake that was likely to have brought Uche to tipping point and she prided herself in bringing the likely solution to solve Sofia's man troubles. What followed was a Hortense endorsed fashion tutorial every morning in front of the mirror that Sofia hated looking into. The intended help unfortunately plunged Sofia's confidence into the dump even further. But one Saturday morning her confidence shot back up and returned her smile because Uche called her. He wanted to meet up.

They met at a quarter past three in the alcove of the McDonalds restaurant on East Lane. She sat there with her face down and saying nothing. He said, "Thank you for coming." But she declined to respond. He stood up. "Would you like any-thing?" he asked.

In an annoyed tone she said "Tea please." When he disappeared she rehearsed what she was going to say or not to say. She wondered how much anger she should show. Nervous and afraid she spun the words round in her head but deep down all she really wanted to know was why he left and what she needed to do to make him stay. In reality she missed him and was miserable on her own.

Uche returned and placed her tea in front of her. Sofia had not registered that he had paid for her tea. He sat opposite her and began to devour his Big Mac and fries. Her belly began to rumble but she squeezed it in. Almost suddenly Uche looked up. "I had a great holiday in the States." He prolonged his grin.

Sofia was baffled. "Where have you been?"

"I just told you. In the States."

"Is that all you have to say to me?"

He chuckled. "What else do you want me to say?"

It felt like as if someone had slit her throat and the blood was sprouting out of the corner of her eyes. "What about the wedding?"

"What about it?" He sipped more cola from his tall cup.

The lump in her throat was hurting as she fought to hold back her tears. "We were supposed to get married."

He paused for a moment. "I'll be back." He stood up to get some napkins. He returned. "If you were in my situation, what would you have done?"

"I'm sorry? I'm not following."

"I was under pressure."

"So the solution was to walk away?"

"Listen a lot was at stake. If you had done what you were told we would not be here right now."

"What are you talking about?"

"I told you, if you dress a certain way, you and I would have no problems."

"Excuse me?" she said. The lump in her throat hardened.

"I was embarrassed. I told you which dress to wear but you disobeyed me."

"My dress? You jilted me at the altar because of my dress. I can't believe this." She buried her head in her hands.

"I told you that I can't stand shabbiness. I told you when you are with me you must look the part. At your age I'm surprised that you have no fashion sense. Did you see the bridesmaids? They were hot. But you were trying to act like old mama."

Her eyes were red but tearless. "But the dress you wanted was too small."

"Every girl that's getting married loses weight for their dress. But you, you prefer to eat chocolate."

"I lost weight Uche. I can't believe you are blaming me and yet you broke my heart with no explanation."

"I did not break your heart. You are such a drama queen."

She was stung. "I'm not a drama queen. I was the one embarrassed and…"

"You think I was not embarrassed? My future wife was looking like a bag lady and you did not care about me or how I felt. I refuse shame."

Uche went on and on about how ungrateful she was and how she did not listen to a word that he said. He said he didn't see how a marriage could be built on such a foundation. Sofia's head was spinning and her heart ached because everything that Uche said was confirmed by what Hortense had said earlier. That she was a poor dresser and it was all her fault. They went round in circular arguments that lasted until midnight. He systematically put her on the defensive until she was tightly spun in a web. From utter exhaustion she gave in. She was convinced that it was all her fault. If it were not for her actions their wedding would have gone ahead.

"I'm sorry. I didn't mean to upset you," she said.

"You're not a bad person. Everybody makes mistakes."

Sofia looked at her watch. "It's really late. I have to go home."

"Me too," he said. Uche made a few excuses then left Sofia outside McDonalds waiting for a cab. She waited in the cold, smarting from the pain caused by her ordeal. Deep down she knew that Uche did not treat her fairly but she believed that she loved him. If he left her, there would be no one else and, she would be alone. So she had to make him see that she was worth living with for a lifetime.

CHAPTER 14

When she opened her eyes her first notice were his eyes.

"Good morning," he said.

The smell of rich coffee and cinnamon became more apparent as she sat up. "Oh my goodness it's morning?"

"Yes it is. You looked so tired so I decided to leave you there."

"I am so sorry. She brushed the throw aside and kicked her legs down whilst nervously feeling for her sandals."

"No need to be sorry."

"Michael I have imposed enough on your privacy." She stood up. "I must go."

"At least stay for some breakfast."

"That's very kind of you, but I think I should go." She found her sandals behind one leg of the solid oak coffee table. Quickly she slipped the backs onto her heels and went to reach for her bag. "Thank you Michael." She walked towards the door.

"Well let me drive you."

"I can't expect that of you. I can get a cab."

"It's just a lift."

"You're my Therapist and I've taken liberty of your kindness."

"Sofia, please wait." She stopped. "Listen, I'm not talking as your Therapist. I'm just a guy who thinks it's immoral to leave you to get a cab. So I insist. You've been through a challenging time and it wouldn't sit well with me if I didn't get you home safely, especially since I have the means to do it." He was pleading with her.

Her exterior melted. "Thank you. Thank you for your kindness."

"Coffee?"

"Yes please." She smiled at him and he reciprocated.

After a second helping of coffee and cinnamon rolls they set off in Michael's car. No one spoke. Sofia had her mind on her phone call from Uche and worried about how he was planning to get into her mind and drive her crazy. Michael noticed the worry on her face. He decided against asking her if she was ok. It was not long before he pulled up in front of her house.

"Here we are," he said.

"Thanks again for everything."

"My pleasure."

She opened the door and stared at her house for a prolonged moment.

She sunk back into the seat. She looked worried. She looked at him then looked at her sandals.

He looked at the park which was a few yards ahead of them. "I was wondering if you could do me a favour?"

She looked at him. "Sure, of course."

"I'm due to see you for your session on Thursday but I've just realised that I have a meeting that my secretary failed to schedule. Unfortunately it's something that I can't get out of."

Reluctantly she spoke. "Oh I totally understand." She waited for the impending abandonment.

"So I was wondering if we could reschedule to another day."

She nodded. "When did you have in mind?"

"Right now, if you can"

Her eyes lit up.

"Is that ok with you?" He turned off the car engine.

Her eyes were filling up with water. "That's perfect. Thanks ever so much." She looked at him, he gently smiled and nodded.

There was a silent acknowledgement between them. He knew that she did not want to be alone and she knew that he had concocted a Therapy appointment cancellation story just so that he could help her once again.

"Are you sure?" she asked.

"Absolutely."

"I'm grateful."

Thirty minutes later Sofia emerged from her house after having gone to freshen up and change her clothes. She looked quite ordinary, not her usual glamorous self. Her hair was tied back with a fuzzy tuft of unruly hair at the front. She wore Khaki shorts, a striped t-shirt, blue Converse All star trainers and a blue canvas over the shoulder bag.

She looked like home and this made him smile but then he noticed signs of worry. When their eyes locked relief flooded her face but then the sadness followed again.

When she reached him he asked her, "Are you ok?"

She waved her hand. "Oh I don't want to worry you with my troubles."

Michael was experienced enough to know that in spite of her saying this, deep down she desperately wanted to tell someone. So he prodded further. "I'm a Therapist and I'm paid to listen to people's troubles." He smiled at her.

She sighed."I thought that I would come out and find you gone. But when I saw you I was so happy but then sad again because I remembered the time when being left behind was my everyday normal. And no one bothered to apologise or explain why they left me."

A part of his heart broke. Overwhelmed, he crossed the line that he promised himself not to cross. "I promise that I will always respect you." His words shot out like arrows that spun in the air and landed where they became scaffolding to hold up her ability to trust.

She felt out of balance because trustworthiness was unfamiliar territory. She said nothing but gratefully walked beside the safe place called Michael.

The weather was beautiful. For a period they just walked over the bridge, through the rose garden and along the edge of the lake. They watched the swans pirouette in the glistening rays of the sun then disappear under the lily-pads for a swim.

"It's beautiful here," he said.

"Yes. I come here a lot."

"Good for relaxation?"

She nodded. "Do you get to go out often?"

"I would love to do this more but I have loads of work most days. I'm not complaining but rest is important too."

"Well the work you do is amazing."

"Thank you," he said. He caught her blushing. For some reason she stopped to look at him. He looked at her. He found her beautiful. He looked at her eyes, her lips and her neck. He saw her kindness and he loved her shy smile.

She too stole a glance and imagined how it would be like to hold his hand and walk along the river bank.

But he had to draw the line. "Let's find somewhere to sit."

She too came to her senses and consented to walking by his side in silence as his client.

He found that he could no longer contain himself. He wanted to know her so he plucked up courage to cross the threshold. "Tell me more about your job."

"Ooo... my job is a long story. I'm a Horticulturist. I love plants."

He nodded. "What do you love about them?"

She lit up. He noticed. "The plants are beautiful but it's the work that it takes to make them beautiful that I love the most. That means getting my hands dirty and the smells. Oh I love the smells. It can take a while for things to grow but I love how it makes me feel."

He watched her as she spoke and listened. He realised that he had found something tangible that he loved about her – passion.

After being caressed by the warmth of the sun and serenaded by the scent of cherry blossoms Michael stopped walking.

She stopped too but longed to carry on as it brought her some grounding balance.

"We could go and sit on the oak benches under the weeping willows over there or we could go to the park cafe. We can continue our session if that's ok with you."

"The weeping willows please," she said.

"Ok then the weeping willows it is."

They chose a secluded area. She sat on the oak log with wagon wheels on each edge. He sat, facing her, on a varnished tree stump. She was comfortable but was not sure about how she would feel about talking about Uche. But decided to plunge in. "You know, he sounded exactly the same."

He switched on his Dictaphone. "Are you talking about Uche?"

"Yes that same cocky sense of self importance." She recoiled. "Oh it makes my blood boil."

"Yesterday you seemed a bit shaken after speaking to him."

"Yes."

"Is that still the case or has anything changed?"

"I was scared. But I feel less worried now."

"Why were you afraid?"

"I panicked. I had this horrid thought that I was going to get sucked into a web that I couldn't get out of." A tear rolled down her cheek. He let her cry because he needed her to have an outlet. She wiped her cheeks with some tissue that he had given her earlier. "When I was freshening up I remembered when I had the miscarriage."

"Do you want to talk about it?" asked Michael.

"I was so surprised when I found out I was pregnant. I had been ill but it never occurred to me that I could have been pregnant. I had trouble breathing. I couldn't walk up a flight of stairs without wheezing. And he would see me struggling but wouldn't help. Instead he called me a drama queen, implying that I was making it all up." Sofia brushed off a fly on her arm. He watched tears roll down her cheek and struggled to not move close to embrace her. "I mean it was glaring me in the face."

"What was? Glaring you in the face I mean."

"It was the fact that he didn't care about me. We were at a train station once. We had to climb a flight of stairs to get to the other side of the station. My chest was pounding and I felt like I was about to explode. But he just kept on walking. When he got to the top of the stairs he turned round and just looked at me." Sofia stopped talking and stared into the distance.

"Would you like us to stop?" asked Michael.

"I will never forget those eyes. They were the most evil eyes he had ever given me."

"How did that make you feel?"

"I felt quite stunned. I couldn't understand why he was treating me that way. But I just couldn't bring myself to comprehend that he actually hated me. That was too much for me at that time. The people at the station were staring at me and at him. I was embarrassed because everyone could see that he didn't care about me. And all I could think of was the shame. They must have thought I was a complete idiot for being with him. After that I lost my baby and instead of giving me a hug he yelled because I hadn't cleaned the blood off my legs when I was in A&E. He said that I should be ashamed of myself and left the room. I thought he had left to calm down but an hour later the nurse came to tell me that he had to leave to go on a work shift. I had lost the baby and he had gone on a shift?"

His heart bled for her but he needed to find a way to bring her out of the painful memories. "Sofia what happened to you was not right. A man who says that he loves you is supposed to protect you and nurture you. Yes you loved him but he didn't love you back and that is less than what you deserved."

She was so grateful that he heard her and he believed her. It was healing to know that he was on her side.

"Is it true to say that any contact with Uche brings back painful memories?" he asked.

"Yes, always. If I can just get rid of Uche I won't remember."

"Is there anything or anyone that you can think of who invokes more positive memories or feelings?"

"You know, it wasn't always bad with him. There were times we would sit and laugh watching our favourite comedians. He had a good taste in movies too. We would binge on Netflix and snacks whilst snuggled under a duvet. I thought we were friends and in spite of the bad ways that he treated me there were some good reasons why I chose him. I wasn't entirely stupid you know."

"And I wouldn't suggest that in any way. What you shared are obviously special memories."

"It was all just a disappointing mess." She thought for a moment. "But to answer your question I have my work. I've achieved a lot that I'm proud of." She began to smile. "And I've made so much progress. I feel stronger and I feel like I'm healing. So it's good to have you around. As my therapist I mean."

He nodded. "Yes I'm a good person to have around. As your therapist I mean." He smiled.

This made her chuckle. "Thanks," she said.

"You have come a long way and you are so different from the Sofia I first met. What I see is a beautiful and strong young woman who is getting to know herself everyday and I'm proud of what she has accomplished." He paused to look at the delicate silhouette around her eyes.

His words were more scaffolding for her heart.

CHAPTER 15

After a brief persuasion Uche and Sofia were married at the Registry office with Peter and Hortense as witnesses. What surprised everyone were Uche's emotions. He cried throughout the vows, was choked at every sentence which set them all off including the officials.

Their reception was lunch for 5, including Ngozi, for a feast of lobster, crabs, tilapia and salmon. They devoured everything then burnt it off at the restaurant dance floor with music from a live band. It was a great day.

They found an apartment together and life seemed to be moving smoothly for them. Uche had turned a new leaf. He was tender towards her. They made good money from his job as an office clerk and her job as a consultant at the local garden centre.

He seemed to enjoy the married life; making plans for how they would decorate their home and plans for how he was going to make Sofia the best dressed woman in town. Sofia was in bliss and was so grateful that Uche had finally come to his senses. He had even managed to get Skye, Sofia's friend who had firmly believed that he was a fraud, to begin to give him the benefit of the doubt. As their marriage progressed she was showered with expensive gifts that came more often than expected and Sofia began to wonder how on an office clerks' salary he was able to afford such lavish luxuries. But she was keen not to ruin her new found paradise by keeping her queries to herself.

Sofia was the only one out of them who had not finished

the diploma in business administration. Depression was the killer. She cried into her pillow more often than swotting for her exams and so she tanked in a very embarrassing way.

The dagger was pushed in deeper when on one occasion she returned home from work at the garden centre to find her husband and Hortense taking selfies in their graduation gowns on the front lawn. They hadn't told her that the ceremony was being held that day. As soon as Sofia approached they stopped the selfies and the hugging and the smiles.

"Finally You are here. I've been calling you all day," said Uche.

"Did you have your graduation?"

"Yes it was a great day. Look at Hortense isn't she looking sweet?"

"Uche, why didn't you tell me?"

"I wanted to surprise you," he said.

"Surprise me by making sure that I wasn't there at my husband's graduation?"
Hortense intervened. "Listen Sofia it was my fault. I was supposed to tell you but I was so stressed with the preparations that I forgot to text you. But don't worry it was a great day. Peter captured the whole event on video."

Even Peter was there Sofia thought. A wave of rejection swept over her as all she could think of was that he didn't want her there. Hortense pulled her in so that she could join in with the selfies. She was stuck in between the well dressed graduates barely smiling, trying to smooth out her green corduroy jacket and clutching on her old grandma bag.

However, after a time those graduation selfies were somehow deleted from phones by mistake and the supposed video of the day had an irreversible fault. The day and the memories of it were never spoken of again. The word *'graduation'* would set Uche off into a rage so the word was completely deleted from their lives to keep the peace.

#

The invitation to Peter and Ngozi's wedding anniversary party came. Sofia could not contain her excitement because she expected to be shown off as the new Mrs Onyeme. She wore everything that he demanded that she wear. If she had protested a violent shouting would have been received. So she complied to keep the peace. "Let's not fight," she said. "We're going to be late." This seemed to pacify him and his exterior would change to that of the happily married man who would surface every time she conformed to the demands.

They arrived at the wedding anniversary party. Sofia looked beautiful but uncomfortable in the awkwardly fitting attire. Her only comfort was that she was about to be paraded as Uche's wife. She hoped that it would be a slap in the face of all those skinny girls that she knew had been making fun of her at their wedding.

However, her expectations were unfulfilled. He left her to sit on her own and her attempts to mingle were met with mockery, "So is he able to eat your rice?"

"I learnt how to make Jollof rice," said Sofia with a smile.

"Uche, this your wife Oyinbo (white skin). Is the Jollof edible?" This was followed by sniggers and chuckles.
Uche failed to come to her defence. "Help her now my sis. Give her tutorial. I'm starving at home."

Sofia was humiliated. All the beautiful single ladies looked at her triumphantly because the man that she snatched from them had not defended her.

One in particular spent an unhealthy amount of time with Uche sitting snugly in the corner of the living room. All that Sofia could focus on was how pretty the girl was; petite and very well groomed. She slapped his shoulder as he gave inappropriate smiles. The longer that Sofia stared at them the tighter her trouser pulled around her waist. The confidence she had felt about her appearance when they had left her apartment was slowly beginning to wane.

Peter came into the room with a crate full of Malt drink bottles. He began handing them round. He spotted Uche and the girl in the corner of the room, giggling. Peter shifted his eyes and saw Sofia looking miserable. He acted quickly.

"My guy. Come and help me carry coke."

"Ah why? You have brought Malt."

"Not everybody drinks Malt. Sofia what drink would you like?"

"Malt will be ok."

"Are you sure? I can get you another soft drink if you like."

"Ah ah. What is the problem? She said she will take Malt," said Uche.

"Abeg (please) open drink for your wife," said Peter.

"Why are you troubling me?" said Uche as he stood up to go to the kitchen. "Sofia what would you like?" he said. "Coke will be ok, thanks." Sofia clocked that the girl was annoyed. Sofia was relieved that her humiliation had come to an end.

"Sofia why not go into the kitchen and talk to Ngozi. That's where Uche has gone," said Peter.

"Are you sure it will be ok. I know what women are like with their kitchen's." Sofia chuckled.

"Hey, come on, you are family."

"Thanks Peter." Sofia made her way to the kitchen at the back of the house. She entered the kitchen as Uche was bellowing at Ngozi.

"Ngozi, Ngozi...The greatest cook in town. What is in the pot for us tonight?"

"As for you I have made a special pot," said Ngozi.

"It can only be assorted meat?"

"Yes now."

"My sis you are the best."

Ngozi looked at Sofia. "Hi Sofia please sit down."

"Thanks. Do you need any help?"

Ngozi protested. "Ah ah Uche get a chair for your wife now."

Uche dashed into the corner and placed the seat next to her." "Sit here Sofia," he said. "Do you want assorted meat?"

"Assorted what?"

"Meat. It's different kinds. Ngozi made some for us."

"Well yes I would love to try it."

Ngozi put an array of fried fish, chicken and cubed beef on a plate. Ngozi was about to serve up another plate. "No my sister. Just one plate," said Uche.

"What about Sofia?" said Ngozi.

"I want to share with my wife. That's love."

"Aw that is so sweet. Sofia did you hear your husband?"

"Yeah I know that is sweet. Thanks Uche."

"Anything for you," said Uche.

Peter walked in just as Sofia was about to put her fork to the delicious looking chicken. "Glad to see you are enjoying yourself Sofia. Is he treating you well?"

"Hey what are you chatting my guy? You know me now. I am the smooth operator. I will treat her well."

"Chairman Abeg (please) this woman is gold ok. Sofia I'm just telling him that he needs to behave and treat you well." Sofia chuckled. "Thanks Peter. He is treating me well." She was trying to follow what she learnt at the church marriage counselling course – to defend your spouse and put on a united front at all costs.

"What do you mean behave?" said Uche as he dug into the piece of chicken that Sofia was trying to pick up.

"Abeg (please) chop (eat) assorted meat and stop talking nonsense in front of your lovely wife," said Peter.

"How are you my lovely wife? Eat some meat," said Uche. Sofia smiled at him then looked at the plate. She was surprised to find just half a piece of fish.

"Eat," he said.

Sofia got hold of the fish. It tasted fishy and spicy. It was ok to part fill her now rumbling belly but she was slightly disappointed that she had not managed to eat the piece of chicken that she had tried to stab into. Ngozi offered to refill the plate however she was too embarrassed to accept it. She had returned to her cycle of comfort eating but she was not ready to show everyone that she had slipped back into her old habits.

The party was over. Sofia and Uche said their goodbyes and got into their car. Sofia turned the key in the ignition.

"Did you see that they didn't have enough food for everyone?" said Uche.

"Well there seemed to be enough to me."

"You're not Nigerian that is why you say that."
Sofia frowned.

"Nigerians need plenty of rice," he said. "Maybe I can teach you how to cook Jollof. We will cook it on Saturday and I will show you how to make it the sweetest way."

"Like all those girls at the party?" she asked.

"Which girls? Those girls don't know anything? Silly village girls."

"Well you didn't seem to think they were silly at the party?"

"What do you mean?"

"Well you left me all alone and you were sitting in the corner with that girl and laughing?"

"She is from my home town and I was asking if she had seen my mum."

"I see. Why didn't you introduce me to her?" She stopped at a red light and waited for him to respond.
He was silent. "Uche" she said.

"We were talking so much about old times that it slipped my mind."

"I was hurt. You ignored me."

"It was not intentional"

"And I was embarrassed."

"Embarrassed by what?"

"Uche I am your wife. We just got married but all you did was sit in the other corner of the room as far away from me as possible and talk to another woman. How do you think that makes me feel?"

"Oh here we go again. Drama queen."

She was smarting. "Don't my feelings count to you at all? At least listen to me." She parked the car and released her seatbelt. She found herself getting wound up. "All I'm asking is for you to consider how I feel."

"I should be able to talk to my friends," said Uche who got out of the car and walked towards the apartment door.

"Talking to your friends is one thing but sitting at the opposite end of a room from your brand new wife for long periods of time? I mean come on Uche. Especially in a room full of your friends is unfair. I was all alone."

"We are just friends. Stop over reacting." He turned the key in the lock.

"I'm not over reacting. Why do you keep saying such things to me?"

"I say them because you are over reacting."

She had tears but they were locked in the vaults of her eyes. "Why did you marry me?"

"Oh here we go again. We are going into the whole I married you for papers argument."

"I never said that. I asked you why you married me."

He left her in the living room. She followed him into the bathroom.

"Eh I need privacy." He shut the door but she bolted in. He sat on the toilet "Are you going to stand there whilst I do my business?"

"I don't care."

"Ok fine." He reached for the toilet roll.

"You still have not answered me."

"What do you want me to say? Is it because the girl I was talking to was fine and hot? Is this why you have brought all these silly questions?"

Her confidence plummeted. Fine and hot he said. He had never used those words to describe her. She looked at herself in the bathroom mirror. She looked up and down the floor to ceiling length of it as it told the tales of her secret midnight binges and of her broken heart.

She gazed for a few moments. Everything was out of place, her face was shiny and the bulges had begun to emerge. She hadn't realised that Uche was still rambling on about how the girl was just his friend. She caught the back end of "I'm not sleeping with her if that is what you think." From that point onwards he went rambling on about how she bought into her friends suspicions of him. How she did not have a mind of her own and how everyone was poisoning her mind against him. He felt he was the victim and could not understand why Sofia would not believe him. He was her husband and his word should be trusted by her.

Sofia's gaze was broken by the strong smell of faeces that wafted past her nose. She hadn't realised that he had left the room and had continued to ramble until he put his head down on a pillow facing away from her on the furthest part of the edge of the bed. She made her way through to the bedroom and sat on the opposite side to him with a lump growing in her throat.

All that she had needed to hear that night was that he had married her because he loved her.

CHAPTER 16

"You have been in that kitchen for ages. When are we eating? I'm starving," said Tom Barton a long time friend and colleague of Michael's.

"Give me a couple of seconds," shouted Michael.

"Smells good though." Tom reached for more salted peanuts and glugged down another mouthful of his cold beer as he sat out on the patio. He saw Michael push through the swinging door from the kitchen and walk out to the patio with two plates piled with steaming oxtail stew, boiled white rice and a crunchy coleslaw salad. Both plates were laid down on the table.

"More beer?" asked Michael.

"No I'm good. This looks amazing."

"One of Clara's recipes."

"She was a good cook," said Tom as he tucked into a succulent piece of oxtail with the meat falling off the bone. Tom noticed that Michael's countenance had fallen and realised that it was because of the mention of her name. "So how are things with you? Life, work...love?"

"You want it all in that order?" Michael grinned. Tom was grateful to see that smile. "Yeah mate."

"I'm all good."

"And the Practice?"

"Yeah I've got my momentum back."

"That's good to hear."

"And you?" Michael asked.

"It's the usual for me. You know; victims of pathological narcissists."

"That is by far the most fascinating of all the cases in this business." Michael spooned some rice off his plate."

"I attended a Co-dependency workshop with Russ Rosenthal."

"Interesting?"

"Yes absolutely valuable. Not every narcissistic abuse survivor should be labelled as a Co-dependent personality. It's not one shoe fits all. Instead a more specific definition would be Self Love deficit disorder. These people are likely to have experienced some form of neglect or narcissistic abuse in their childhood and when it comes to adulthood they feel most comfortable with individuals that subject them to the abuse they experienced when they were a child.

"It's familiar territory I guess. Attracted to it like a magnet," said Michael.

"Exactly."

"So what's the therapy?" Michael asked.

"It sounds simple but in the scheme of things it becomes the most powerful weapon that these people will ever have."

"Which is?"

"Self discovery and self love. Looking in the mirror, finding your real self and loving the person you see."

"Hmm...," said Michael.

"This child somewhere along the line lost their sense of self," Tom sipped on his beer.

"Or they never had it in the first place..." added Michael.

"Exactly. For some reason they never got to develop a sense of self because of trying to be the person that they thought would be most lovable."

"The Ignored and Neglected child," said Michael.

"Yes. The neglect helps the child assume that they are not lovable so they morph themselves into who they think is pleasing. And in that process of morphing and re-morphing they lose themselves. These kids are quite intelligent because they have learnt to adapt themselves and blend into the environment they are in, no matter how harsh the conditions."

"It's like looking into a mirror and seeing no one there. No reflection at all." Michael looked at the plant that he had seen Sofia admiring the day she visited his home.

"That's right," said Tom.

"A painful position for a child to be in but fascinating in that it's a journey of finding themselves and loving that person that they find." Michael looked thoughtful.

"I tell you the workshop is worth going on."

"Absolutely. It's exactly what I need to get a fresh perspective for one of my clients who could be a classic example of Self love deficit." Michael put down his knife and fork. He had cleaned his plate. "But let me ask you. Is it then a case of the person willing themselves to the point of self love through affirmations maybe?"

"Not exactly. For these clients affirmations are difficult to do because their most painful memories of what happened to them in childhood are locked away and they simply can't remember what happened or why they self hate. It's difficult to persuade themselves that they are lovable until they recall and address what happened to them."

"Hmm... painful," said Michael.

"Indeed. So it takes a session with a highly skilled Hypnotherapist to help them to unlock the vault. Whatever surfaces from the vault is then dealt with in their psychotherapy sessions."

"I like that; getting to the root. Fascinating."

"I will send you the details for the course. Mate this food was delicious." Tom had cleaned his plate too.

"There's plenty more."

"No I need to be able to walk out of your house and not crawl out."

Michael chuckled. Tom drank the last of his beer.

"More?" asked Michael.

"No what I need is a strong coffee."

"Me too."

"So I've got to ask. How about love life? Are you seeing anybody?"

"Here we go again."

"It's a simple question mate. Are you putting yourself out there? Or is there anyone that you have your eye on?"

"It's complicated," said Michael.

"What do you mean it's complicated?"

"It's not that simple."

"Mate all you need is a good woman. Not a complication." Michael nodded.

"What about the woman that you saw at the Chelsea Flower show? You seemed quite keen on her."

"Yeah I know. I was...I am."

"The Chelsea Flower Show starts tomorrow. People who go to those places are often repeat offenders."

"Repeat offenders? What do you mean?"

"What I mean idiot is that most people who like plants would probably go again and again. So you might bump into her."

"Tom I don't think..."

"Don't think mate. Just go. And if you do go then that's a sign that it's not just your head involved. If I know anything about you it's that this woman, whoever she is, has really taken you. I haven't seen you like this since..."

"Since Clara you mean? It's ok mate. We can say her name. I'm coming to terms with what happened."

Tom nodded. "Follow your heart Michael."

CHAPTER 17

The sweet scent of the rose garden was little relief to Sofia's aching ankle. She feared that she might have sprained it whilst edging in to get a closer look at the rare species of Hydrangea in the award winning garden on display at the Chelsea flower show. This was her yearly event for inspiration and stress relief. For many years she had walked the gardens alone. Uche had never taken an interest. He always made excuses on the day and would wiggle his way out of going. Sofia would drown the pain in the beauty that the gardens displayed. This year was no different. She was alone again trying to nurse an injury. She walked over to her wooden bench underneath the Bonsai Olive tree, sat down and relaxed under its shade. It was her yearly ritual to walk around the gardens then to sit at her wooden bench to rest. She bent down and gave her ankle a massage for some light relief. Then sitting up she drank in the peaceful sound of the water fountain that was behind her.

Someone came and sat down beside her. She shifted along and put her brochure on her lap. She was not too keen on sharing her little piece of heaven with a complete stranger but she had to comply.

"Hello, Sofia."

She was startled as she was not expecting to hear her name being called, especially not at the Chelsea flower show. She turned to look at the stranger sitting next to her. Her cheeks began to pink up.

"Michael."

"How are you?"

"I'm alright. What a surprise."

He set his brochure down on the bench. "It's good to see you."

"Thanks it's good to see you too." She smiled and took in his wonderful friendly smile and suddenly her world was alright.

"Enjoying the gardens?" Michael asked.

"Yes it's beautiful. And you?"

"I absolutely love it."

"Is this your first time?" she asked.

"No. We used to come here every year."

"We?"

His eyes caught hers. "My wife and I."

Her eyes were slightly glared as she tried hard to hide her surprise laced with disappointment. "Oh, I didn't realise you were married."

"She died a few years ago."

"I'm so sorry." She put her head down and looked at the butterflies on the green platform shoes she was wearing. She felt sad for him but angry with herself because she felt that she had been selfish. There was a brief silence.

"Her name was Clara."

She looked up. "What a beautiful name."

"We would come every year. She loved it and after a while I began to love it too. When she passed I stayed away I plucked up the courage to come back. It was one of her wishes that I continue coming to the show so this is me trying to keep that promise."

She nodded. He was grateful for the obvious and kind attention that she gave him.

She wanted to ask how she died and how he had been coping but she could not bring herself to speak.

He helped her. "Let me show you something."

"Ok."

He stood up and she followed. Miraculously the ache in her

ankle had disappeared.

They walked side by side in silence with the fresh breeze flowing through the gathers of her dress. He led her straight down and then guided her to take a left. Walking a little further they were embraced by the scent of lemon and Bergamot from the lemon tree garden.

"You know in all the years that I've been coming to Chelsea I have never bothered coming down here," she said.

They reached the entrance of a very tranquil place. He led her down the white marble paving stones. Either side was a pool with lily pads floating on the surface. She took in the purples, greens and blues. He watched her take in the beauty. She took a left and he took a right.

"I'll meet you in the centre." He smiled playfully.

She smiled too. "Ok." She stopped to look at a spiral brass statue. It looked like an orange peeled in one. She put one hand on it to steady herself so that she could slip off her shoes. The soles of her feet were embraced by the coolness of the paving. Her eyes took in the soft palate of flower colours; the blues, lilacs and soft peach on a white canvas of shrubbery.

Slowly she reached the centre where there was an array of pink roses. To the left Michael was standing by the floating shelf on the gardens concrete wall. In the centre of the shelf was a single bonsai juniper tree.

"Juniper," said Sofia.

"What?"

"You're standing by a Juniper." She pointed at the bonsai.

"Nice," he said.

An interesting feature was a copper hanging seat for two. She sat on the green and copper coloured cushion and began to sway from side to side. He watched as she swayed. She looked happy. He sat on a seat sculptured out of a rock and waited.

They sat in that moment with no one saying a word. She was in a place of content with a slight breeze caressing her cheeks. The weather was just right. The mood was just right. It was perfect to allow one to off load the burdens. His content was seeing her at peace and allowing her to sway..

"Sofia"

Startled, she turned to see who was calling her. Michael was also set out of balance by the alarming call.

"Is that you Sofia?"

"Stuart" she said.

"What's all this then? You're enjoying all this without me?" Stuart shook his head as all six foot of him walked towards the copper hanging seat. He was smart casually dressed. A crisp ironed shirt, no crease in sight. Every item of clothing had a label of repute. Everything was in order, nothing hanging out or sagging. He presented with carefully manicured hair, beard and nails. The latter showing no sign of his Landscape gardener profession. He embraced her with Cocoa butter, cafe latte skin and a scent that suggested sophistication. He noticed Michael sitting on the rock but focused on Sofia.

"What are you doing here?" she asked.

"I'm a Landscape gardener. So what do you expect?" He gave the brightest smile that Sofia could not resist."Have you just arrived?"

"No I've been here for a bit. I'm here with..." Sofia had tried to begin to introduce Michael when like a gentle wind he interrupted her. "It's beautiful here. I come every year just to lap up the exuberance." For a while he carried on about the technicalities of landscaping and the intricate details of horticulture. Sofia was attracted by the knowledge and care that he took to describe every detail. She was almost going into a trance drinking up his kind politeness and obvious attractiveness when she noticed Michael in the corner of her eye. Immediately she came to her senses. She began to feel bad about how rude she had been. Michael had now stood up and mimed the words 'I should go now.' She was torn between not knowing how to interrupt Stuart and being worried about how Michael would view her if he left without her introducing him. She toyed between the two opinions then suddenly a wave rose from within her.

"Sorry to interrupt you Stuart. Let me introduce you to

Michael."

"Who's Michael?" asked Stuart.

"Come, Michael," Sofia said.

"I should be going now Sofia." Michael walked towards them and stood by Stuart.

"We haven't met. I'm Stuart."

"Michael Marshall."

They gave each other a strong handshake.

"You are?.."

Sofia was anxious about what Michael would say."

"We're associates."

"Oh I see. Sofia and I are friends." He put his hand on Sofia's shoulder which made her a tad bit uncomfortable but she wore it well."

Michael saw her discomfort. "It was lovely to see you Sofia."

"Thanks for everything Michael."

He gave her a warm handshake. He always seemed to manage to ground her and bring her to a place of peace. But he had to leave.

"Nice to meet you," said Stuart.

"Likewise," said Michael and he walked away.

As they watched him walk away Stuart nodded. "Nice guy."

"Yes."

"Should we have lunch?"

"That will be lovely," she said. They walked with arms interlocked towards the cafe.

As Michael walked away he tried hard not to give in to the urge to look back. He failed and then had to deal with the churn in his stomach caused by the sight of Sofia walking away, arms interlocked with Stuart.

He struggled for months trying to convince himself that he needed to do away with the Therapist- client crush that he was developing. He toyed with the possibility of referring Sofia to another therapist to avoid him crossing any professional lines but each time he decided against it as he could not leave her. He thought hard about whether the crush could be something more and that it was likely that his heart was not telling him lies.

He pondered on the first time that he had seen her at the Chelsea Flower show. He saw her in the distance. He was attracted by her beauty and touched by her loneliness. He watched her sit under the Olive Bonsai and wondered who she was and what her name was. He remembered that the courage to walk up to her and strike up a conversation was futile. Then again he remembered that two weeks after the show he had bumped into her at the garden centre. She had knocked over the thyme and he had picked it up for her. In her polite and shy way she thanked him, once again without eye contact. Then her steps were too quick and he was distracted by his neighbour Mrs Potts who needed help to shift her Hydrangea onto her trolley.

He turned around and she had gone. It was a missed opportunity to chat and offer to buy her a coffee at the garden centre cafe.

He was amazed that his path had crossed this beautiful woman's again but he had failed to make himself known to her. However, when she walked into his practice as the Sofia Blackwell who had booked an 11'o clock psychotherapy session with him he was certain that this woman in some way was to be a significant part of his destiny. He was just yet to understand what part of his destiny she was meant to fill.

CHAPTER 18

Stuart and Sofia's relationship began to blossom in an unexpected way. He was kind, he was thoughtful. If she needed a box to be lifted he was her arms. If she was tired and needed a meal he would jump in as the chef. He did her groceries and offered to be her 'on call' bouncer in the probable event that Uche would decide on an 'out of the blue' appearance at her door step. He was touched by her history and promised that he would try to right the wrongs done to her.

They would sit sipping wine whilst discussing every herb under God's beautiful sun. They would analyse the tantalising flavour of lovage in a chicken sandwich, the attractiveness of borage in patio pots and the versatility of mint. He was funny and he was witty and she found it very hard to resist his constant invitations to drive down country roads to view his vastly growing portfolio of landscaping. She loved his company and was grateful that he filled the days that were previously lonely and empty. He was there for her. She only needed to ask and he was there. It was an utter surprise to her as she was finally beginning to feel she was in the unfamiliar territory of happiness.

Stuart had grown up 'alone' in a household with a very angry Evangelical father. Reverend James Green believed that order, cleanliness and obedience were akin to Godliness. Anything short of these standards was a sin punishable by humiliation.

His wife Sophia was agreeable, timid and obedient. He was instantly attracted to her. It was difficult to tell whether he was attracted to her agreeable face or her agreeable manner which was at most times painfully annoying. It was a manner which gave access to the abuser. She was a girl that had lost herself and had a strong desire to be loved.

James set out to tell her that they were to be married following a courtship. He barked the order and she complied. His suave manner had hooked her. His handsome face had trans-fixed her and when he gave her his arm she became the admir-ation of her friends. The courtship led to a flamboyant wedding at the village parish and subsequently an ordination that led James into the priesthood. She was only 15 but Sophia could not have been prouder as the Mrs Reverend James Green.

They lived in the picturesque town of Port Antonio, 60 miles from Kingston. Life was simple. James spent his time at the parish whilst Sophia learnt how to bake under the watch-ful eye of her mother-in law the Reverend Mrs Green Senior. However, money was scarce and jobs were few and far between. The offerings in the collection plate that was handed around every Sunday were only enough to run the church and give the Reverend Senior and his wife a modest living. They could not afford to employ James as a vicar and so he needed an income of his own to take care of his young wife. The Caribbean hard-ships caused a righteous dissatisfaction to grow in James and his young ambitious friends.

Then the opportunity of a lifetime came. Their tickets had been paid for and their suitcases had been packed. James had preferred to go ahead alone and then to send for Sophia later. However, the bellowing anger of his father made him to decide otherwise.

"No son o' mine is crossing the waters to fornicate with every woman in sight. I will not have the sin of the flesh lurking in my house. Do you hear me?" bellowed Reverend Green Senior.

"Yes Sir," said James almost cowering.

"And what's to happen to Sophia? Give that idiot of a girl

two seconds and she will find herself in bed with any nonsensical fool who will promise her an 'I do'. I will not have shame in my house. Do you hear me?"

"Yes Sir."

"Now Sophia is as stupid as they come but she is your wife and you are taking that girl with you," he shouted as his spit sprayed all over James face.

"Yes Sir," said James as he trembled and tried to purse his legs to prevent the urine from trickling down. But this was no help at all as James saw the angry look on Reverend Greens face who had noticed the growing patch of wet on the front of the trousers.

That is how Sophia found herself with James on board the HMS Empire Windrush on their way to England for the 'good life'. On the 22nd of June 1948 they arrived at Tilbury Dock Essex.

However, their exhilaration upon arrival was swiftly snuffed out by the hardships they faced. Door upon door was closed in their faces. There was no work and there was no accommodation. Their constant worry was how they would survive. They had left the caress of the sun and the coolness of coconut water for what? Is what Sophia would constantly moan. And James would lash back with descriptions of her poverty-minded, ungrateful behind. They would constantly argue whilst sharing settee upon settee in the homes of well wishing Jamaicans that they met at the local church in Tilbury.

Eventually James found work in a lumberyard which paid enough for a room in a half burnt down building in Brixton. Sophia subsequently found work as a seamstress with a pay packet that was more rewarding than his. He downplayed it and told her that the reason for the pay difference was because her skin was as 'white' as porcelain compared to his 'Arabica coffee bean' complexion. Sophia brushed it off and enjoyed the new found progress of being able to pay for sugar. However, the stress of the cold, the low pay and the constant rejection because of the colour of their skin drifted them apart. Their relationship consisted of James barking like a dog and Sophia standing at obedient attention.

James took to drinking and philandering. If Sophia plucked up the courage to confront him she was rewarded with a beating and a warning that she should never question the integrity of a Reverend.

He made it difficult for her to make any meaningful friendships. The only women allowed in their home were the women that he secretly bedded behind her back whilst they pretended to be her friends. Her life was lonely, only surrounded by the criticisms of her husband.

However a glimmer of hope appeared when 25 years later Sophia fell pregnant at the age of 40. It seemed to be what their marriage needed as James became more attentive, more homely and insisted that they go to church every Sunday. Nine months later their son was born and they named him Stuart. Sophia then died during childbirth when Stuart was 12 leaving Stuart and his younger sister Dorcas to be raised by James who had gone up the ranks to become the Associate Pastor of the Calvary Church of God in Christ.

When Stuart Green met Sofia at the garden centre he was smitten and when he learnt that her name was Sofia (similar to that of his mother) he fell deeply in like such that he wasted no time to tell her that he thought she was beautiful and wanted to get to know her better. He was a matter of fact, no beat around the bush kind of man and Sofia liked it. She was drawn to him even more when she learnt of the sadness of his childhood and how he lived in constant fear of his father. The sadness of how alone he felt touched her heart especially when she heard about the unreasonable cruelty of his step mother Prudence and how he and Dorcas became outcasts when their baby step sister Daisy was born. They found common ground and to them this became love. She was tired of infatuations that would go nowhere. She had come to the place of reality and this discarded the fantasy of Michael Marshall. Stuart was real and attainable. And most importantly, compared to Uche, Stuart was a complete breath of fresh air.

CHAPTER 19

Sofia kept looking at the test kit on the kitchen counter and ever so often she would shift her gaze to the door, waiting for Uche to walk through it. He had said that he would be a little late but Sofia was slowly getting wound up. She looked again at the test kit wondering about how her conversation that evening would pan out. As she considered many thoughts she heard the key turn in the lock. Uche walked in and threw his over the shoulder bag on the counter. "How far?"

"Hi Uche."

"You are still awake?"

"Yeah. How was your day?"

"Long." He picked up his mail from the mail tray and flung his keys in. He sat down on the settee next to her with a letter opener. He reached over and fondled her. She smiled at him but she hated it when he did that. She did not know why but it made her cringe. She loved her husband but she did not know why she was, at most times uninterested. But she pretended well.

She stood up to avoid him from going any further. "Are you hungry?" she asked.

"Yes. What is there to eat?"

"Rice and chicken. Do you want some?"

"Yes but I will get it myself." He never liked being served any food. He washed and ironed his own clothes. That is how he wanted it so that is how they lived.

"Ok then." She sat back down.

As he began to read his letter he fondled her again. He put the letter down and asked her if she had taken a shower. She felt sick but responded to let him know that she had. She moved in closer to give him greater access to reach her.

"I have something to tell you," she said.

"What is it? I love you," he said as he moved in closer.

"I think I'm pregnant."

He looked at her, stopped touching her and reached for the TV remote on the coffee table.

"Uche did you hear what I said?"

"I'm not hungry. I ate some Ebba and eghusi (mashed cassava and meat stew) at sister Tolu's house. It was sweet."

"Sister Tolu? Why did you go to sister Tolu's house?" Sofia felt jealousy begin to seep in.

"Listen I am her brother in Christ and she needed some help with a broken shelf. She had nobody else so I offered to help."

"So out of all the men in the church you are the only one who can fix a broken shelf? Why is a married man visiting a single woman at this time of night? Why Uche?"

"She's a single mother. Not a single woman."

"It's the same thing mate."

"It's not. Anyway it's over and I'm now here with you. But sorry I can't eat your food."

She was smarting but decided to remain focused on the topic at hand. "Well can you at least respond to what I told you."

"What?"

"I told you that I'm pregnant Uche."

"Are you sure?" He put the TV remote down.

"Yes of course I'm sure." At this point Sofia was in a whirlwind of emotion. She had no idea whether he was happy about the news or not.

"You did the test?" he asked.

"Yes I did."

"Do you have it?"

Sofia walked over to the counter and picked up the kit. She

came and thrust it into his hand. He looked down and saw the word *'Pregnant'* in blue. He heaved a big sigh. Her heart was beating fast.

"You have to do the test again."

"What?"

"I said you have to do it again."

"What do you mean do it again?"

"I mean just what I said because I'm not accepting this."

"Not accepting what? Are you not accepting that we're having a baby? Or what is it Uche?"

"I said do the test again. I don't believe that it's accurate. I'm just considering your age. If you were younger I would agree."

"Uche I've done the test four times. I just didn't tell you."

"What? So you kept something like this away from me?"

"I wanted to be sure before I said anything."

"This is unbelievable. You hide this from me but you expect me to believe whatever you say."

"Uche I am your wife and I am telling you that I am pregnant. Why can't you trust that?"

"You hide the pregnancy from me and you expect me to trust you. You are just trying to trap me."

"Trap you? What are you talking about? How can I trap my own husband with a baby? For goodness sake Uche we're going to be parents."

"Do the test again." He reached for the TV remote.

She had lost her energy. "Why do you treat me like this?"

"Like what?"

"Why can't we just be normal?"

"Normal? You don't know how lucky you are."

"Lucky?"

"Do you know that Peter constantly complains about his wife? He thinks Ngozi is ugly."

Sofia frowned. "That's not true."

"What will you believe? He didn't want to marry her. He had to marry her out of honour because she was pregnant. But that's not me. Were you pregnant when I married you? You don't know what you have. Somebody actually wants to be with you but you dramatise and twist everything. Somebody says do the test again and you fly off the handle. Are you ok in your head?"

At that point she felt numb. He had spun her around in knots. She was exhausted and did not know whether he wanted her to get food for him or whether she had remembered to tell him her good news. Then she couldn't understand why she had suddenly felt a strong dislike for Peter. She was certain however, that she had become very unhappy. She looked at him. He responded with indifference and picked up the TV remote again to flick through the channels.

She stood up and went to bed. She wanted to cry but she couldn't. The tears just wouldn't flow.

CHAPTER 20

Three months later Hortense heard her telephone ring in the living room. She had left London and found a good job and an attractive two up, two down house in Lancashire. It was something she had always wanted – a house with rent she could afford all on her own. She did not hesitate to take up the opportunity as Sofia had gone off to rent a flat with her husband.

She picked up the receiver. "Hello."

"Hortense it's me."

"Sofia, long time. Is everything ok in paradise?"

Sofia breathed heavily down the phone. "I lost the baby." There was a silence longer than usual. "Hortense are you there?" The line went dead. Sofia rang the line again. There was no answer. She dialled the number again. This time there was an answer.

"Oh I'm so sorry I had to hang up. My boss was on another line. Right now we are doing a very important project so I've been on call. Without me they can't sanction things so I had to take the call. So how are you? Some of us are no longer important to you. When was the last time we spoke? Since you got married you have been distant."

Hortense and Uche had fallen out after the graduation. According to Uche, Hortense had disrespected him and was therefore no longer welcome in their home. Sofia had tried to smooth things over but Uche would not budge. Hortense had said good riddance and told Sofia that she would never set foot in their marital home unless Uche, her sorry excuse for a husband, came to Lancashire to apologise. The latter was unlikely thus Sofia spent most of her married life alone as Uche's friends never became hers.

"I haven't been distant," she said. "I guess it is married life," she explained. "And I'm sorry I have not called," were the words that firmly placed her on the defensive shelf again.

She felt guilty and decided that she shouldn't mention her baby again. She was in the hospital emergency room and didn't know who else to call. Uche had taken hours to leave work saying that he couldn't find his manager to ask for permission to be by her side. When he finally showed up at the hospital Sofia found herself being embarrassed and apologising to the nurses for his indifference. She behaved as if it was her fault that he did not care. No sooner than he had arrived he left after an embarrassing argument with her. He was mortified that she actually had the "guts" to present herself before the Consultant with bloodied legs. He wondered how a woman of her age could not find the sense to wash herself. "Do you know what this does to me as a man, as a husband? Why are you putting me under this stress? My own wife is stinking. Me, Uche Chidinma Onyeme should face this kind of embarrassment? God forbid." He squeezed his lips, called her dirty and then walked off in a huff. "I'll be back," he said. "I'm sorry," she said but he had gone. Two hours later she found a text from him. *'I have to leave. I will see you tonight. Sorry working.'*

That is how Sofia found herself alone wondering who to call. She dared not tell Skye as she would have immediately gotten on the next flight home. Sofia didn't want to ruin her holiday. So she was left with Hortense. However, judging from her conversation with Hortense it was clear that Hortense had not heard what she said so she made light casual conversation with a very large lump in her throat. "I just thought I'd say hi to you."

"Well thanks for calling Sofia."

"Ok goodbye Hortense."

"By the way I'm sorry you lost the baby."

Before Sofia could express her surprise that her friend had indeed heard her, the line went dead.

When she got home that evening she limped to the bathroom. As soon as she opened the door she slumped to the ground feeling defeated. All over the floor was a pool of her blood in a coagulated mess.

CHAPTER 21

"Congratulations You are a father now. Did we ever think this would happen when we were kids?"

"Thanks man."

"So how is Ngozi? I'm sure she is sleeping now."

"Yes she had a tough time but she is resting now. She did a good job."

"Ok Peter. We will find time to visit you guys and the new addition."

"Ok thanks my guy. We will see you and Sofia soon."

"Hey Sofia." Uche called out to Sofia who was in the kitchen. She had been secretly eating a slab of chocolate cake that she had bought from Greggs earlier that day. She had returned to binge eating. Nothing fit her and her self esteem had plummeted to seemingly a point of no return. She swallowed quickly and hid the cake slice at the back of the cupboard.

"Yes Uche," she gulped down a shot of diet coke and a tablespoon of martini. After losing the baby the taste of martini rosso was the only thing that encouraged her to face her day.

"Good news."

She popped her head round the living room door. Her eyes were sunken with dark circles. Her hair was dishevelled. "What's the good news?"

"Peter and Ngozi have given birth"

She was a mixture of emotions. She was genuinely happy for

them but couldn't help but to remember her own painful loss. "That's great news" she said. "Boy or a girl?"

"It's a girl."

"Lovely. Have they named her yet?"

"We will attend the naming ceremony two weeks from now."

"Naming ceremony?"

"Yes its Yoruba custom to hold a celebration to name your child. I guess we will find out the name then."

"Ok that's great."

Sofia's life had definitely taken a few turns. Unable to cope with the loss of the baby, she lost her job. This meant she was at home and financially dependent on Uche. She was frequently left alone. She barely had money for anything. Any requests for money were met with excuses. He lived the lavish lifestyle with designer clothes, expensive gadgets and trips to America. She was left behind to suffer alone in the spare bedroom that he forced her to move into. He needed "space" and would only summon her into his room for her to perform her marital obligations. But she could never bring herself to tears. Instead she stared out the window like a wounded animal, bearing the agony. She stared hard and long as if waiting for him to come back as a transformed man who at the least loved her.

He wanted time alone to relax. And each departure would be swiftly followed by showers of gifts to pacify her and to prove that, even though he had punished her, he still loved her in his own peculiar way.

The recurring theme was that Sofia would be rewarded for her pain. Signs of happiness were crushed. Pain was welcomed by gifts.

He wanted to chip away at her confidence one chip at a time until she was nothing. Because when he looked in the mirror all he could see was Uche, reigning supreme. There was no room for anyone else. Other people were just the fuel to satisfy his unhealthy appetite for their lives. Sofia was his supply and he had well and truly depleted her.

He would confuse her to avoid confronting questions about suspected infidelities with attractive co-workers. Her queries were met with, "It's all in your head," or "I am here trying for a baby with you. But it's not enough. You accuse me of having an affair. Is it because she is good looking?" he would say. This would always cut her to the core.

Then to make her walk on more eggshells she was in constant fear of losing her home. They were evicted twice and his excuse was her unemployment.

Eventually they moved in with Peter and Ngozi where the insults moved up a notch. Hi mantra was Sofia was not a good cook, or she was terrible at cleaning. Then to top it all it became about how she could not get pregnant.

The dehumanising treatment brought Sofia to her tipping point. She had had enough of the constant disrespect. For a while Hortense had taken it up on herself to be in Sofia's ear. Late night calls for hours telling Sofia that she was being used and that Uche did not care for her. Hortense was of the view that if Sofia didn't do it first Uche was surely going to leave her. Hortense took on the *'leave Uche project'* with venom that even Sofia felt was a bit excessive. "Make sure you leave after he has gone to work," she said. "When he gets home he will find the shelves of your wardrobe empty. That's what that bastard deserves."

CHAPTER 22

Sofia moved into the second bedroom of Hortenses's two bedroom house. Just as Hortense had envisioned Uche came home to empty shelves.

Peter and Ngozi had been out and had not seen Sofia leave. When they arrived home they assumed that she was in her bedroom watching television and chewing on biscuits.

Uche was in disbelief but he knew exactly where she had gone. All night Peter and Ngozi were trying to pacify Uche who had been pacing the corridors planning what he would do to Hortense.

"Sofia has not got her own mind. She allows that single woman to poison her. Hortense is jealous. God forbid if I meet that woman in the street. Who does she think she is trying to break my marital home?"

"Uche calm down."

"What do you mean calm down? My wife is missing; all because she was giving her ear to that idiot."

He rang Sofia's mobile several times with no response. Then he began ringing Hortense. His blood began to boil as she was not responding either. He rang and rang until finally there was a glimmer of hope.

"Hello."

"Can I speak to my wife please?"

"She's not here."

His voice was raised. "Hortense, can I speak to my wife please?"

"I said she's not here."

"Where's my wife?"

"Did you not hear what I said? I'm not Sofia's keeper."

"You are a manipulative snake. Peter this woman is a snake."

"Uche calm down," said Peter in the background.

"Who are you calling a snake?" said Hortense.

Uche shouted. "I said bring my wife to the phone."

"I'm not scared of you."

"Bitch"

Hortense became a viper. "Oh no you can't call me a bitch and get away with it. I'm no bitch."

"Idiot Marriage wrecker Because you have no man of your own you come to destroy others."

"You wrecked your own marriage that is why your wife walked out on you. So now you are blaming me? You are the idiot."

"Hortense God forbid, what I will do to you."

"Listen baby I'm from the Caribbean. Don't threaten me."

"Idiot." He shouted. "Who is a baby? Hey? Don't come against me oh You lie, you manipulate and now you are poisoning my wife against me. May God pour hot coals on you If my marriage is destroyed...." The line went dead. "Hello Hortense. Hortense," he shouted. "She has hung up on me. That bitch is in trouble." He paced up and down.

"Cool down Uche. Please," said Ngozi hoping that a female voice would pacify him. His volume turned down a notch. "Ngozi that girl. She is a snake. I know that Sofia is there. I could hear her in the background."

"I never liked that Hortense. The way she would speak to Sofia did not sit well with me," said Ngozi. The baby began to cry and Ngozi left to attend to her in the bedroom.

"My guy, don't get wound up over this Hortense. It's your wife that matters."

He began to tap his foot on the floor. This was a long standing habit that indicated that he was getting incredibly annoyed.

"Do you still have the number of that faith healer?"

"Yes why?" Peter inquired.

"I go do fire prayer tonight to get that witch out of the way. Hortense is a witch."

Peter giggled with caution. "Easy my guy, easy."

"If we were in Lagos just one or two guys would be sufficient to mash her up. She wants to challenge me? A married man? God forbid." He clicked his thumb and middle finger. He leant forward, grabbed a handful of roasted nuts that were on the coffee table and began to chew ferociously whilst staring at the wall intently and deep in thought.

"Easy, Uche. Cool down. Remember immigration. Any slight mistake would mess you up. Don't ruin your future over this girl Hortense. Anyway why is she so hot on meddling in your marital issue?"

"Is it not Sofia who tells her everything?"

"Well that's women for you. They talk. But this Hortense her vex(anger) is on another level. I hope you have not been messing around with her."

"Me, Uche Chidinma Onyeme who is a married man messing around with someone like Hortense? God forbid." He clicked his thumb and middle finger and mimicked a spit to the ground to signify his disgust.

"Ah Why not? 'She get fine body' (she has a fit body). 'Use im brain' (stimulate your imagination)," said Peter.

Uche looked away. "That woman stinks. I don't sleep with stinking woman and on top of that she is a witch." He mimicked a spit to the ground again.

"My guy, I think you have sampled her. Because her vex is on another level." Peter began to chuckle.

"Abeg (please) help me get phone card. I need to call my sister in Nigeria. I need her to call Sofia."

"Ok but what I know is that Sofia loves you. Just try to speak to her if you can. I think she will come around. Every marriage has problems. I think you can solve this one. What you need to do is give that girl a baby. That will keep her mind occupied."

"Are you mad? Sofia is so fat now but you want to put 'belle' (pregnancy) on top of it. You want to kill me? Then you want me to come squeeze my own 'pikin'(child) with your own in this small flat? God forbid." They burst into laughter.

CHAPTER 23

Sofia had lain on the bed all night drenching the duvet with her tears. Her eyes had turned from a bright red to an off purple because of the hours that she had been crying. Hortense knocked on the bedroom door asking to come in.

"Come in Hortense."

Hortense pushed open the door dressed in her flamboyant, pink, furry night gown. "What do you want for breakfast?"

"Hortense I really appreciate what you..."

She interrupted "Don't mention it. That's what friends are for." Hortense sat on the bed next to Sofia. For a few minutes they sat and gossiped. They laughed, talked about how rude Uche was to Hortense and then laughed some more. Sofia felt like it was old times with her roommate. This took her back to the times when she thought that she was happy.

"You have to leave him," said Hortense. "Look at the state of you Sofia."

"What's wrong with me?"

"I mean look in the mirror." Sofia stood up and looked at her fuzz-ball dishevelled hair and grubby clothes.

"What do you see?"

"An unhappy person." Tears pooled in her eyes.

"Well what I see is a woman that has been chewed up and spat out."

She managed a slight grin. "I'm not dead yet."

"This is not funny Sofia. You need a new life. I'm not telling you to leave him but this is not doing any good for you."

She nodded.

"Right. You are getting up and going to the job centre."

"Job centre. Ah yes."

"You need income to get your own place. Start afresh without that idiot."

"You're right. Thanks Hortense."

"Come down. I'm making eggs.

Sofia stood for a while staring into the mirror before she made her way down to have something to eat.

Two months into staying with Hortense, Sofia had still not managed to secure a job that she was qualified for. She couldn't even get the menial jobs. One cleaning job rejected her because of her lack of experience, all others rejected her because she was 'over qualified'. This caused her confidence to plummet. Her weight over exerted the scales no thanks to the midnight cake binges organised by Hortense who was always conveniently on a diet when it was time to eat them. Sofia could not fight the temptation and would fall for it every time. "Help yourself," Hortense would say. "Next time I will get you a Victoria sponge if you like." Sofia would always respond with "No I really shouldn't," whilst falling for the temptation to pick up another slice. Coupled with this were the steadily increasing insults that she had been historically used to but it seemed that Hortense had breathed in a fresh new wind that had intensified her jabs.

"I'm sure it's the way you dress. I'm surprised you didn't get the job." She would follow this with, "I would offer to take you to where they can do your hair but only when you start working."

This would always come after Hortense had returned from work, "Are you sure you cleaned the whole house? It usually takes me 30 minutes but you have been here all day. I know you are not used to cleanliness but just try." Then especially after Sofia had finished surveying herself in the mirror came, "Uche is obviously into slim girls."

There was the shouting, which was a level that Sofia had never experienced. "I'm trying to help you" she yelled. And if Sofia dared to defend herself with her usual "I know you are really helping me but I'm sure that things will work out," Hortense would work herself up into a sweat. "That's insulting. That's really insulting. Why would you speak to me like that? How can things work out with that monster? You want to go back and have babies in that hell house?"

"I'm not saying I will go back Hortense. I'm just saying."

Hortense would slam a baguette on the kitchen counter and this would make Sofia jump. "Think of all your friends who have sacrificed to make your life better." Hortense would top this off with stomping to her bedroom and slamming the door, making Sofia jump each and every single time she did it. Books would be slammed on the floor. Shouting sessions would emerge because of the dust left on the staircase. Hortense had worked hard and succeeded at throwing eggshells all over the floor for her to crunch over.

Sofia started getting headaches. She would jump at any sudden noise and would be terrified of any spots she may have left on the bathroom floor or kitchen sink. She became obsessively concerned about her appearance; at a much higher level than when she was with Uche. She was compelled to ask Hortenses's' opinion of her choice of fuzz-ball hairstyle or her choice of cleaning product for the ground floor of the house. Afraid if Hortense would complain about the amount of milk she had poured in her tea and then subsequently give her a lecture about the cost of things and that "You don't care anyway because you sit around here getting fat. When are you getting a job?"

The jabs were endless. Slowly but surely she had found herself in another prison of total lockdown. Hortense had become another woman. Or maybe Sofia was finally beginning to see Hortense for who she really was and for the first time in a long time longed to return home to Uche.

CHAPTER 24

Hortense was so elated when the news came that her mother's Visa to travel to the UK from Jamaica had been granted. Her mother was to stay for a two month holiday.

Sofia was genuinely happy for Hortense and hoped that her mother would be the answer to pacifying Hortenses's' increasingly hot temper.

The day came when Mrs Ambrose was to arrive. Hortense had stayed overnight in London so that she could make it for her mother's 6am arrival at Heathrow airport. Sofia had remained behind in Lancashire under Hortenses's strict instructions to clean the house from top to bottom and to heat the food at 1.30pm ready for their arrival. Hortense had cooked a cheesy macaroni bake, jerk chicken, tomato cucumber and scotch bonnet salad, coleslaw and a sorrel punch chilling in the fridge. Sofia was allowed to make the apple pie and vanilla custard because she felt that by the time her mother had taken her fill of jerk chicken it wouldn't matter if the dessert was not up to scratch.

The doorbell rang. Sofia's heart had been racing all morning but it kicked up a notch at the thought that Hortense had arrived with her mother. Sofia had a sense of guilt that she had been living in Hortenses's house, virtually for free, and only able to contribute her job seekers allowance that had only recently started trickling into her bank account.

The guilt had been nurtured by Hortenses's eggshell slinging efforts and nurtured by Hortenses's friends who would come to the house constantly asking when she was leaving. They would cast disapproving eyes at Hortense when Sofia offered the unsatisfactory response of, "I will soon be on my feet and hopefully get my own place."

Chenai was the worst offender as she had made it her profession to make sure that Sofia knew just how much of a freeloader she had become.

Sofia had wondered why these friends had never become hers in spite of the number of years that she had known them. They were close to Hortense and favoured her. But there was a silent contempt for Sofia which made her wonder whether they were being fed little, white lies about her. These suspicions would enter her mind from time to time but were swiftly ignored because Sofia refused to allow herself to believe that Hortense could do such a thing. Nonetheless, as a result of their treatment of her she felt like a freeloader and was worried that Hortenses's mother would be angry at her for taking advantage of her daughter.

The front door opened. "Welcome home mummy." Sofia heard Hortense from behind the door. She bolted in whilst dragging two large suitcases.
Sofia jumped to the rescue. "Let me take those," she said.

"Oh thanks Sofia."

"No problem." Sofia squeezed and heaved her muscles so that she could take charge of the heavy suitcases. She was not going to be defeated by them because she had to prove that she could work for her dinner.

"Just put them in my room," said Hortense.
Sofia darted up the stairs with one suitcase. When she came back down the front door had been shut. She heard voices in the living room. Hortense and her mother had headed for the lounger. She grabbed the second suitcase, hoisted up her buttock muscles and dragged it up the stairs. When she came back down the living room door was open and she caught the back end of their conversation.

"It's ok Ma you can have a shower before your meal. You will be with me in my room. It is the door to the left at the top of the stairs."

Sofia butted in, "Hortense I cleaned out the spare room today and mum can have that room. I can sleep on the floor of the utility room until I leave; which should be in the next few weeks."

Hortense was silent with a look of surprise on her face.

"Welcome Mrs Ambrose. I'm Sofia. I've heard so much about you." Sofia moved in to shake Mrs Ambrose's hand. As she got closer there was an immediate waft of air.

With sudden haste a maroon curtain rolled out from the ceiling and hit the floor with a disturbing thud, dislodging a pile of dust that began to irritate her nose. The full length of it swayed from side to side swirling the dust into a cloud. She pulled back her outstretched hand, confused by what was happening. Mrs Ambrose and Hortense had disappeared.

Sofia watched the curtain as the swaying picked up speed. From behind was a sound of wailing. She found an opening in the curtain and moved in to peer at who was crying. As her hands touched the gathers they flew apart like the parting of the red sea. With her heart racing she walked through. In the midst of a thick cloud of smoke hundreds upon hundreds were sitting in neat circular rows from the tallest to the shortest and crying. In the centre was a coffin. At the side of the coffin she saw Nouara, dressed in rags and being held back by a man. It was Max.

"Mum" she said.

Nouara looked at Sofia and said, "That woman needs to leave." Nouara stretched out her hand and knocked Max over. Her fingers were pointed in a direction. Sofia turned her head to look at what her mother was pointing at. Max looked in the same direction and spoke. "Just leave Hortense. Please"

In front of her Mrs Ambrose stood tall and majestic with immaculate clothing. Everything was neat and tidy and in place. She looked much younger and smelt like the rose garden at the nursery that Sofia used to work at when she was happy;

when it was before Uche.

The woman had her hand stretched out for a shake. "Call me Hortense," she said. Memory banks quickly zoomed back in time to the moment where her world had begun to crash down. Her father had died and she saw her mum at her most vulnerable state. The very woman that had caused her mother so much misery was right in front of her. As their finger tips touched her mother disappeared. So too did the coffin and the wailing people. Sofia was back again in the living room standing in front of Mrs Ambrose with their hands interlocked in a shake and her face a very cold pale.

"Call me Hortense and I thank you for your kind consideration. Or perhaps you can call me Mrs H to avoid confusion." She chuckled. "That name has been in our family since the slavery days. From the time that Master Wilberforce named my great, great, great grandmother. She was born on a slave ship you know. She had an African name but they changed it. They said that as a baby she always used to crawl away from the cotton fields and after a panic they would find her rolling up with the apples in Master Wilberforce's garden. So he changed her name to Hortense which means 'of the garden'."

"I see. What a lovely story," Sofia said trying to hide her enormous discomfort resulting from her recent revelations.

"I hear you are a bit of a gardener yourself."

"Umm well I'm a Horticulturist."

"Same thing isn't it?"

Sofia chuckled. "Maybe it is."

As Mrs H sat down Sofia took the chance of a quick recap. Here she was; the object of her father's philandering, the thorn in her mother's flesh and the reason for her totally substandard, unhappy childhood. Then Sofia's heart bled for her mother when she remembered how in comparison to Mrs H her mother was indeed a very poor dresser.

CHAPTER 25

Sofia hit it off with Mrs H much to Hortenses's annoyance. She made Sofia laugh. She was a very charming and a 'no beat about the bush' kind of lady. She was very attractive and made regular express efforts to ensure that her nails, hair and makeup were on top form.

She started to take Sofia on walks all the way down to the river and back again. "Eat fruits Sofia" she would say. "Come on take a few days and eat just fruits all day and watch the weight fall off, instead of all these pills that they dish out nowadays. In my day all they told us was to climb up the mango tree, pick a few oranges and eat them at breakfast, lunch and dinner. If you do that Sofia we will begin to see your shape reappear. Eat as much as you want, but just fruits."

"Thanks Mrs H," she would say gratefully as the weight piling on her bottom was beginning to be a major cause for concern. Mrs H on the other hand was a fine, strong specimen perfectly sculptured. Even with the lines beginning to surface under her eyes she looked, young, healthy and beautiful. Sofia could understand why her father may have been attracted.

She had known from a young age that her father had a wondering eye but had always thought that he was just messing around and would eventually come to his senses. She remembered the day that she caught her dad coming out of his bedroom in the early hours of the morning with a woman half his age whilst her mother was fast asleep in the next room.

It was easy for her to understand her mother's pain as her mother's life had played out in her own. Where her husband had preferred others over her.

"Sofia I don't mean to pry but erm..." Mrs H paused "Don't be offended," she said again.

"Not at all. Please feel free to pry." Sofia smiled but behind the facade was a panic. She was worried that Mrs H had remembered the funeral. She was worried that there was going to be awkwardness.

Sofia had toyed with the idea of coming clean with Mrs H by telling her that she had seen her before at her father's funeral and that her mother had requested for her to be physically removed from the place. But the opportunity to come clean never surfaced.

"Well I noticed a ring on your finger but you are here living with us."

"I assumed Hortense had told you."

"You married?"

"Yes I am." That admission opened the lid on the shame she had kept in the jar of embarrassments. She was ashamed because she had failed at basic human relations.

She refused to succumb to the cliché *'everybody makes mistakes'* because to her, her life circumstances were not a mistake but a complete nightmare.

"I see. So where is he?"

"I left him."

"Why you do that?"

"I was just tired of the way he treats me."

"So you're just teaching him a lesson before you go back to him?"

Sofia was surprised by that comment. She was surprised that Mrs H had concluded that she was definitely going back. The reality was that Sofia had not thought that far. She was terrified of the prospect of being alone. Divorce was not an option that had entered her mind but she knew that his treatment of her was not right and should not be allowed to continue. Her leaving was akin to putting a plaster on a stab wound. She had no idea what she was doing. She was just making it up as she went along. "No I'm not going back," she said trying to sound confident."

Mrs H chuckled. "I see. Well I'm sorry to hear that. But are your parents happy with it."

She tried to hide the pain. "My parents passed away," she said.

"I'm sorry to hear that my dear."

"Thank you. It's ok."

"Your family name is Blackwell isn't it?"

She felt nervous. "Yes it is.

"You know I've come across many Blackwell's in my life-time. My neighbour in Jamaica is a Blackwell as well as half of the people that live on the street close to the coconut farm in my town." She chuckled.

"Really?"

"Yes really. What's your daddy's name?"

Sofia decided that there was no way Mrs H would connect the dots as it was such a long time ago. She decided that it was safe not to lie, or so she hoped. "Kingston."

"Kingston?"

"Yes Mrs H. You know we really should be getting back."

"And your mother's name?"

Sofia had let the cat out the bag so there was no point in conceal-ing anything anymore.

"Nouara," she said trying to moisten her parched throat with the bottle of water that she had held in her hand with sweaty tightness.

"Nouara?" Mrs H looked straight ahead, right through Sofia. The smell of rum laced with cigarette smoke lingered in the air. She could hear the faint sound of Bob Marley's "Stir it up... little darling..."

The intoxicating sound of his voice lingered. "Hortense I've already explained this to you before," he said. In a vision he came and stood right in front of her. He smelt the same. He wore his favourite chequered red shirt that she had bought for him at

Christmas.

"Kingston," she called out.

He carried on speaking as if he had not heard her. "This can't carry on," he said.

Those words pierced her as she remembered exactly how it felt when she heard him say those words for the very first time. That's when Mrs H saw the spitting image of herself standing in the corner of the room wearing the pink form fitting dress that she had adjusted to fit her hour glass figure. She had adjusted it to impress him and to entice him not to make the decision that, for weeks, he had been telling her he would make. She was several years younger with tears streaming down her face and wondering why the man who had told her that he would leave his wife for her was breaking everything off. She had given up everything for him. She had left the prospect of a new job in London and had turned down a good offer of marriage for a love affair in Dorset.

The most handsome man she had ever known had told her that he loved her and would marry her. Mrs H bled for her younger self.

"What does she have that I don't?" her younger self asked.

Kingston tried to reason with her. "I'm a married man Hortense."

"That never stopped you before. I gave up everything Kingston. Everything....I could have been married to Dean by now."

"So now you're blaming me? I never forced you not to marry the man." Kingston turned and looked at Mrs H, her older self. She looked back at him and felt the betrayal that she had felt all those years before. The young Kingston kept on walking until he walked right through her. Her younger self fell to the ground and curled up in a ball of bellowing cries until she dissipated into a puff of smoke. The smell of rum and cigarettes lifted. The record playing 'Stir it up' came to a screeching halt and Mrs H was once again standing, facing Sofia.

"Are you ok Mrs H?" Sofia asked.

"Yes I am dear. We should get back." She smiled a painful smile and led the way. Sofia decided against asking if Mrs H knew her parents because she was afraid of hearing the obvious answer.

"I never knew your parents by the way."
Sofia tried to process her shock.

"Did Hortense ever tell you about her dad?" asked Mrs H.

"Not really she just said that she never knew him."

"Well her dad died when she was two years old, so that's right she never knew him."

"Oh I didn't know. Hortense never said. I just assumed..." Sofia felt really sorry. "I'm really sorry."

"Well that's life. Thank you. Hortense is a hard nut to crack. She doesn't like to talk about it."

Sofia walked silently behind Mrs H feeling that she may have misjudged her friend harshly. Behind that seemingly mean persona was a girl who was hurting.

"Has Hortense ever seen photo's of your parents?"

"Erm yes. I think I've shown her a couple of times."
Mrs H stopped. "She's seen your daddy?"

"Yes I had loads of family photos in the flat that we shared."

"And how did she respond?" Mrs H continued walking.

Sofia remembered the day that she had decided to send her relationship with Hortense to the next level. She showed her the family photos then recalled how annoyed she felt when Hortense made some rude comments about her family's physical attributes. However, Sofia found it odd that Hortense had no photos of her own when they had agreed to have a family photo sharing time.

"She seemed ok Mrs H. I did feel a bit guilty though because she never grew up with her dad but I had loads to share about mine."

"I see. Yes it has been tough for her but she tries to hide it behind being rude to people. Somehow she feels that no one will get to the bottom of what's really happening."

"And what is happening if you don't mind me asking Mrs H?"

"She's in pain is what is happening. But pay her no mind," Mrs H said as she walked down the pathway back to the house in silence.

They never spoke about the matter again. Sofia resolved that Mrs H was not the woman that she had seen at her father's funeral but just someone who looked very similar.

When the two months came to an end Mrs H took Hortense into the kitchen and closed the door shut. They were in there for half an hour. There was silence then occasional times where Hortense could be heard saying *"That's my choice to make,"* and *"Why should I."* After a longer silence Hortense emerged from the kitchen with a face laced with anger on top of an underlying fear. She brushed past Sofia and went to drag one of the suitcases out the door. Mrs H emerged. She looked a little worn out. She stood tall and straightened her dress.

"Sofia Blackwell it has been a pleasure meeting you. Whatever choice you make be sure to have no regrets because regrets are a bitter pill to swallow." She walked out.

#

When Kingston Blackwell met Mrs H he was actively looking for a spark to switch things up because the life at home with Nouara was becoming bland. He argued with Nouara everyday telling her that her suspicions of him having affairs were just her imagination running wild. He swore his innocence but Nouara could not shake the feeling that he was being dishonest. He left her alone for days on end and this drained her. She lost her youth and her beauty began to fade. Ultimately Kingston had grown tired of her. Nouara carried the regret that she had left all that she knew and everyone that she loved to follow a man who had become a stranger to her even though they shared a home and two children who had unfortunately been caught up in the whirlwind of their toxicity.

It was a Friday evening when Kingston was just chilling with Max in Cocoloco, one of the very few Afro-Carribbean clubs in downtown Bournemouth. She stepped in. Mrs H was totally stunning. She commanded attention and Kingston was hooked. He wasted no time and walked up to her for a flirt.

She divulged information at a swift pace. He found out that she was engaged to the man who walked over to where he was talking to her, confidently re-claiming his territory and making Kingston back off. The man was a medical student at Bournemouth University and not impressed that his girl was being chatted up. However, in the following weeks Mrs H had made appearances at the club alone since her fiancé, Dean, had travelled to London for a Medical school placement. He saw the open door and took the opportunity to charm her. He worked on her for three weeks until the weaknesses in her character succumbed and started a full blown affair with him. Both selfishly dived in forgetting the rings on their fingers. He told her that he loved her and that he would leave Nouara so that they could build a life together. She had fallen in love and at top speed broke off her engagement. Next she was turning down a good job at a leading London hospital as a nursing assistant, all for the love of Kingston.

But as soon as she had given up everything for him he became hot and cold. Intimate one day and hardly reachable the next. He drove her mad, filled her with anxiety and she had not realised that he had become her addiction. Every day she wanted to know when he was going to leave Nouara and in turn he would make the empty promises. Every day she wanted to see him. There were days when he would want her and days when he needed space.

Then the day that changed her life forever, came. It was a simple but painful conversation where Kingston plainly told her that he would not be leaving his wife. He coldly warned her not to contact him as she would sorely regret it if she tried to ruin his marriage. Her efforts to make him change his mind were fruitless as he had completely become cold towards her.

Hortense tried to get Max to persuade Kingston to change his mind. Max, although fond of Hortense and well known for doing anything she asked him, told her that he could not come against a marriage. '*It was what God put together and who am I to stand against God?*' is what he told her. He also reminded her that he had told Kingston a long time ago that it was a bad idea to get involved with Nouara, '*But that old fool paid me no mind. So I'm sorry Hortense.*'

Broken hearted she moved to London to start a new job. Whilst in London she reconnected with her ex-fiancé Dean Ambrose. He still loved her and was willing to forgive all. They married with a small ceremony in Hackney, a two tier white marzipan frosted fruit cake and a bottle of pink Champagne. Dean's friends insisted that she was going to break his heart again but he would hear none of it as his heart was set on her.

Dean was a man of few words, never seen to make quarrel with anyone. Disagreements were dealt with dignity behind closed doors. Dean's closed door events became quite the talk of the town when Mr and Mrs Ambrose had found their way back to live in Dorset because of a job offer that the well known Doctor could not turn down. He paid no thought to the idea that he was returning to the Lion's den that had devoured his relationship the first time around.

It was then no surprise that in spite of just brief public sightings of the two together in a supermarket or in a bank, the rumour that quickly surfaced was that his wife was carrying on with Kingston.

Nouara was convinced that the rumours were true and spared no breath to nag and plead with Kingston about breaking her heart. Both Kingston and Hortense denied everything. Kingston laughed it off whilst Hortense assured the man that she had once lied to before that she would "never make the same mistake twice."

The significant moment came when Dean Ambrose called for a closed door event with Kingston Blackwell. He had suffered no end of humiliation with the gossip reaching his professional circles. He had had enough of Kingston's manipulative manner; a manner that enjoyed giving fuel to the gossip and winding up everyone's feelings.

The conversation lasted 30 minutes. Kingston emerged from behind the white varnished door to Dean's office. He had the usual manipulative grin lining his face but one could tell that it was held up by scaffolding that was trying to hide an intense fear. Kingston was terrified but layers of historical pride refused to allow him to admit it.

No one knew what transpired between Dean and Kingston but what was evident was that there were no longer frequent sightings of Kingston meeting Hortense in Supermarkets and if they did meet Dean would be present and Kingston would offer a mere, very respectful 'hello'. It seemed that the whole messy situation was well and truly over. Kingston seemed to have reformed and was trying to work on nurturing his young family. Things seemed to be on the mend when Nouara found out that she was pregnant with their second child Sofia.

Simultaneously Hortense and Dean were expecting their first child. However, this happiness was not long lived in the Ambrose family. Hortense miscarried.

CHAPTER 26

Uche had determined that he would not give up until Sofia was back by his side. Without fail Sofia received a stream of texts as a morning motivation to get her to pack her bags and go running back to him. The texts were a confused mess of up and down, hot and cold and love and hate. 'Come back home' he would say in a text. Sofia would respond with 'Leave me alone," Uche in return would lash out, 'Ungrateful human being.' She would respond again with 'Leave me alone' and his response 'You can't manage alone. Everything you have came from me. Look at you. That high level of success is just not in you. If it were not for me where would you be?' This would be followed by a long silence as Sofia nursed her wounds. It worked all the time and all that he needed to do next was to re-confirm what she already believed about herself. That she was nothing and nobody wanted her. After the long silence and after Sofia had wiped away her tears another text would appear on her phone in the fashion of 'Come home. You know I love you' Sofia would not respond then the final hook would be thrown in 'It was supposed to be a surprise but I will tell you now...I have rented a brand new place so that we can try for a baby'. It was a simple case of reminding her that no one else wanted her and that he was the only one who would love her. It was the perfect bait to lure the self hating, love starved young woman.

After Mrs H left, Hortense had morphed into a more difficult version of herself. Everything that Sofia did would annoy her. She was annoyed that Sofia had left toothpaste marks on the sink and annoyed that there were footprints on the white fake cashmere rug. It got to the point where Sofia would get nervous whenever Hortense opened the front door returning from work.

Hortense was angry that Uche had been sending her texts and trying to persuade her to leave.

"You'll regret it if you go back to him," she would say.

"Maybe I should at least try to make things work with him," was Sofia's attempt at justifying her intentions.

"Don't make me upset. After all he's done to you. I can't believe it."

"Hortense I just left without any explanation."

"What did you need to explain? You wanted to explain that you were leaving because he is an abusive bully? I'm lost Sofia."

"I think I should go back to him and..."

"What."

"He's got a new place Hortense."

"I can't believe this. Without any consideration for how I feel about this."

Sofia was a bit alarmed by that comment but had no time to process it.

"After all I have done all you think of is to go back to that animal of a man."

"Hortense I appreciate all you have done for me but I think it is time for me to go now. And give you your space back."

"You don't think I am worried about how he will treat you? You don't have to leave." In the several weeks that Sofia had stayed with Hortense this was the first time that Hortense was absolute about wanting her to stay.

"I appreciate you Hortense but I need to..."

Sofia ducked as a sharp flicker of white sped past her eye. A loud crash almost deafened her ear. In slow motion Sofia's head turned towards the loud noise that had spread all over the white washed wall. Hortense was shouting some words. Sofia turned back to look at Hortense who had the most angry snarl plastered on her face and glaring eyes that were reddening up in their corners. Fear gripped Sofia as she was trying to process what was happening.

In the far corner of the room she saw a young girl sitting on the floor with her head buried in her knees. The little girl was terrified and trying to escape the argument that was happening between the man and the woman that were standing a short distance away and hurling insults at each other. Sofia recognised the red Papa Smurf t-shirt that the girl was wearing. It had always been her favourite t-shirt that she would wear whilst watching the Smurfs and devouring a bag of marshmallows, picking the white ones first and demolishing the pink ones later.

It was the night that her father had slapped her mother and bloodied her nose after she had thrown her cup of tea which had missed his ear and crashed on the white washed wall. Terrified, the girl crawled to the corner of the room with a trail of marshmallows following her and praying that her parents would just stop. She buried her head in her knees and Sofia remembered how she had felt anger towards her mother for making her father angry. If she had not made him angry she would not have had a bloody nose and there would have been peace in the house. Sofia began to cry.

Just as quickly as they had appeared the young Sofia and her parents had gone. What was left was the brown stain on the white washed wall. Hortense had thrown her hot cup of tea that had narrowly missed Sofia's ear and crashed on the wall. Hortense walk off in an angry huff.

The whole thing was paralysing but in that moment she was convinced about what she needed to do.

CHAPTER 27

U che opened the gate to the new two up, two down house with a white washed picket fence and a lime green door. Sofia wiped her shoes on the thatched door mat that had the words 'Welcome Home' written on it in black calligraphy style letters. Every single one of their footsteps was heard on the polished mahogany floor. It was smaller than what they were used to but it was clean and pleasantly in character with the style of home that Sofia loved; warm and cosy.

"What do you think?" Uche asked, looking uncharacteristically nervous.

She looked at him not knowing what to say.

"It is £200 cheaper than our last place." He walked towards the back of the house. "There is a garden," He turned the key in the back door lock. He ushered Sofia through the door.

The garden was of a reasonable size, suitable for her potted herbs and fruit trees. She stood for a moment looking at the grass. Uche seemed to have changed. He seemed apologetic for everything that had happened and here he was offering Sofia a new fresh chapter that they could embark on as a couple. She thought hard as she surveyed each blade and their shade of green.

She felt sad and she felt tired. All she wanted to do was to rest. She wanted to close the door without worrying about what or who was behind it. But her choices for the right door were very limited. She had decided to leave Hortense and days of feeling scared and alone and opted for moving back in with Uche. He promised that things would be better and he promised that he had changed. Sofia made her decision based on that promise alone but as she stared at the grass she had a strange feeling that she was jumping out of being scared and alone and leaping into terror. But since she had no one and nowhere to live, terror would be her only option.

"It's lovely," she told him. "Let's move in." She smiled and morphed into the agreeable role that she had become so accustomed to playing.

CHAPTER 28

Much to Sofia's surprise the white picket and the lime-green door had offered up bliss in a most unsuspecting way. Uche seemed to be trying with an enrolment in a local anger management course and helping to dig up the dirt for the bonsai apple trees in their back garden. This all secured the perception that he was attempting to burn bridges.

Sofia was happy for the lighter atmosphere however, he still had a reign on what she wore, where she went and who she spoke to on the phone. It was still the same old mental sabotage. He told her that her friends did not care for her as much as he did. That she should be very careful about Skye. That Skye was well meaning but she was not married and would not understand their relationship. He pointed out how he had repeatedly caught Skye referring to Sofia as being 'dim', a comment that surprised Sofia as she had been friends with Skye since childhood and had not once ever heard her friend refer to her in any derogatory way. As always she took Uche's comments with a pinch of salt, but it was hard not to develop a suspicion of everyone around her.

Then there was the over the top character assassination of Hortense who in his view was the 'Queen of vipers'. He reiterated that if Sofia was not careful these friends would destroy everything that she had. *'They'* were not like *'them'*. Everyone else was beneath *'them'* and the success that *'they'* had achieved. His view was that Sofia did not have a mind of her own but he would make sure that she was protected against everyone who was jealous of her. The white picket fence house soon became the place that bred the idea that no one else but Uche was trustworthy. And Sofia found herself alone and afraid.

#

A tough interview at the farm laboratories of a local supermarket chain yielded a job in Sofia's favour. She was delighted as this meant she could get out of the house, see more than their four walls and hear more than Uche's repetitive mono-tone voice.

Uche was more than eager for her to go to work because of the mounting bills and unnecessary financial commitments that fed Uche's insatiable appetite for fashion and gadgets. It was a satisfying enough position, managing the supermarket chain's strawberry crop, ensuring suitable yields and work to improve the quality of the varieties.

She made friends with Jacob who was also a Horticulturist. He was kind and was willing to listen to Sofia's endless chats about her herb garden, the mould in the upstairs bedroom that she was struggling to get rid of and then occasional spurts about her husband which were awkward but necessary for her to let off some steam.

He made her laugh with his endless news about the trips he had made to the countries on the list of his never ending world tour. He was knowledgeable and well travelled and kept persuading Sofia to at least put a few stamps on her passport. He believed that it would do her a world of good and bring back some of the gorgeous colour to her cheeks.

She felt that travelling abroad was a world out of her reach but she couldn't understand why. Uche on the other hand had easily picked up his passport and travelled to distant lands, leaving his wife behind telling everyone within earshot that he needed 'time to himself'. This would give Sofia countless amounts of embarrassment. Her husband was in the custom of taking holidays without her. In fact he had never been on any holiday with her. This caused those who were in the bad habit of mocking her to jeer 'so he's off again without you?' Sofia would expertly hide the pain and mounting shame by laughing it off with a quick response 'I sent him off as he was getting on my nerves. I need time to myself.'

He would then return with 'guilt gifts' as Sofia would call them. He had an odd way about him when it came to giving her gifts, which no matter how beautiful they were had a peculiar 'aura'. It seemed that they were coming from a place which was not love. Sofia could never put her finger on it excepting that the gifts had an agenda which, in a cruel way, was self-serving. The clothes were always a size smaller. If she didn't fit into them he would tell her that she needed to lose weight to wear them. Everything that happened to be the correct size was nothing like what she would have chosen herself but she wore them because that was his prescription – doctor's orders.

Jacob was Sofia's breath of fresh air. He was not intense. He just loved life and this is something that Sofia was missing. Her life had been spent stressing herself over an uncertain future whilst forgetting to enjoy the day that was right in front of her.

It was on a day that Jacob was discussing his happy vibrant life that Sofia just broke down in tears. They had been in the lab discussing a cross pollination strategy. Sofia had walked over to get a folder of their charts. Jacob had brought up some yield graphs and pie charts on his laptop for Sofia to have a look at. When she sat next to him she could not hold it in anymore. Jacob had to hold her to stop her from falling off her chair.

He took her to *Amakele*, their regularly frequented coffee shop at the bottom of the village. They often had lunch in *Amakele* which was the pink and light blue shop in the alcove of Hovers Yard.

Over Cappuccino and a vanilla frosted slice Sofia divulged her life's worth of bad marriage tales. He comforted her with kind words and more importantly he listened intently. Just being in the presence of someone who was not judging her or telling her that what she was saying never happened was healing in itself. They talked for hours. It is here that she found out that Jacob was a Christian. But his Christianity was happy and loving; a concept that was miles away from the Christianity that she had been exposed to.

Jacob looked at his watch and realised that it was late. He encouraged her to go home for the day. He could do that because he was her boss. Before he left he reached down in his man bag and fished out a little hard covered brown book. The book was worn around the edges. If it had not been for the hard cover it may not have survived the years of wear that it had endured. He handed it to her.

"Promise me that you will read this."
She smiled. "What is it?"
"Read it."
She nodded. "I will. Thanks." She took the book. The title caught her instantly. She held back another episode of tears. The title read: 'You are Good Enough' by Yolanda Burns.

Sitting in the bus on the way home Sofia pulled out the little brown book. She read the title again and surveyed it for a while. She looked out the window pondering on whether that statement was true; was she really good enough? The track record of her life begged to differ. She opened the book and went to the opening line. *'The first thing that I want you to know is that the sooner you get to know who you are and start loving yourself, you can say goodbye to being unhappy.'*

CHAPTER 29

In the month that she had known Jacob he introduced her to volumes and volumes of books that she devoured. These books had words that were beginning to move the cogs in her brain. The little cogs were being persuaded that there was some value to the life of Sofia Blackwell Onyeme. When she looked in the mirror the feedback she was getting was different. She combed her hair different. Powders and colours and fragrances began to pile up on her dressing table and each morning each of them landed on her body. Her shopping was less frequent for food. Instead different items of clothing began to replace the grandma items clogging up her wardrobe. This was followed by the new development of the everyday burpees, sit-ups and lady press ups which were sucking her into her God-given shape.

None of this escaped Uche's notice. She saw his reflection in the mirror every time she did a burpee or surveyed the fitting of each new outfit she wore to work. There were no 'you look good' comments or no 'well done comments. Instead there was the look of intimidation. Sofia looked and felt amazing and this made him nervous.

#

Sofia waited for Skye to emerge from Baker Street Station. She had not seen Skye in months and was eager to see the face of her childhood friend. Jacob, who was standing next to her, looked at his watch.

"Don't worry she will be here," Sofia said.

"I'm just checking what time it is. We need to get on the next bus if we are to make it on time."

Sofia tried to ring Skye's line. The hustle and bustle on the street made it difficult for her to hear the ring tone so she moved away closer to the statue of Sherlock Holmes. It was no use as too many double decker buses with roving engines lined up behind her and the din from the rowdy French students taking photos with Sherlock made it impossible to hear anything. She walked back over to where Jacob was standing. She tried to tell him that she couldn't hear anything but Jacob paid no attention to what she was saying. In a sense he was transfixed. Sofia looked in the direction that Jacob was looking. She recognised what had caught his attention. She quickly looked back at Jacob and smiled. He was taken by Skye.

"Skye," yelled Sofia. Jacob was startled by the yell but at the same time happy that the object of his attention was the very woman that they had been patiently waiting for.

"Oh come here," said Skye. They locked in an embrace for a period. Skye gave her friend a long needed squeeze. Sofia held back the tears as Skye gave her a piece of home, a piece of her childhood and a piece of the time when dreaming and hoping carried so much expectation.

Skye pulled from the embrace and surveyed Sofia from top to bottom. "Oh my goodness you look amazing. I love that top. This, I mean everything about you, is absolutely gorgeous. I am going to steal that perfume from you."

"Thanks Skye," She had a smile that oozed confidence and highlighted her strong beauty.

Jacob cleared his throat a little so that the women were aware that he was still standing there.

"Oh how rude of me." Sofia turned to face Jacob. "Jacob this is my friend Skye."

"Hello Skye." Jacob held out his hand for a shake.

"I know you."

Jacob looked puzzled "You do?"

"How come?" Sofia asked.

"You're the guy I saw earlier wearing the yellow t-shirt with a question mark on it and demonstrating an unhealthy relationship with his watch." Skye grinned. Sofia looked at Jacob and for the first time noticed the striking yellow t-shirt with a question mark on it. She also noticed embarrassment creeping all over his cheeks; a state that she had never seen the always cool and collected Jacob in.

Jacob cleared his throat again."I was looking at the time." He felt that he needed to explain himself but when he had let it out he wished he hadn't as he felt even sillier than before.

"We should go," Sofia took Skye's hand and led the way to the bus stops. Jacob followed behind. Skye looked back and asked "So why the question mark?"

Jacob smiled a little. "It's to grab people's attention."

"Well you caught mine." She looked back at him again and smiled. He smiled back. Skye put her arm around Sofia's shoulder and whispered. "Well he's nice. Where did you find this one?"

"He's my boss."

"Oh. So I need to be on my best behaviour then."

Sofia chuckled. "Yes, please be."

Sofia was walking with a slight limp that Skye noticed.

"What's wrong with your leg babe?"

"Oh I think I sprained my ankle."

"Sprained it? How?"

"I was at the flower show and as usual was not looking where I was going. Then bam I bumped into this guy. It was so embarrassing. I ended up mangled around his ankle. You know that yellow bag you gave me? Well it went flying and so did I. Just embarrassing."

"Well what did the guy that you bumped into say?"

"He was really nice about it. Helped me up, got my bag for me and was apologising and yet it was my fault."

"Hmm… he sounds nice. Was he cute?"

"No idea Skye. Who wants to be eyeball to eyeball with someone at your most embarrassing moment?"

"Wait you didn't talk to him?"

"I did. I just didn't look at him. I apologised and dashed off. The dash is probably what made my ankle worse."

Skye shook her head. "Next time you bump into a knight in shining armour make sure you get a look at him."

"I'm married Skye."

"What has being married got to do with checking out whether the guy who has been polite to you is cute or not? I mean honestly?" They laughed.

On the bus Skye enquired why Jacob needed to grab peoples' attention. After an awkward misunderstanding where Skye thought that Jacob used his shirt to attract women to re-gurgitate chat up lines, it was understood that Jacob innocently wanted to strike up conversations with people to discuss the meaning of life. He considered himself an Evangelist and had a passion for sharing his faith and new found peace after inviting Jesus Christ into his life. Skye was intrigued and was eager to have the conversations which they planned to have over coffee the following week. More so than the conversations Skye was eager to spend time with the very attractive man.

Skye had spent quite a lot of time in Canada following the dream relationship with Tim their high school friend. Skye and Tim had always had a tumultuous relationship of breaking up and getting back together and then breaking up again. Their reason for breaking up would be an argument over money or other women. Their getting back together would be over them convincing each other that they were meant to be together.

Tim was not a difficult man to live with. In fact he was quite caring. His only fault was an inability to commit to Skye or anything else for that matter. He went from job to job and from woman to woman and breaking Skye's heart in the process. But for some reason Skye could not let go. She felt that she had to save him.

This all ended when she started attending personal development evenings with a friend who was always in her ear telling her that she deserved better. After a year of attending several 'Trent Shelton Motivational evenings' she made the decision to leave him. She packed her things and got on a plane and moved back to England.

She rented a flat in Hemel Hampstead and began to work on a life-long dream, to own a novelty hand bag store, whilst she worked in bars as a waitress by night.

Sofia felt that this evening in particular would be perfect for Skye. Jacob had invited her to the Zane West SLS tour. It was a Self Love Seminar. Jacob had two free tickets that he knew Sofia would make good use of.

They got off the bus at the British Library and made their way to the Knowledge Centre theatre.

Zane West was a 6 foot tall slender athletic man. He dressed simply but smartly. It was no doubt a shock when he showed the audience his yesteryear photos as a teenage overweight and depressed person barely able to perch on his high school classroom seat. *"That was me,"* he said. He grabbed their attention.

"In life you are going to come across so many people who will tell you that you are less than. They will show you your flaws and point out your inadequacies. Ultimately they are trying to let you know that YOU are NOT good enough. But I would like to suggest to you tonight that in the midst of all those haters and naysayers there needs to be one person who will go against the grain. That person needs to stand up with courage, SHOUT OUT from the rooftops and tell you that YOU are GOOD ENOUGH. That's it. All you need is ONE person. That one person will make you a winner in spite of all the opposition. But here's the catch. For this to work, that one person has to be YOU."

Sofia caught a tear that had rolled down her cheek.

CHAPTER 30

Attending motivational talks and personal development seminars became a bit of an addiction for Sofia. She gained more of an awareness of herself and her situation. This gave her the courage to conclude that the way she was being treated by Uche was not right. It was not love.

It was the night that Sofia had just finished another Zane West Self Love Seminar that her life would take a sharp turn. She parted ways with Skye and Jacob, who had officially become a couple that was fast falling into love, and made her way home.

She passed through the turnstile at Watford Junction station and stopped to buy her usual steaming cafe mocha that was always sure to last the length of Leavesden road.

She got home. The lights were on meaning Uche was at home. She heaved a sigh because as per usual Uche had neglected to bring the bins back in. He never took them out and he never took them in.

After completing her weekly bin routine she turned her key in the door. As she opened it an immediate assault from Uche's shouting hit her. She stood back, intimidated by the bellowing, but then noticed that it was not being directed at her. She entered the front room. The violent yelling was coming from the back.

"Easy. Easy." Sofia distinctly heard Peter's voice. She opened the door.

"Tell this bitch to leave my house." There was the most

demonic snarl that Sofia had ever seen plastered all over Uche's face. Peter had been trying to restrain him from lunging at Hortense who was standing in the corner of the room hurling insults and all forms of derogatory terms.

Sofia stood in shock as Hortense hurled obscenities at her husband.

"Bloody liar," said Uche as Hortense described every aspect of his married man anatomy with such astonishing detail.

"Me? Sleep with you? You are stinking woman. You stink. We don't mention it because we are gentlemen. But this room is reeking. I'm not attracted to that. I'm a married man."

Sofia's eye caught Uche's but he was not moved by her presence. Peter then noticed Sofia who was bright red in the face and extremely annoyed.

"Oh blow. My guy, Sofia don come (Sofia is here)," Peter said.

Hortense turned around and faced Sofia. There was a silence.

Sofia's eyes had welled up with tears and her entire being had been filled with a rage that she was finding difficult to contain. She looked at Uche. "What is going on? Hortense why are you here?"

"What do you mean what is going on? You are the one who brought this bloody liar into our marriage."

"The biggest liar on the planet is calling ME, Hortense Ambrose, a liar. What a joke."

Peter stepped in. "Hortense I think you and I should leave. Sofia is here and I think we should let them sort this out as a couple."

"Don't speak to me. All you are is a flying monkey. Everything that bastard says you do. You have known for years that he's been cheating on her but you bat a blind eye. All the time being nice to her and yet you've been stabbing her in the back. That's why I'm here to expose the game."

Peter was indignant, "No need for name calling here. You don't know me bitch. I was trying to be a gentleman but obviously it's too much for you. You want men who treat you like trash."

Uche interjected. "You are the one who stabs people in the back. Is Sofia your friend?" He pointed a finger at her.

"Hortense what is going on? Why are you here?" Sofia asked.

Oh you got me fired up now," Hortense looked at Sofia. "I'm sorry to break it to you Sofia but this bastard of a man that you foolishly keep coming back to has been sleeping with me behind your back and laughing at you in the process."
Sofia looked at Uche. "What?"

"Idiot," bellowed Uche. This made them all jump. "Idiot. Get out of my house." Uche lunged towards Hortense. Hortense took a step back. Peter jumped in between them. Uche was pointing straight at Hortense with his eyes wide and nostrils flaring. "Peter I go kill this woman o. I go kill-am (Peter I am going to kill this woman. I will kill her.)"

"Easy, easy. Cool down." Peter pulled him to the side of the room.

"That's it flying monkey. Do your job well. Acting like you are innocent when you knew all along."

"Please leave me out of this craziness," said Peter.

"The secret is out Sofia. He married you and yet he was sleeping with me all along. Every single night after work and lying to you that he was doing extra shifts. Boom. Who is the bloody liar now?" Hortense looked over at Uche in triumph without any care for the hearer in front of her.

Sofia felt sick.

"I said get out of my marital home," said Uche.

"Uche is this true? Are you kidding me?" Sofia asked.

"Well I'm not kidding," said Hortense who folded her arms.

"You see what you brought into our home?" Uche looked at Sofia. "A stinking witch who practises witchcraft to break marital homes. She is jealous of you and you are so blind." He began walking up and down the room. Sofia started to get confused as she felt herself being spun in another of his webs. But then she stopped spinning to ask, "Is this true Hortense?"

"Why would I lie?"

"She is jealous of you." Visible beads of sweat had accumulated on his brow. His shirt was drenched.

Hortense spat like a viper. "We slept together on your wedding night."

Sofia fell back onto the settee. The tears that had been hard to cry over the years now began to flow. Uche had both his hands on his head. "Hey," he shouted. "Hey, the devil is a liar."

"Come on Hortense that was below the belt," said Peter. He looked at Sofia. "Sofia I'm really sorry about this. I didn't know."

Uche interjected. "My guy, you didn't know what? It's all lies."

"So it was lies when you told me that you were just using her but you really loved me?" said Hortense.

"Shut up. Just shut up. Idiot. Shut up. Dirty stinking idiot. Nonsense."

"Cool down," said Peter.

"Cool down for what? My marriage is dying here and…" "Did you sleep with her or not?" They were all taken aback by the bellowing sound of Sofia's voice.

"Shut up. I'm your husband but you dare to accuse me of sleeping with that idiot. So you and your so called friend want to put me in a corner to humiliate me. Not me Uche Chidinma Onyeme. I'm a married man, an honourable member of society and I will not be brought down to your level."

Peter looked on, quietly surprised by the behaviour of his friend. He thought that surely the easiest response to his wife's question should have been a 'no'.

"Did you sleep with Hortense Uche?" Sofia asked again.

"He can't answer you Sofia because he knows I am telling the truth."

He spat like a cobra. "Nonsense. You see, you come here trying to destroy me not knowing you have come to destroy yourself. None of you would know the truth even if it were placed right under your noses. Bitch, don't ever cross me again." He pointed at Hortense again trying to intimidate her then he turned to look at Sofia. "You see Sofia, that bloody liar is an imposter." He shrugged his shoulders then gave Hortense an angry look. "Who are you really, Hortense?" His arms were out with hands outstretched mocking Hortense and pretending to wait for her to answer. Hortense looked nervous and remained silent. "Sofia I will tell you the true version that you were not willing to see in this so-called friend of yours. I'm not beating about the bush anymore. You stab me, I stab you. Hey Black-well, are you paying attention? Hortense is your sister. Your dad was not a responsible man like me." He grinned. Peter looked in shock at his friend who was denigrating his own wife.

"How dare you?" Sofia said. "How dare you?" She felt anger rise within her as the integrity of her beloved father was being attacked.

"You are talking of me daring? I don't dare. I just talk."

Peter interjected. "Uche I don't think this is the right place or time to talk about this."

"No Peter let him talk," said Sofia indignantly. She looked at Hortense who had a tinge of remorse beginning to settle on her forehead. "It seems that there's been a lot of talking already behind my back. But right now my back is not turned." She looked at Uche, with eyes that were livid.

"Thank you," he said. "You see this woman that you call a friend told me that she hates you."

Sofia looked at Hortense with pain. "Tell me something that I don't know sweet heart."

"I'm not your sweetheart," said Uche.

Peter was confused by Uche's comment.

Sofia smirked. "Now, that I know. I'm just your wife."

Hortense interjected "I told you no such thing."

Uche smirked with mockery. "And you think I'm the one who is the liar. Number one, her dad is your dad. Number two, she says she hates you because you grew up with him and she did not. You see? She is out to destroy your marriage because she wants everything you have. You stole her father is what she said." He raised his eyebrows and looked triumphantly at Sofia and then to Hortense.

"Sofia do not listen to him. He is lying to you. I'm sorry but what I said is true," said Hortense.

Sofia took in a deep breath and looked at Hortense. By now tears had been quietly streaming down her cheeks in black puddles as they carried the mascara down from her lashes. "Did you have an affair with my husband?" she asked but in a quiet tone.

"So you want confirmation from a marriage breaker instead of confirming with your husband."

Sofia remained silent, waiting for a response from Hortense.

"Unbelievable," Uche snorted.

"Did you have an affair? It's a simple question Hortense." Hortense reluctantly opened her mouth. "Yes."

Sofia grabbed her chest and bent over. Some tears fell directly from her eyes to the ground wetting the wooden floor. She straightened herself up as Peter came behind her guiding her to a chair. "No thank you," she said.

"Bloody liar," Uche shouted again. "Sofia I am your husband and I have told you several times that a man like me is hard to find. I am a married man and I will not be lied about in this fashion. I am an honourable member of..."

"Oh shut up Uche. Shut up."

Uche went quiet.

Sofia took one step towards Hortense who moved one step back. "What is he saying about my dad? You knew my dad?"

"Sofia it's all lies."

"Then why did he talk about my dad Hortense."

She was nervous. "Uche will say anything to hurt you."

Uche put his hands on his head. "Hey, people can lie. Bloody liar. So you didn't tell me that that man is your dad?"

"Just shut up Uche," Hortense quipped.

Sofia screamed. They jumped. She came up closer to Hortense who became very nervous. "You know the relationship I had with my dad. You know how much it hurt when he died. I shared these things with you as a friend. But you were laughing at me behind my back with MY husband. Hortense how could you? Tell me why I shouldn't rip your heart out now? Tell me," she shouted.

"Sofia calm down. I never said anything about your dad," said Hortense.

"Then who should I believe? You? Why should I believe you?" She took the pot of lavender that was on the window sill and smashed it against the wall as she screamed. Splinters of terracotta scattered all over the floor.

"Take it easy Sofia," Peter urged.

"SHUT UP," she yelled.

"Or should I believe you Uche? You have been a liar from the start. The pair of you have manipulated me and lied to me for what? What did I EVER do to you hey?" She waved the piece of sharp terracotta that was still in her hand, making them all visibly nervous.

Uche tried to look nonchalant. "You are seriously asking such a question. You should believe your husband not a marriage wrecking snake."

"I don't believe either of you. In fact I don't care if either of you is telling the truth. I've had enough of this. I'm done." There was a silence as Sofia walked to pick up her bag. She moved towards the door then turned and in a swift move threw the remaining piece of terracotta in Uche's direction. He ducked looking very afraid as she looked like she intended to clip his ear. She missed then rushed to get out.

Uche gathered himself then in a surprisingly soft tone asked her to stop. "Where are you going?"

She looked back at Uche then at Hortense. A shadow of grief overwhelmed her. Why couldn't she have reacted more viciously? They had cheated on her. They had lied but all she could do was to throw a piece of terracotta. The truth is she felt guilty. She knew exactly what they were both like but she carried on with them. She let them abuse her but never stood up to them. To her their confessions were a mere confirmation of just how embarrassing her weaknesses were.

At that point all hope was lost. It was like the day that Regina and Langton had conspired to crack the lens of her brand new binoculars that she got from her dad for her 8th birthday. Regina was supposed to be her friend but she teamed up with her brother to hurt her. Sofia never understood it then and she still could not find a way to understand why they hated her so much.

In turn she was aware of and tolerated the hate of Hortense and Uche but she did not understand what she did to them that was so bad for them to want to repay her in such a way.

"I'm going out for some fresh air," she said then slammed the door behind her.

CHAPTER 31

Michael had moved his psychotherapy sessions to his home where he had built an amazing extension to his garden. The therapy room looked out over his attractive flower garden which was an idyllic setting that offered tranquillity and calm. He sat in the conservatory waiting for his 11.am appointment. He was waiting for Sofia.

After she arrived they were sitting opposite each other. Michael was waiting and giving her time to find her place of calm. Today was a big day. She had agreed to talk about her deepest hurts. It had taken her a year but she felt that she was ready and Michael felt that she was ready to take that next step.

"Ready?" he asked.

"I am." She took in a breath. He nodded to encourage her. She began. "When I left him it was hard because I had nothing but my job. I slept rough for a while, taking showers at train stations. I'm sure that everyone at my workplace noticed I was wearing the same clothes for a minute but they were kind about it. I always had these overwhelming offers for lunch which I gratefully took." She stopped to wipe some tears away.

Michael was touched. "It must have been a very challenging time."

"It was but I kept going because I had begun to see that there was better waiting for me if I didn't give up." She clasped her hands together. "These words were constantly ringing in my mind – YOU ARE GOOD ENOUGH. I would rehearse it on the night bus, in McDonalds having a cuppa at 5am and everywhere I could get a chance to sit and think."

"So you were fighting for your life." He shifted in his seat.

"I was Michael. I was fed up of pain. I listened to people like Zane West and he was speaking about a beautiful life that I had never experienced so I fought because I wanted it. But I must admit that the hardest part was when I filed for divorce. I had sworn that this would never happen to me. I didn't believe in it. I was 'old school' you know; that marriage was forever, 'til death do us part'. Filing for divorce meant that I had changed and that scared me." She looked at him and he still had the re-assuring look that beckoned her on. "In my faith, forgiveness is a big thing and for days I pondered on whether it was the best thing to forgive Uche for everything and just remain his wife. But I realised that living with Uche meant agreeing to con-tinued abuse. I knew he was not going to stop." She paused and took a sip of her elderflower water. "He was furious for months. Endless texts buzzed on my phone and he would bump into me in shopping centres and shout at me to no end. Then he would start the hot-cold thing. After shouting at me like a dog he would turn into a mouse begging me to come back, begging me to give 'us' another chance. It was laughable really because there was no 'us' it was just him. It was just Uche and what he wanted. I didn't exist. He had sucked the life out of me..."

"But maybe, not all of it?" Michael added.

"You think?"

"Well you still had enough life left to think about what was best for you."

"I guess I did." She released a small smile.

"Yes you filed for divorce."

"Yes I did."

"Why was that important?"

"I had to show myself that I was valuable. All my life, I just used to let things be. People could treat me anyhow, speak to me anyhow and I would never stick up for myself. I thought so little of myself that I would put myself in situations where people could devour me at will. My divorce was me sticking up for me, because no one else was going to do it. Leaving him was forgiving him, in my eyes because with the anger that I had in me I could have done something worse. But ultimately it also became forgiving myself for all the wrong choices I had made."

"You took a bold step."

"I did and I'm still doing it. This counselling is all part of me saying that I matter." Tears began to roll down her cheeks again. "You know Michael. I never mattered. Everyone else was important except for me. I was the bottom of the pile and the 'nobody' in the crowd."

"But you managed to make a bold statement that Sofia does matter. She's valuable and she's beautiful."

She smiled a shy smile. "I did Michael. I did and you have been a great part of that. I'm so grateful for you."

He nodded. "So where is the Uche Chapter of your life now?"

"I closed it."

"How so?"

"I filed a restraining order recently because of a manic chain of texts that he sent me."

"Wow."

"I just didn't want any more incidences of him calling me up and trying to mess with my mind. He called me a week ago and tried to repeat what he did last time and so I gave it to him. I told him that I was not scared of him and told him to back off. After hanging up I filed the restraining order. That chapter of the old Sofia is gone. I'm not his doormat anymore." She felt courage rising up within her. She gulped down the elderflower water.

"That is inspirational." He looked at her with admiration.

"Thanks Michael." She blushed. He noticed.

"So what does your next chapter hold?"

"I'm really excited about life. But at the same time I'm worried."

"What worries you?"

"Making the same mistakes."

He nodded. "Life can never guarantee that there will be no mistakes but what we can do is spend our time trying to learn from our previous ones. I call it failing forward. This means you fail but still move forward because you're learning about what made you fail and gaining wisdom about how to overcome the past.

She smiled. "I like that. In fact that's really profound."
He smiled too with his award winning smile that she loved so much. "You could spend this next chapter finding out about Sofia and falling in love with who she really is. Who you are is enough."

Pools of water erupted in her eyes as those words landed on her chest. "Yes," she said.

"You have come a long way. Take time to allow yourself to heal. But you're doing great."

"Thanks Michael."

"You're welcome." He looked at the clock and readjusted himself in his armchair.
Sofia looked at the clock. "Oh is it that time again?"

"I'm afraid so." He smiled.

"I hate it when our sessions end."
He wanted to say 'me too' but quickly reigned himself in.

CHAPTER 32

With her new found confidence she became more and more attracted to Stuart who was increasingly becoming a strong presence in her life. He made her happy and she felt that she was ready to allow him into her life. He was upfront in telling her that he wanted more than just walks in the park. He told her that he was a forever kind of person.

Their relationship sweetly progressed into a friendship. In the time that she had known him it was the longest time that she had ever laughed.

He was polite and charming. He wined, dined and showered her with gifts. There was no drought of affection, instead a tsunami of devotion. He made her feel special and she knew that a fresh new chapter of her life had begun.

"I'll pick you up tomorrow. Early though," said Stuart over the phone.

"How early," she asked.

"7.30 ish."

"Stuart that's early."

"Yeah I'm sorry about that but I want us to get there early."

"But does it have to be 7.30?"

"Ok how about a compromise. I'll get to you by 8 am."

"Ok Stuart I will be ready."

The Next day Stuart rang her bell at 7.30am. She was

ready but surprised that Stuart had broken their arrangement.

"You're early."

Stuart seemed surprised. "Oh you're ready."

"Yes. Should I not be?"

"Ok. Can't a brother get a hug?"

She smiled and pulled him in for an embrace. When he let go she noticed the glassiness in his eyes. "I love you," he said. She was taken aback. Not once had he made that declaration. It was always implied but this time it was clear as day.

It touched her heart as she watched him eagerly wait for her response. "I love you too," she said.

"You look good," he said.

Her confidence exploded. "Thank you. I guess I will be the admiration of all when we go out." She did a little catwalk and mimic pirouette which he supported by swinging her around in a twirl.

"Yes but not dressed like that," he said.

The pirouette dissolved into a broken march. She was stunned. She laughed to break the tension. "I thought you said I look good?"

He was silent for a brief moment. This unsettled her. But before she could register anything he grabbed her by the waist and pulled her close to him.

"Of course you do darling. What I meant was I'm taking you somewhere special so you have to wear that dress I bought you."

The lines of concern on her forehead dissipated. "Do you mean the black dress?"

"Yes I want my girl looking stunning."

She had a playful smile.

"You're beautiful," he said.

"So are you," she said.

"Now go and put on that dress." As she walked away she turned her head to look at him. He blew her a kiss. At that point she knew she was in love.

He drove her to the Lake District where he got out his hiking boots and backpack.

"Are you having a laugh?" she asked.

"What do you mean? Isn't it beautiful?"

"Well of course it's beautiful Stuart but I'm in fish net tights and heels."

He looked at her and giggled. She felt her annoyance rising but she did not want to ruin the day.

"Listen don't worry I've got it sorted." He pulled out some hiking boots from his backpack. "These should be your size."

"So I'm taking off my heels to wear those?" She had one eyebrow raised.

"Look, trust me. It will all make sense soon."

They walked for what seemed like hours. She followed behind him whilst he methodically led the way. Her legs began to ache. Her tights had become all but a piece of string.

"Stuart, can we stop for a moment? I'm knackered."

"We're almost there."

"Almost where?"

A sweat broke out in her armpits and a sour taste filled her mouth. She no longer felt confident in her dress.

He picked up speed as he began to climb up. She was getting tired of it but she didn't want to complain.

They got to the top. She felt awful and made it for the nearby bench to sit down.

"Gets your adrenaline flowing doesn't it?"

She offered a small smile but she was deflated and really wanted to go home. "Do you have any water in that backpack?" she asked.

"Oh damn. I thought that I had packed some water in my bag. I'm sorry we can only get some when we get back to the car."

Her throat was parched but she didn't want to make him feel bad. "Oh well. It's ok. I'll get a drink when I get back."

"The view is beautiful isn't it?" He looked at her.

"Yes it is," she looked out and tried hard to hide the pain

that was slowly rising in her heart. She turned back to look at him. She found him kneeling on the floor with a little jewellery box in his hand. She frowned. Her heart was racing. His eyes were glassy and his eyebrow was upturned in the cute way that always made her heart melt. "Stuart what are you doing?" She could barely bring out the words as her saliva was not enough to moisten her dry throat.

He opened the jewellery box and revealed a ring encrusted with diamond and ruby in the shape of a heart. "Will you marry me?"

She grabbed her aching knee, looked at the ring and then looked at him but could not bring herself to say anything.

CHAPTER 33

Michael rushed to the door when the bell rang. He pushed the heavy oak.

"Oh you're early," he said. "Come in. We can have some tea. I had just put the kettle on."

"Oh I'm not staying for long."

He shut the oak door and had a slight frown on his forehead.

"Not staying? But our session is in..."

"I know. That's what I came to talk about."

He was taken a bit by surprise but very eager to hear what she had to say.

"Do you want to reschedule? If so that's ok. But you didn't have to come all the way down to change it. You can always ring. It's no trouble at all. Let me get my diary." He walked towards his study.

"No Michael. It's not that. I..."

He walked back. "What is it? Is everything ok Sofia?"

"Oh no, of course everything is ok."

He had his hands on either side of his waist. "Well I'm glad to hear that."

"I just wanted to let you know that I won't be coming for therapy anymore."

He was not expecting to hear that. "I see."

Anxiety began to fill her voice. "I know it is short notice but I will pay you for this session. It's only fair."

"It's fine about the payment. Don't worry about it. But what brought you to this decision, if you don't mind me asking?"

"I feel I've come a long way..." She paused and found him nodding in reassurance. She carried on. "I'm happy. Things are going well for me. I'm in a relationship and..." She looked at him. His eyes were glassy because she had hurt him. He was embarrassed so his cheeks went pink. He smiled to reassure her that everything was ok.

"He's a good man Stuart is..." She found herself going on the defensive. "He's real supportive and I feel he's a good person for me."

"Well I'm pleased for you...genuinely. You deserve peace."

She looked into his kind eyes and saw the sincerity. It was a gem that she had seldom seen throughout her life.

"So what's next?" he asked.

She felt that she had to explain further."It's just that Stuart is a strong Christian and he doesn't believe that Therapy is a reflection of faith. So he has been working through things with me." She sounded apologetic. "We pray loads too."

"There's nothing more comforting than a good prayer," he said as he tried to ease the tension that he saw building up.

"Thanks Michael."

He nodded. "I'm a Christian too and I respect your friend's views but I see therapy as part of your walk of faith. It's almost like you are working your way to your healing."

"So you think I'm doing the wrong thing?"

"I absolutely respect your decision and I'm happy that you are making a strong step towards working things out yourself with your friend's help."

"Thank you Michael, you always make me feel good about myself."

"Are you sure you don't want to stay for tea?"

"Oh no, I can't. He's waiting in the car outside."

"I see." He looked sad but tried to maintain his professionalism.

She walked and tried to open the heavy oak door. He rushed to her aid and swung the door open. They stood at the open door.

"Well this is it then," she said.

He smiled a painful smile. He held out his hand. She reciprocated and held out hers. Their hands touched for a momentary eternity. His eyes were glassy as were hers. She lingered almost as if waiting for him to rescue her. She breathed in deeply then put her free hand on top of the handshake. His exterior began to melt.

"Goodbye Michael," she said.

His eye caught the glimmer of the refracted light from the rubies encrusted on the ring on her finger. He winced slightly.

She noticed what had unsettled him. She looked at the engagement ring and then at him.

"All the best Sofia," he said.

She gently let go of his hand and walked away.

As he watched he knew that he had lost her.

CHAPTER 34

It was a Saturday. Michael was at home. It was an appointment free day that he had set aside to have a long needed rest.

He had had a week of going through his emotions and analysing how he felt about Sofia. It bothered him that she was engaged to Stuart but he could not bring himself to doing anything about it. He refused to over step professional boundaries. He was employed as Sofia's Therapist and was not prepared to manipulate her vulnerability in any way.

He pondered on the first time that he had seen Sofia at the Chelsea flower show. Again he nursed his regret for not having acted. He felt that if he had acted Sofia would not be in the arms of another man. He would have taken care of her. She would not have needed to sign up for therapy because he would have loved her back to life. However, a black line was thickly drawn between him and making Sofia the love of his life when she turned up for her first 11 o'clock appointment.

He got to the bedroom at the back of the house. He opened the door and slowly walked in. His hand swept over and caressed the photo frames that were displayed on the mantel piece and the dressing table. He picked up the hair brush and put it to his nose. It still had hints of her scent. When he placed it back down he blinked. As he blinked big tear drops fell from his eyes and fell on the turquoise jewel earrings. He stooped to pick them up. They were Clara's. He squeezed them in the palm of his hand and kissed them.

For several hours he sat on the floor wrapped in Clara's burgundy shawl. The bottle of red wine had tipped onto the cream rug but no stain followed as he had drunk it dry. His bloodshot eyes were heavy with sleep but he continued to clutch on to the photos of Clara, many of which were strewn all over the floor. He looked at the photo that he was clutching. It was his favourite one. She had the smile that had made him fall deeply in love with her. He closed his eyes and quite unexpectedly to him his belly began to bubble. He doubled over, face down on the floor as the most painful sobs escaped. He body writhed in pain as he cried like a wounded animal.

The next day he woke up blinded by the rays of the sun that had pushed through the gaps in the curtains. He looked at his watch. It was morning and he had fallen asleep on the floor. His head was pounding as he picked himself up and gave himself a long stretch. He walked out and Clara's shawl fell from off his shoulders.

Fifteen minutes later he returned to the room with a black mug of strong coffee in one hand and several flat packed boxes snugly tucked under his free shoulder.

Within the next hour there were boxes all over the room all labelled *'Women's Shelter'*. He methodically folded Clara's clothes neatly and placed them in the boxes until all the closets and drawers were bare. When the last of her photos and other belongings had been packed and the boxes labelled, he sealed them with duck tape. He took the box with the photos and made his way to the attic. He placed the box down next to the old drapes that they had picked out for their very first apartment. More tears streamed down his cheeks as he bent to kiss the box. "Bye sweet heart," he said.

The boxes with the clothes filled his Land rover. After donning his blue tinted dark glasses to conceal his baggy, tear drenched eyes he sped off down the road.

CHAPTER 35

Months later in New York City.....

April Stevens was one of the finest Chocolatier's in Manhattan. After her father died she continued running the family chocolate shop on 5th Avenue. Coco Crumbles had churned out buckets of worthy chocaholic treats over the years and April's expert chocolate crafting skills had contributed to their allure.

It was close to Valentines, the busiest time of the year, so she was working around the clock to ensure that the growing appetite for chocolate treats was satiated.

"Julio the front shelves need to be filled with almond pearl drops," she said.

"I'm right on it Miss April. I just got to get more stock from the back."

"Ok. Everything looks great and smells absolutely divine. Good job," she said as she adjusted the bow on the golden wicker basket of assorted fruity liqueurs.

"Thanks Miss April but this is all you."

"We're a team Julio. I couldn't do it without you." Julio smiled and went to the back of the store to get the almond pearl drops.

April noticed that the gentleman who had entered the store had been wondering around for a while and had not made any selections. April decided that it was the perfect time to go and ask if he needed any help. She judged by his expensive shoes, quality leather over the shoulder bag and what she detected as a Ralph Lauren sweater that he was a man of sophistication looking for a quality gift for his significant other.

"Good morning Sir," she said.
The man turned to face her. She was struck by the beauty of his hazelnut eyes. His smile screamed of gentlemanliness as it softened the cleanest cut beard that she had ever seen.

"Good morning," he said.

"Have you managed to find what you're looking for?"

"I'm open to suggestions."

"Well we can tailor your gift to who it's for. Would it be for your wife or girlfriend?

"None of the above," he said.

"Oh. Mother or sister maybe?"
He chuckled. "No again. I came in here because I heard that it's the best chocolate shop around. What do you recommend?"

"Absolutely. Our Hazelnut praline drops are popular or our newest line, the Berry Blancmange swirls. I'll get you some samples to taste."

Almost immediately April had come back with a pretty black box with 4 shiny heart shaped chocolates set in four gold coloured parchment paper cases. The box was placed on a diamond studded silver plate.

"Thank you," he said as he took one of the Berry Blancmange swirls. He took a bite and allowed the sweet to saturate his tongue. It was a very pleasant sensation. "Delicious. I mean really delicious."

"Thank you, I appreciate that." April was pleased.

"Very good. I'll take a box of these and throw in some of those pralines too."

"Absolutely. Are you from England Sir?" She began to expertly fill the pretty pink Coco Crumbles box embellished with the gold painted *CC* logo. She tied a professionals bow around the box until she had the most stunning finish.

"Well that's where I've lived for a long time but I am originally from Zimbabwe."

"Oh my goodness I would love to go to Africa one day. Are you on vacation?"

"It started as a vacation but I fell in love with the city and well I'm here to see what life has in store for me."

"This city is definitely beautiful Sir." She handed him the pretty box.

"Thank you. That's lovely."

"Thank you for your business Sir and we hope to see you again."

"With chocolates like this that shouldn't be difficult."

"You're too kind."

"By the way, my name is Michael."

She held out her hand for a shake. "I'm April and I'm the owner."

"It's a pleasure to meet you April and you have a great place here."

"Thanks."

"Thanks again. You take care." He smiled one last time then left.

#

"Welcome to today's show. I'm your host Mackina Shaw and what a line up we have for you today." *'Applause and cheers'*
"Our first guest needs little if any introduction. He is America's 'Couch Therapist' and USA today's 'Dr Heart throb'. As a Registered Psychotherapist and Motivational Speaker he's become an overnight social media success with millions of views a day for his 'Mondays with Dr Mike' videos. He is one of my absolute favourites and I'm super excited about today. Please help me welcome to the show Dr Michael Marshall." *'Applause, cheers and whistling'*

Michael walked onto the set in the midst of the uproar of applause. He hugged and kissed Mackina and then sat down in the armchair facing her.

"Dr Mike welcome."

"Thanks Mackina and it's such a pleasure to be here. I absolutely love your show."

"I really appreciate that and we are super excited to have you here."

"Thank you so much."

"Now Dr Mike most of us are aware of your amazing success as a Therapist. We love your shows, which I love and watch regularly…"

"Thank you I appreciate that."

"And I'm sure other people have too. In fact let's take a poll. Dr Mike, cross your fingers." Mackina cheekily grinned.

"I had them crossed before I came out," Michael chuckled.

"You did? Well you should have nothing to worry about. America loves you…. I hope" Mackina chuckled again and Michael tried to control a belly laugh. "I'm just kidding Dr Mike…Ok let's take the poll. Push the green button if you have ever watched a Dr Mike show and red if you have not."

A drum roll and background music began to play. Following a loud siren a recorded voice bellowed 'The Results are in.'

"Ok here we go. Show the results on the screen," shouted Mackina.

The studio audience exploded as 100% in green flashed across the screen.

"Dr Mike 100% of our audience have watched your show. Anyway I absolutely had no doubt about that."
Michael pursed his hands together like in a prayer and thanked the audience and Mackina whilst bowing his head slightly as he thanked them. The applause eventually died down and Michael was evidently humbled by the response that he received.

"That's a testament to the millions of people that you have helped. But as I was saying before, your success is evident but what we always like to hear in order to understand you better is to know the man behind it all. We would love to hear a little bit of your story."

Michael adjusted himself in his seat. "Wow where do I

start."

"Just start at the beginning, Michael. We don't mind." Mackina grinned and fluttered her eyelids jokingly.

Michael chuckled. "Ok um..."

"Let me help you. We know that you are from Zimbabwe and you were a Psychotherapist in England. You had your own practice but at some point came to the US and started what is now an amazing Social media following. But what made you leave everything behind in England?"

"That's a good question. I started the Psychotherapy practice with my wife Clara. The practice thrived for a while and then we got pregnant. Our life was just as you would want it to be, which was happy. But then we lost the baby. Clara had a late term miscarriage and that was the first of the blows to our little paradise. Clara didn't fully recover..."

Michael stopped to clear his throat. The studio silence was thick. "Excuse me," he said before he continued. "She didn't fully recover after the miscarriage. I had to reduce our work in the practice so that I could make time to take care of her. Unfortunately things got worse and we found out that she had cancer. Everything just crashed at that point. Then after a short while she passed away."

There was not a dry eye in the studio as Michael relayed his story.

"Michael I am really sorry for your loss. I believe we had heard about the passing of your wife but I don't think we knew that you lost a child too. This is a total shock to me."

"I've never really shared that publicly. But as time has passed I've mustered the courage to talk about it more."

"And we applaud you for it. We can only imagine how challenging life must have been." Mackina added trying to professionally hold back tears as people began to clap for Michael to acknowledge his bravery.

"Her name was Amanda Grace."

"Beautiful name," Mackina said.

Michael nodded. "After losing my wife and daughter life was

169

incredibly difficult so I decided to go travelling. One way of coping for me is leaving the place that hurts. Some people might call it running away but I prefer to call it respite. Some people need the space to gain the strength needed to carry the weight of the challenges they face." He stopped as applause erupted again in acknowledgement. "Anyway I travelled for a while and I studied. To cut a long story short I did return to England, I faced those challenges and I re-opened the practice."

"Ok so fast forward you decide to leave your practice again and you come to America and your life just explodes into success."

Michael was nodding.

"So in step with what you said before, when you left your practice were you leaving the place that hurts? Had someone or something hurt you?"

Michael hesitated.

"Is it complicated?" asked Mackina.

"A little bit. There's a long story and a short story."

"Give us the long version Michael. We have time. We have waited a long time to meet with you and you have our undivided attention." She batted her eyelids again which made Michael chuckle. This made the audience chuckle and this blissfully eased the tension that had built up earlier.

"I'll give you the short story."

"Why can't you give us the long one Michael?"
Michael turned a slight pink in his cheeks. "The short version is easier for me to share."

"The short version is easier for you to share? Was it a girl Michael?"

Michael chuckled again. "No," he said.

"Only we wouldn't want you to get in trouble with April."
A photo of April Stevens appeared on the screen. They both looked at the screen.

"She is absolutely beautiful," said Mackina,

"She definitely is," Michael added.

"How long have ya'll been dating?"

"It's been a few months. April is a great girl."

"Is she a keeper?"

Michael cleared his throat.

"This is not the time to clear your throat Michael. We don't want April banning you from eating her chocolates, which are divine by the way."

Michael laughed. "Absolutely, she is a keeper." 'Claps and cheers were received from the audience whilst Michael fought to hide how embarrassed he was.

"But I'm not letting go of the long version. We are your die- hard fans Michael and we deserve to know. Clear your throat Michael." They laughed and the audience laughed.

"Ok, ok. I had learned that in order to move forward some-times you have to leave the past behind. I hadn't fully left the past behind so I had to physically do something. I closed the practice and I decided to go on vacation and I came to New York."

"Dr Mike, I still feel that you've not told us the full reel of the long story. But we will have to get you to promise to share with us next time because I know there will be a next time. But right now we're out of time." A roar of sighs filled the room. "I know time flies fast in here. We're gonna have to bid Dr Mike farewell. Dr Mike it's been an absolute pleasure to have you on the show. Ladies and gentleman Dr Michael Marshall has been amazing." The audience erupted with applause and cheers. Mackina stood up as did Michael and he gave her a hug and a word of thanks.

CHAPTER 36

"Hello everyone I want you all to raise your glasses to my future wife. She's stunning, hard working and obedient. She's more than any man could ask for."

There were several clinks of glasses going around the room as the guests toasted the newly engaged couple. Then a round of applause and three cheers as the sister of the groom knelt on a dining chair so that everyone could have a better view of her as she spoke. "My parents were on the HMS Windrush boat that came from the Carribbean to England. They had nothing but worked very hard to build a life here. And I know that they would be proud of you bruv (brother) just as much as Daisy and I are."

"Thank you sis," said Stuart with tears welling up in his eyes. "Now I've got to say something. Thanks Dorcas. You're my sister and you mean the world to me... and you Daisy. When people look at my life they see my money, my car and my house. Yes I am very wealthy. I've worked hard for it as I'm sure all of you have even though you are not as wealthy. But that is not what it is all about is it?" We are Christians and our job is charity which is giving to others. But my sister and I didn't get given a lot. Especially after my mum, God rest her soul, died. It was like we were orphans even though our father was alive. We became step kids..." Stuart stopped as he caught Sofia's eye who was quite bewildered as to what he was trying to say. She also felt the tension as his half-sister Daisy felt quite uncomfortable as it seemed that a silent rant was being directed at her in the middle of an engagement party. Stuart got the gist of Sofia's stare and wrapped it up. "What I mean is that your life can change in beautiful ways when God crosses your path with beautiful people. To Sofia everyone." Stuart made quite an uncomfortable sharp bow in front of Sofia. From one perspective he was honouring her but from another perspective the bow had the suspicious look of mockery.

"To Sofia," everyone shouted.

Sofia blew him a kiss and thanked everyone that was celebrating her.

She definitely looked stunning in the silver sequin camisole, figure hugging leather jeans and diamante studded white pumps. Her hair was sleeked up in a ballerina bun and her face was sculpted and designed to perfection much to Stuarts' approval. He liked to show her off but Sofia got the sense that he was in fact showing off the ring as he held out her hand to anyone who came close to talk to her. It perfectly complimented her gorgeous manicured hand.

Sofia was having a good time but at the back of her mind she was trying to process why she had the sense that she was being lifted up and then immediately pulled down throughout the evening.

The party was mainly friends from Stuarts' church who all seemed to have the same DNA that churned out the up, down, hot, cold environment. Within a split second a compliment of *'You look amazing, what a stunning figure you have'* would be instantaneously flipped into *'But I expect to see you at the church slimming club on Tuesdays. The girls and I will help you for the big day. We must not disappoint Stuart.'* Then to crown the insult Stuart would interject, *'Thanks sister we need all the help we can get'.* This was a confusing comment from someone who constantly told her that she looked fine and didn't need to worry about how she looked. However, she dismissed it thinking that Stuart was merely trying to please those nosy busy-body church mothers.

Then whilst serving a generous helping of blackberry pudding Sofia overheard the group of bible scholars who were discussing the topic of divorce and how it was a sin that they detested. These were people who knew full well that Sofia was a divorcee and they succeeded at laying a carpet of eggshells for her to crunch over. These were people who were gorging on their engagement cocktail sausages but clearly did not approve of their union.

However, normality was restored to the party when Skye arrived with Jacob. They were now married and enjoying every moment with each other.

The three of them enjoyed the food and drink and belly aching jokes. The only thing that slightly annoyed Sofia was that Stuart could not spend more than two minutes with them without getting up. However, in spite of Stuart's yoyo behaviour the evening as well as the wine went down well.

CHAPTER 37

Skye and Jacob were at home ready to enjoy a quiet evening together on the couch by watching a movie and binging on avocado and cashew dip with vegetable sticks.

Jacob came in with a tray of nibbles and coffee mugs and placed them on the coffee table before he softly collapsed onto the lounger close to his wife who was fiddling with the remote. Jacob began to serve a plate of crudités for Skye when the front door bell rang.

"Who could that be?" asked Skye.

"Don't know. Not expecting anyone." Jacob pushed back the curtain and looked out the window. He looked puzzled. "It's Sofia."

"Sofia?" asked Skye.

"Did she tell you she was coming? Jacob went to the front door.

"No, and she usually calls. I hope everything is ok." Skye became worried.

"Well we're about to find out," he opened the door. "Hey old girl what brings you here?"

"Hi Jacob. Oh you're here?"

"In the flesh," said Jacob.

"Oh dear have I got the wrong day? Hi Skye, did I get it wrong?"

"Oh babe, were you thinking about our girlie day? That's supposed to be next week? Come in love."

"Oh gosh it's next week. I am so sorry," said Sofia.

"Easily done," said Jacob

"Ok I'm leaving and I will see you next week. Sorry."

"Don't be silly come in and have a cup of tea," Jacob beckoned her to come in.

"No, I don't want to take you two's time."

"You've come all this way so might as well have a cuppa and a bickie at least."

"Come on Sofia. It's lovely to see you." Skye pulled her in for a hug. Skye noticed that her friend had been holding back tears.

Sofia and Skye made themselves cosy in the second reception room whilst Jacob served them up two hot steaming cups of tea and a plate of Jacobs crackers sandwiched with chocolate spread. "I'll be in the front room," said Jacob as he closed the door.

"I will be going soon. I saw the crudités in the living room."

"Don't be silly. Take your time. Besides it will give that husband of mine a chance to watch the cricket. I just can't understand the game and I don't have the patience for it."

"I can tell it's your couch night so I'm not going to ruin it" She took a big gulp of tea.

"Easy with that. You don't want to burn your throat."

"You have a great husband Skye." Sofia sighed a little.

"I do indeed...why the long face?"

"It's nothing. Maybe I'm just tired."

"Is everything alright with Stuart?"

Sofia adjusted herself in her seat.

"Have you had a row?" Skye asked.

"No, of course not."

"Then what is it?"

"I don't think we're right for each other."

"You mean you and Stuart?"

"Yes me and Stuart."

"Honestly I'm surprised. I thought you guys were..."

"I know. It's confusing."

"So what happened?"

"I can't explain it. It's just a feeling."

"Could it be cold feet?"

"No I don't think so."

"So have you broken things off with him?"

"No I haven't. I'm just trying to figure out what to do."

"You know I support you whatever you decide."

"But what do you think of him?" Sofia was eager for Skye's response.

"Well I don't know Stuart that well. He seemed to make you happy so he ticked all the boxes for me. But then again when you have Uche as a point for comparison anyone would be an angel I guess." This made them laugh. "But seriously what are you going to do? You have to at least tell him how you're feeling."

"I want to take Hypnotherapy sessions."

"Hypnotherapy? Ok so do you have a therapist already?"

"My last Therapist gave me a recommendation."

"Will you tell Stuart about it?"

"No."

"Ok. Can I ask why?"

"He won't approve. That's why I stopped my last Therapy sessions. He thinks Therapy is for people who lack faith and he insisted that I stop. But now I know it was the wrong decision. I believe in Therapy. Michael, my last therapist helped me work through so many issues and I felt so much better for it. I shouldn't have listened to Stuart. So I'm asking for your help. The Hypnotherapy sessions are online and I need to use your laptop, and if you don't mind, in your house because..."

"Babe you know I'm here for you but I don't think it's healthy to keep things from your partner especially something like this."

Sofia began to look flustered. "I'm terrified of losing him Skye especially if I'm wrong. This very well could be cold feet but I want to be sure. I'm thinking the therapy could help me to understand myself better. Help me to figure out why I keep attracting the same sort of man. Remember Sam?"

"Yeah I remember him. Jerk."

"What about Mark and Andrew?" Skye was nodding as Sofia continued. "I mean all of those guys were creeps. But I stood my ground. I never let them near me. But with Uche I don't know what happened. I knew. He made me nervous the first day I met him. But I got confused. I got hooked and maybe being older I was scared of being alone for the rest of my life. And I'm terrified that I might be doing the same thing. Stuart is the first guy since Uche but he looks exactly like him."

"Like who?" asked Skye.

"Like Uche. I feel like Stuart is Uche but with a mask on. He's more refined but cruel. He is the intelligent kind of cruel."

Skye squeezed Sofia's shoulder. "Those are really strong words. I had no idea you felt this way babe."

"How would you know with me constantly trying to cover things up? That's my problem. I'm always trying to patchwork things that should stay torn." She buried her head in her hands.

"I think the therapy is a great idea. Maybe it will help you to sort out the difference between what's real and what's not. Use the spare room for as long as you need."

"I need you to promise not to tell Stuart."

"I won't but I will need to tell Jacob."

"Yes of course. Thanks Skye." They lingered in an embrace.

CHAPTER 38

Week after week Sofia showed up at Skye's door. She would bury herself in the spare room for 45 minutes sometimes for an hour. There were days when Skye would hear sobbing from behind the door but she restrained herself from going in because she had promised to give her friend some privacy. But it was agonising to see her friend come out the room with bloodshot eyes and then sitting with a cup of tea in an uncomfortable silence.

Two months into the sessions Sofia's Therapist recommended that online therapy was not the best for her as he felt that she needed hands on after care which could not be done online. He recommended a Therapist in London. Her sessions subsequently moved from Skye's spare room to a couch in London. As she gained perspective into her situation and gained more self confidence she decided that keeping all this from Stuart was no longer serving a good purpose.

Every Thursday Stuart and Sofia would meet at Starbucks for coffee and she decided that when Stuart walked through the door it was time to tell him.

"Hey babe," Stuart came in and hugged her. He wore French connection tweed with a back t-shirt and trousers. On his wrist was a designer watch and on his feet dark Timberland Bradstreet Chukka boots. He smelt divine. His smile would cause anyone to melt. There was nothing not to like. "Have you ordered?"

"No just got here." She put down her phone.

"You smell good. Is that the one I just got you?" he asked.

"No it's something different but thank you so do you."
He started walking towards the queue."What drink do you want?"

"I'll have a flat white. Thanks babe."

"Nothing to eat?"

"No, not hungry."

"Ok babe." Stuart stood up and went to place their orders and pay for their coffees.

He came back with her flat white, his cafe latte and an enormous slice of vanilla cake and two forks. She looked at him. He shrugged his shoulders. "You can share it with me if you change your mind."

He cut off a generous piece of the cake with his fork and popped it in his mouth as Sofia took a sip of her drink.

"Oh babe you're missing out. Come one have a piece."

She shook her head. "Babe I need to tell you something."
He was nodding. "Ok but I've got something important before you tell me."

"Ok Stuart you go first."

"My sis called me and she popped the question."
Sofia was confused. "Popped the question? What do you mean?"

"She wants to know if we have set a date."

"For what?"

He tapped on her head. "Hello. Is there anybody in there? The wedding darling."

She pushed his hand out of the way. "Oh the wedding. Yes of course. So what did you tell her?"

"I told her I'd discuss it with you."
She was nervous. "I see."

"I was thinking May."

"But that's just two months away."

"The quicker the better for us to become one don't you think."

"Babe I wanted to tell you something."

"What could be more important than setting our wedding date?"

"I'm seeing a Therapist."

He put his fork down. "What?"

She was trembling. "I said I'm seeing a Therapist."

"Babe I thought we talked about this."

"We did but I thought it was best for me."

"So you started without checking with me first?"

"I knew you wouldn't approve."

Signs of fuming began to collect around his mouth and eyelids. "How long have you been seeing the Therapist?"

She cleared her throat. "Three months."

He threw down his napkin. She flinched. "Is it that same Therapist? Michael whatever his name is?"

"No."

He stood up. "I'll take you home. We shouldn't be discussing this in public."

She followed him to the car park in silence. He opened the car door for her and ushered her in without looking at her. He turned the key in the ignition and sped off down the motorway.

"I'm really sorry," she said.

"Sorry for what?"

"For not telling you."

"Well why didn't you?"

"I've already told you why."

"So what is it? Is it an urge to talk to another man?"

She shook her head. "My therapist is a woman."

"And you think that makes this ok?"

"No. I just believe that this is something I needed."

"You don't even know what you need babe."

"What do you mean?"

"I mean exactly what I said. You don't know what you need. Ok so this is it. You went through a very abusive relationship and I get that it traumatised you but I am not that guy."

"I don't think you are..."

"Babe you think I don't see you dodging me and second

guessing whether you want to be with me in spite of all that I have done for you? But I'm patient enough to know that you're going through it. You're bound to see that psycho in me because your mind is still playing tricks on you. It's all in your head babe. It's all in your head."

She was stunned. "I think..."

"You see that's the problem babe. You're thinking too much. You should stop thinking and put your trust in God." He started to raise his voice. "How many times do I have to ask you where your faith is babe? Trust me you don't need some Muppet getting you to lie on a couch and talk about your feelings all day. If you ask me you should stop this therapy thing right now."

"But it's helping me Stuart."

"I should be helping you. I am going to be your husband Sofia. Isn't my opinion important to you? And have you forgotten that I actually love you Sofia. This is not a joke that you can just switch off just because your mind is playing tricks on you." She tried to touch his shoulder which he shifted quickly but tried to pretend that he was changing gears. "I don't doubt that you love me and of course your opinion is important to me. You are important to me," she said.

"Then you better seriously reconsider this Therapy thing. I know I'm right." He parked the car outside her house. She opened the door to get out. "I'm coming tomorrow morning and we are going to hash this out. We have got to put things right." Without looking at her he said goodbye, sped off down the road without waiting to make sure that she had gotten into the house which was his normal custom.

CHAPTER 39

The next day she had a cooked breakfast ready when Stuart arrived at 7.30am. They sat and ate in silence which is something that they never did.

Stuart wiped his mouth with his napkin.

"More coffee?" she asked.

He shook his head. "No thanks." He shifted his chair backwards. "So have you had a thought about what we talked about yesterday?"

"I have." She took his plate and cutlery and began to scrape the leftovers into her plate.

He scrunched up the napkin he had finished with and placed it on top the scrapings she was shifting onto one plate. "Good. You can phone that therapist today and cancel."

"I'm not cancelling Stuart."

"So you didn't hear a word I said?"

"I heard every word."

"Then stop this foolishness."

Sofia became indignant. "You know what? I couldn't figure out what it was until you spoke yesterday."

"Figured out what? Why it is that you feel like ending our relationship? Why you think we're not right for each other? For goodness sake Sofia, are you 12? I said I'm not him. Can't you get it out of that imagination of yours that runs way too wild?"

"My imagination? You never consider my opinion about anything and yet you want me to consider yours." She slammed the fork onto the plate.

He looked at the plate. "Yes I do Sofia."

"When I told you that the Therapy was good for me you didn't listen."

"Because I know what's best for you."

"But this is my life Stuart. It's my life."

"What do you know about life? This relationship is the best thing that has happened to you in months, in years even, but you are willing to ruin it because of the tricks your mind plays on you. You're letting Uche destroy everything good. He's moved on with his life but you are still stuck in the past." He pulled the pile of plates towards him. Sofia wondered what he was doing. "I mean what have I not done for you? Is it not money or clothes?"

"And I appreciate it all," she said.

"Well I don't see that appreciation. All I see is that I'm being blamed for what another man has done. I try so hard, maybe too hard sometimes, to show you that I'm not Uche."

"I don't mean to hurt you."

"You don't mean it Sofia but it damn well hurts."

"I'm really sorry. I don't mean to...I just..."

"Honey every time you go to a Therapist all I will be thinking is Uche is still on her mind taking over and taking control. Consuming and occupying every facet of her mind and that drives me crazy that that idiot still has a hold on you. If I could erase all that you went through I would. But I can't."

"I know you can't. But I just want a way to sort out what I feel in my mind. I want to get to know me and be sure of what I want."

"So you're unsure about me?"

She hesitated. Her heart melted as she saw the desperation in his face. "No I'm not unsure about you." She lied.

"Then let me be your therapy. Let me be the one that you run to for a shoulder to cry on or someone to talk to." She was silent. "Please Sofia?"

She pulled him in for a hug. "I will think about it ok," she said.

He pulled away from the hug, stood up and took the dirty dishes to the kitchen. She turned to the window looking worried.

CHAPTER 40

On one of their regular girlie meetings Skye was eager to talk to Sofia. Early that day Skye had asked Sofia to come to the coffee shop a little earlier than usual as she had something important to say to her.

Throughout the day Sofia wondered what it could have been. She pondered on whether Skye was pregnant or whether she and Jacob had finally made the decision to move to Birmingham.

"Ok spit it out then," said Sofia eager to hear Skye's news. Skye sipped on her chamomile tea. "Stuart came to see us."

"Stuart? When?"

"A few days ago."

"And?" Sofia asked.

"Babe he was in bits."

"About what? What do you mean bits?" The tea burnt her lip.

"He was in bits over you. The man was in tears and I really felt for him. He is worried that you're not coping."

"Not coping with what? The guy doesn't want me to go to counselling but he wants to go behind my back telling people that I'm not coping."

"Sofia he's not just a guy going behind your back. He's your fiancé and that's a big difference. He loves you and wants to help."

"I know I need help but he won't let me go for counselling."

"You haven't been listening to him Sofia."

"I'm the one not listening? Phew how quickly tables are turned."

"Look he wants to help you. He wants to be in your life. And from what I've seen I believe that he loves you and wants the best for you."

"And I appreciate that but..."

"But you're not listening. He's not Uche Sofia. He's Stuart, the guy who has fallen madly in love with you. He told us everything that he's planning to do to help you with your journey. It's like he really understands what you went through and wants to be there for you. Every step he said."

"But what about what I want?"

"I think that when we've been hurt our mind gets clouded sometimes. We don't know what we need."

"That's exactly what Stuart says."

Skye looked a little guilty. "Yes he said that to me too. Maybe what you need to do is look a little closer at what's right in front of you instead of looking elsewhere. He's a good man."

"It's counselling. Not another man Skye."

"I think it's a good excuse."

"What do you mean excuse?"

"You're afraid of being with someone that's the real thing."

"No Skye I really don't think that..."

"Sofia, I've known you for years. Get out of your own way and don't ruin the best thing that's ever happened to you. Sorry to be harsh but I say it as I see it. We got to know Stuart a little better the other day and I'm only saying this because I love you. You're so wrong."

Sofia felt cornered and her lip hurt like hell.

#

Sofia was headed to Skye and Jacob's house. They had invited her for lunch and a talk. Skye had said that she was not happy with the way that they had left things the previous week at the cafe.   Sofia was happy because this meant that her friend was willing to repair the rift that seemed to have appeared in their friendship.

She was excited. Skye had promised her oxtail and mash and she had brought her homemade hot rolls and a bottle of wine. She rang the door bell. The door opened and Sofia found herself startled.

"Hey babe,"

"What are you doing here Stuart?"

"I thought I'd surprise you. When you told me you were going over to Skye's I tried so hard to stop myself from going into hysterics." Stuart grinned. She was not impressed.

She walked into the hallway and Stuart took the rolls and wine out of her hands.

He frowned. "Wine?"

She had a tinge of guilt across her forehead. "For Skye. It's her favourite."

"For Skye? But she's pregnant."

"She's pregnant?"

"Yes she's pregnant. You didn't know?"

"No I didn't."

"Well I've known for weeks." Sofia felt that she could have been mistaken by the fact that she saw a cruel grin quickly sweep across Stuart's face and disappear just as quickly as it had appeared.

"I'm surprised she didn't tell me." She turned away from him to hang her coat up on the peg.

"Well you've probably been too busy in counselling." This hurt her. She swiftly turned around to address him.

"Hey babe. Good to see you." Skye appeared and ruined the mini verbal attack that she had planned for Stuart. Skye pulled Sofia in for a hug. Sofia switched her annoyance to a smile.

"Be gentle with the mummy to be," said Stuart looking

triumphant.

Skye pulled away. "Oh you've told her."

"Yes I had to. She brought you some red wine." He shook his head.

"Oh thanks darling. Ordinarily this would go down like a treat. But not for the next nine months." She chuckled.

"So it is true," Sofia said.

"Didn't you believe me babe?" Stuart asked.

She ignored him. "I'm so happy for you love. That's grand news. Why didn't you tell me?" She hugged her warmly.

"We've been so busy. We're trying to get the nursery ready and Stuart has been marvellous at landscaping our garden. He's a gem by the way."

"You're doing their garden?" She asked Stuart."

Stuart looked pleased with himself. "Yeah it's a gift for the baby. They'll need a good play area. Skye and Jacob are family so it's the least I could do."

"I see. That's lovely."

They walked into the living room where Sofia hugged Jacob and gave her congratulations. Stuart walked out into the garden where he continued the barbecue. Jacob began hugging his wife and Sofia for the first time felt like an outsider.

She followed Stuart into the garden. He was roasting the sausages and the chicken, basting them here and there whilst watching Sofia.

"Do you want a drink babe?"

She shook her head. "So when did you start working on their garden?"

"I don't know. Two to three weeks ago."

"Why didn't you tell me?"

"It's a job babe. We don't normally discuss who I do my landscaping for do we?."

"But this isn't a regular job is it. Skye is my best friend. You didn't think to mention it?"

"Look if you're suggesting that I'm trying to come between you and your friend, you're wrong."

"I'm suggesting nothing of the sort."

"But you're angry?"

"I'm angry about what Stuart?"

"That your friends see me for who I really am; a good guy."

"This is absurd."

"No darling what's absurd is that you are determined to paint me as the villain. You really want me to turn out bad because that's what you're used to."

"I see what you're doing. You're trying to turn my fiends against me because I refused to listen to you. Is this my punishment?"

"I don't know what you're talking about."

"I'm not stupid Stuart."

"I help your friends, actually our friends to do up their garden and I'm the enemy?"

"Yes you do them a few favours and swan in like the saviour of the day and they are putty in your hands. Oh Stuart this, and Stuart that – he's a good guy..."

"But he is babe," Skye interjected.

Sofia turned around embarrassed that Skye had overheard her rant.

"Sofia, Stuart was just trying to help. We're not putty in his hands. In fact we're all trying to help you."

"Trying to help me with what? By ignoring me and totally disregarding my feelings? Is that how you're helping me?" She was raising her voice.

"Why don't we all calm down," said Jacob.

Skye held onto her belly. "Well, I'm not calming down. Not this time. I've had enough of this. What do you mean by totally disregarding your feelings? Your feelings are all we have ever heard Sofia. Ever since we were kids it's always been about Sofia this and Sofia that and whoever was doing something bad to you. Never about me was it? Good old Skye, like clockwork, flying in to hear about your endless woes. But I always used to wonder why you couldn't shut up and just look at the bloody person looking at you in the mirror. Granted, people like Uche were nasty but you let it happen to you Sofia. Every time you let them do it. And you always went back for more. You could never see that it was your fault. And now you're too pig headed to see what good you have in front of you. And I'm sick of it Sofia. You carry on with this foolishness, this guy will leave you. I'm sorry to say it but that's what I think and damn it I won't blame him." Jacob pulled Skye away.

Sofia was taken aback. "Wow. Is that how you really feel?"

"I'm sorry Sofia. I've said my piece."

"God Skye, you can't tell me that you believe that it was my fault. I cried in your lap for days." Sofia was left standing in the middle of the garden stunned.

Stuart began to remove charred pieces of sausage and chicken that had been burnt to charcoal.

Sofia walked back into the house and passed Skye and Jacob who had taken refuge in the living room. They watched as Sofia grabbed her coat. Stuart entered the room.

Jacob tried to call out to her. "Sofia, please wait. Maybe you should go after her Stuart."

"It's best to leave her when she's like this."

"He's right," said Skye.

Sofia walked down the road heartbroken and embarrassed.

CHAPTER 41

S ofia arrived at work early. She had not spoken to anyone since the incident at Skye's home. Jacob had been on leave and she was not looking forward to sitting next to him in the office upon his return to work. It was undoubtedly going to feel very awkward.

She had spent the week crying herself to sleep, writing poems about her miserable life and wondering whether returning Stuarts' engagement ring in the post was too harsh a reaction.

She walked down the hallway and straight to the lab. She was determined to get stuck in to meet the deadline for the launch of *Diana* the new strawberry variety.

She turned the light on, slotted in her ID card and headed for her desk. To her surprise her desk was empty. She rushed over to take a better look. Her files and notebooks were gone, in fact the table had been wiped down taking away all the memories she had etched in since starting her job. She began dialling the desk telephone when the door was pushed open.   Smeeta the office administrator walked in.

"Smeeta you're just the person I need to solve this riddle."

"Morning Sofia. A riddle, did you say?"

"Yes my desk is completely cleared out. Any ideas why?"

"Oh yes, the new boss from America wants to be close to Jacob. They have back to back meetings scheduled so instead of looking for a room to book they felt that they would use your office for the period that he's here. And they didn't want you to be disturbed because it's a busy week ahead for you."

"I see,"

"When he gets in I'll ask him to come and apologise since it was short notice."

"No, it's fine Smeeta. Thanks for letting me know."

Smeeta led the way to office 201 where Sofia found her belongings piled on a black office desk that had seen many Christmases.

No sooner than Smeeta had left and she had begun to re-arrange the files on her desk Jacob popped his head around the door.

"Hello girl," he said with a smile that was slightly displaced.

"Oh hello, I thought you were on leave."

"I am. I've just popped in to meet the big boss. How are you?"

"You mean the man that has hijacked my desk?"

"Ah yes. I'm really sorry for the way that was handled. Head office totally lost their knack on this one."

"I'm not too bothered though. It will give me chance to catch up on the preparations for this week."

"Yes big things ahead. But seriously, how are you? I didn't like the way we left things."

She placed the files down. "I am totally embarrassed for the way I behaved. I shouldn't have walked out."

"Skye feels equally as bad. Maybe you girls should hash it out."

"I would love that. I was just angry because Skye was right. I have been extremely selfish. She has always been there for me, more than I've been there for her."

"Well maybe you could tell that to her in person. Patch things up."

Sofia smiled. "I will."

A bellowing American accent filled the hallway. "Jacob is that you?"

"Got to dash," said Jacob to Sofia.

"Mr Cruikshank, welcome."

"Now you know, I always insist on you calling me Tyler."

"Of course. Welcome back Tyler. Good to see you."

"Big week ahead of us."

"Indeed." Jacob led the way as Tyler followed. He took one glimpse into Sofia's office and caught her eye. He was a tall Afro- American man in a suit and bow tie with box cut hair and manicured nails. As he passed her door Sofia stood up to get a better look of the big boss as he followed Jacob down the hall in a military fashion.

Sofia began going through her numerous emails. As she was constructing a response to head office regarding timescales for *Diana's* launch party, an email from Stuart popped up. The title was 'is this a joke?' The sharp tone of his voice jumped out at her.

She hesitated and pondered whether she should open it or not. Opening it meant that most of her day would be consumed with thoughts of the damage behind that email. This was valuable time that she needed for the launch. She deliberated briefly then with one swift click she opened it as she could no longer take the suspense.

'What? Is this supposed to be a joke where I open a letter with my name on it and inside is a ring that I gave my fiancé. What do you want, a round of applause? Should I be laughing now or what? Just because you can't handle the fact that your friends know who you really are....'

"Miss Blackwell I presume?"

Sofia was startled. She looked up and saw the American boss standing in front of her. She minimised her email.

"I'm sorry I didn't mean to make you jump."

She stood up. "Mr Cruikshank, Welcome. Please take a seat."

"Please, call me Tyler."

She nodded. "Come and sit down Tyler. Would you like

some tea or coffee?"

He looked around her office before answering. She followed his gaze. He was looking at her 100% genuine leather Italian handbag. "Water please," he said.

She walked over to the mini fridge and bent over to open it and grab the bottle of water. She knew that he was watching her. She turned around quickly. He was still standing and surveying her. She looked straight at him and observed. His hairline was the top half of a square. The curls in his hair were arranged in shiny distinct patterns. Everything was in a straight line, rigid and controlling.

"Please sit down Tyler," she said as she sat down.

He placed the bottle of water on her table. He caught her eyes before loosening the top button of his suit jacket. He took it off slowly, turned around then bent over to hang his jacket on the back of the chair. He grabbed the bottle and sat down. "Umm Mauve I like it."

"Excuse me?" she said.

"Your nail polish. Attractive."

She looked down at her nails and frowned.

"This office suits you. I'm glad."

She allowed him to continue.

"We needed the office for senior staff. Not to say that you are not qualified. I urged them that you are perfectly capable at your job and completely qualified to be involved in this ground breaking event. So please don't put yourself down because of it."

She noticed a slight grin which quickly dissipated. She looked directly at him and swallowed the temptation to make him aware that it was her name in the papers and it was she who had done all the ground work to make the company shine. Instead she swallowed hard and chose diplomacy. "Of course. I can use this quiet space to get all my work done."

"Have dinner with me," he said. He took a big gulp of his water. Sofia noticed the attractiveness of his face.

"That's very kind of you to ask but I will have to decline."

"I'm a good listener. You look like you need a good shoulder to rest your pretty little head. I have good shoulders."

"That's very kind of you but…" There was a knock on the door. Jacob popped his head round.

"Sorry to disturb. Tyler the Zoom meeting has started."

"That's my cue." He left without looking at her or saying goodbye. Throughout the day he did not acknowledge her at all. It was a day of indirect belittling and insults all because she has rebuffed his proposition.

At the end of the day she was happy to leave the office and walk down the cobbled street that had the refreshing scent of strawberries wafting the air all the way to the train station.

When the train came she was eager to find her seat in order to sit down and read the numerous messages that had been causing her phone to vibrate all day.

"Someone's eager to get hold of you," her colleagues had commented earlier.

"It's just twitter notifications," she told them. But the reality was that Stuart Green had been firing text messages and calls throughout the day. As each message pinged and pinged and pinged she fought to hold back her tears. She tried hard to drown them out and remember Michaels voice in her head 'Don't react. Don't go on the defensive." After the 10th ping she switched the phone off and rushed to the toilet, passing by Tyler Cruikshank who was trying his hardest to break her down.

She sat down on the twin seat in the 5th row and pressed the button on her phone to assess the damage:29 missed calls from Stuart Green,52 text messages from Stuart Green, and 2 missed calls from an International number that she did not recognise. Despite the knots in her stomach and a familiar terror which surprised her she opened the messages.

Why aren't you answering my messages?

Pick up my calls please.

You're being rude

Why are you doing this to me?

You posted my ring back.

Who does that?

*I just called you. Why didn't
You pick up?*

*Is this how you treat me after all
I've done for you?*

*Now you're showing your true
colours?*

Well it's all becoming clear now?

I told you I'm not Uche.

*You told me that guy did nothing
for you. So how can you compare us?*

*I gave you everything.
Things you were not used to.

*Tell me did Uche give you the bags,
the perfume, the makeup? Did he
take you on holidays?*

Come on I'm waiting for you to tell me.

*What about the holidays and introducing
you to my top notch friends? But
I get no thanks for that.*

*I can't believe that you
have sent my ring back.*

*So you're saying it's over?
After all we have been through.
After all I've done for you.*

*So when you said you loved me
were you lying?

*You just do what you feel like
without considering me. It's
all about you.

*Skye was right. All you think
about is yourself. What about
everything I have invested in you?

*Who were you before I met you?
You were a simple woman afraid to
be herself. I had to think for you
but this is the thanks I get.

*I know you're getting all
these messages. So why aren't you
responding?

*I sent you several messages earlier
today but you have not responded. Is this
how you treat your future husband. Is my love
not enough for you?

*All I have ever done is love you
and this is the thanks I get.

*I love you Sofia. I truly love you.

*I want to be with you.

*Please call me when you get this
message.

*I just called you 9 times Sofia.
If this is not love then what
do you call it.

*A man calls you several times. He
Texts you and tells you he loves
you but you ignore him. What more
do you want Sofia.

*So you want to be alone for the rest
of your life licking your Uche wounds?
Do you know how hard it is to get
a man like me?

*What do they call people like you?
Ungrateful is the word. You told me
yourself that nobody wanted you.

*You don't even get along with your own
brother. Where is Langton today? And who is to
say that Uche actually treated you
the way you said he did. Out of the goodness
of my heart I was willing to take your word for it.
But this is the thanks I get? Unbelievable.

She couldn't read anymore. She constructed a text message
trying to fire back about her brother in the fashion of it was
none of Stuarts business regarding her relationship with
her brother. She deleted it and threw her phone in her bag.
In a rage she took it out again and began to construct a text
about Uche in the fashion of how dare Stuart insinuate that
her ordeal of abuse was all in her head? She wrote a long
note about how she was emotionally abused for years and
yet he, her so called fiancé had tried to block her therapy.
As she wrote reams and reams of trying to defend herself
and defend her actions and how she was now entirely sure
that her decision to return the ring was the right thing she
stopped and looked out the window. She watched the view
of the trees pass by in the fastest slow motion she had ever
seen. She looked at the text and deleted it as she listened to

Michael's voice in her head. "Try your hardest not to defend yourself. Just delete."

She pressed the 'delete all' button and watched as all the venom was cleared from her phone. She flung it in her bag. She relaxed back and stared out the window. She couldn't cry. She was just numb.

CHAPTER 42

The day of *Diana's* launch came. All the preparations had been made. She had worked hard alongside trying to dodge numerous Stuart Green attempts to get hold of her.

He had sent another ream of texts that she deleted. He had left roses at her doorstep and tried to intercept her shopping at the local supermarket. However, all his attempts had failed.

Then there were the unsolicited angry looks from Tyler Cruikshank whenever they passed each other in the hallway. To say she was exhausted was an understatement.

By 7pm guests were flooding into the venue. The decor was beautiful with a strawberry and foliage theme and Sofia looked stunning in her diamante gown.

She glowed as the host and completed the task with the utmost professionalism. Jacob and Skye looked on with pride whilst Jacob propped up Skye's overarched back with cushions and rubbing her bump every now and then.

Skye and Sofia had managed to patch things up. They met at their usual coffee place to embrace and apologise. They made their admissions to each other and promised to start again on good ground. Sofia was grateful for the reconciliation but was sober enough to realise that her friendship with Skye would never be quite the same again.

The evening went well but she had not anticipated that Stuart would show up at the event. Of course he still had the ticket as her plus one.

When her eyes spotted him she picked up her glass of wine and gulped it down in one. She lifted up the edge of her diamante dress and in a slight speed made her way to the ladies. Sitting on the toilet she took two deep breaths and pumped her inhaler. The inhaler was a new development that was prescribed by her G.P. to help to relax her.

She stood up tall, washed hands in the basin, dried them and creamed them to soothe the rash that was developing at the back of her hands. After a few sprays of her fragrance she placed a tablet under her tongue which began to fizz. She arched her back, smiled and walked back into the room.

"Hey Sofia," Stuart was standing with a plate of strawberries. "Talk to me."

"Stuart this isn't the place."

"At least speak to me. You didn't give me a chance to have my say."

"I will."

"When? I've called you all week but nothing."

"Listen, not here. Please. I will call you."

"Why don't I believe that?"

She was standing in a corner and he was in front of her. She saw no gap to fit through to the rest of the room or to where Skye and Jacob were sampling the cheeseboard.

"I said I'll call you Stuart."

"I send you flowers but it's not enough. Or maybe you never got them?"

"I got the flowers."

Tyler Cruikshank walked past and caught her eye. He still looked angry.

"And you couldn't think to call and thank me? Or a text even," said Stuart.

"I'm sorry Stuart. I have a lot on my mind right now. And besides, you know that I have never been one for flowers. So why give me flowers?"

He ignored her. "You gave me back the ring Sofia. Does that

not mean anything to you? We are getting married. I would say that should be at the top of your priorities." He moved closer to her.

"I can't talk about this right now."

"Why? You owe me an explanation."

She moved to the side and he followed. She moved to the other and he followed again.

"Can you get out of my way please?"

"Hey. Who are you talking to like that?"

She tried to push past him. He grabbed her arm.

She pulled away. "Let go of me Uche." She had shouted and everyone was looking at them.

He looked around at all the eyes staring at them then back to Sofia. "I told you that I'm not Uche. Have it your way," he looked around again to the very curious faces. "It's over Sofia," he said in a volume that ensured that all the spectators could hear then he walked out.

She was numb. He was embarrassed. The only face she saw was at the back of the room. It was Tyler Cruikshank with a look of triumph plastered on his mouth.

It was a work event, so she couldn't leave.

#

A new chapter of her life had begun. She was alone again as they had officially ended their relationship.

Her days were quiet. She kept herself busy at work, rarely coming out for lunch or a chat. When Tyler Cruikshank returned to America she was given the option to return to her old office but she opted to decline. She had become accustomed to the beautiful view of the farm and the waft of fresh strawberry air that lifted her spirits every time.

The waters were beginning to settle after writing an apology to management for her conduct at the *Diana* launch party. The apology was accepted and was returned with a minor slap of her wrist.

She had also begun to recover from the humiliating experience of Stuarts sisters who came to collect the bags, shoes and new dresses in boxes and bags still unopened in her closet. "If she wasn't going to marry him then she didn't deserve them," they said in a very annoyed way. These were her possessions but Sofia chose peace and silently allowed them to go through her home collecting items, some of which she had bought for herself.

He cancelled her gym membership which had been a birthday present and without notification cancelled a mobile phone contract which inconvenienced her for a period until she paid for another. However, in spite of the humiliating break-up she carried on strong and had her Therapy as a great support. In reality it was the only thing that kept her going.

Several weeks later, she was working hard on an article for Culture Horticultural Magazine, when Smeeta came into her office with a slight tap on the door. She pulled down her reading glasses over the crown of her nose.

"Hello Smeeta. What can I do for you?"

"Hello to you too dear. There's a Mrs Ambrose here to see you."

"Mrs Ambrose?"

"Yes she says she knows you."

Sofia looked at her watch. "Ok please send her in." Smeeta disappeared whilst Sofia stood up and looked out over the beautiful view. She took in a deep breath and squeezed her hands. She thrust her hand in her bag and fished out lipstick, a mini-brush and a compact mirror. With her hand in a slight shake she eased over her baby hairs with the mini-brush. Her lipstick popped out and was used to cream up her lips to a matte burgundy pout. After a few inspections the three items were thrust back into the bag.

"Sofia."

She turned around. "Mrs H."

Mrs H noticed a smudging of burgundy in the corner of her lip. "It's been a long time my dear."

"It has but you look well Mrs H."

"Thank you dear. I'm sure you have been eating 100% fruits. You look amazing."

"Thanks Mrs H." She smiled and tried to hide how nervous she felt.

"Can I sit down?"

"Oh yes of course. Please forgive my manners." Sofia pulled out the chair for her.

"Oh, there is nothing to forgive. How have you been?" Mrs H straightened out her crisp blue skirt and placed her satin ultramarine blue gloves on the desk. The bodice top with different hues of blue lined her figure to perfection and the peacock feather fascinator finished the look with elegance.

"I've been well Mrs H. Tea?"

"Thank you Sofia. I would love a cup but I have something delicate I need to discuss with you. Is there somewhere more comfortable we can go to discuss this?"

Sofia looked at her watch, looked through her diary and thought for a minute. "Well you could come with me for lunch."

"Perfect."

They walked together down the path towards Amakele cafe. A rash began to flare up on Sofia's arm."

"Are you ok?" asked Mrs H.

Sofia didn't answer.

"What's the matter with your arm?"

"Huh?"

"Your arm?"

"Oh sorry, I was miles away. I might have brushed some nettles. It just feels a bit stingy.

Mrs H reached down in her bag. "Here. Use this." She handed a tube to her.

"What's this?"

"Jamaica's best bee balm."

"Bee balm?"

"Yes it should help with the itching?"

"Thanks." She opened the cap and lifted it to her nose for

a whiff. The peppermint smell was accompanied by a strong stench that came from her armpit. Her nostrils flared as she noticed the sweat stains on her shirt. She squeezed then rubbed the balm on her arm.

They got to Amakele and picked a table. Sofia excused herself and went to the bathroom whilst Mrs H perused the menu. In the bathroom Sofia washed her hands and looked in the mirror. A shine had surfaced on her face making her look tired. She reached down into her bag and reached for the watermelon deodorant spray. She sprayed both underarms twice each until the pong had been drowned. Then she proceeded to powder her face. She took one last look in the mirror then made her way back.

"So what brings you here?" Sofia asked over salmon, chips, salad and ice cold elderflower water.

Mrs H swallowed. "I won't beat around the bush."

"I appreciate that. How did you find me?"

"I read an article in Culture."

Sofia nodded. "Did you hear about Hortense and my husband?"

Mrs H looked down. "I did?"

"So you must know that I know that Hortense is my sister." She lost her appetite then used her napkin to rub the corner of her eye that was going red.

Mrs H put her knife and fork down. "I think I should explain a few things. I had an affair with your father."

Sofia looked down.

"But we loved each other." Mrs H looked at her.

"I don't think that's something I should be hearing?"

"The last thing I want to do is embarrass you. When I fell pregnant with Hortense I was married at the time to Mr Ambrose but he couldn't have any children or so we thought."

"Hortense is my sister then?"

"I don't know."

"What do you mean you don't know? Mr Ambrose couldn't have any children but you had an affair with dad. That clearly makes my dad her father."

Mrs H looked away.

Sofia joined the dots in shock. "Oh God."

"I'm not sure who her father is. I was going through a lot back then. I hooked up with anyone who would listen."

"Does Hortense know this?"

"I told her everything."

"That's not the version I heard. To me it seemed that Hortense was convinced that my dad was hers. At least that's the version she told my ex."

"I'm really sorry for what you had to go through."

"Mrs H I'm not the one who you should be apologising to. You do remember my mother don't you?"

"God rest her soul. I tried to."

"So you admitted the affair to her?"

She hesitated. "Your mother was a difficult person to..."

"She wasn't difficult. She was distraught because her husband was cheating on her and flaunting it in her face."

Mrs H put her napkin down. "I'm sorry for that. I was selfish. My husband was very controlling. Everything had to be done in a particular way. I'm sorry to say but when I met your father he made me come alive."

"But he was married."

"I know. It was wrong but I cared for him. When we first met I was only engaged. I really thought he would leave Nouara for me but he wouldn't do it. He said that he loved your mother."

Sofia shook her head. "What kind of love is that?"

"Well, love enough not to leave her for me. It crushed me. My fiancé had left and I had nothing and no one. I finally went back to my fiancé. We married and I miscarried the child that I was certain was your dads."

Sofia was in shock. "You had a miscarriage?"

"Yes I did...At some point your dad and I rekindled our affair but this was after I gave birth to Hortense. My husband was a very cold man so I looked elsewhere for comfort."

"Your comfort ruined the lives of other people."

"I've already said that I was selfish. I was young and foolish. Passion was our priority back then."

Sofia looked annoyed. "And your poor husband who had to put up with it all."

"He knew that other men were getting me pregnant but he forgave me each time because he said he loved me." She brushed a tear away.

Sofia raised her hand for the bill. "I'm going to have to get back to work."

Mrs H nodded. "Of course and I thank you for your time. I just wanted to apologise for what Hortense put you through. It was not right."

"I forgave Hortense a long time ago Mrs H. I just refuse to speak to her... You know it's uncanny that the little piece of paper that Uncle Max gave me all those years ago resulted in such revelations. Totally weird."

"Uncle Max? Is that your father's friend?"

"That's him. I told him I was going to London and he knew of someone who needed a flat mate so he gave me the advertisement slip. That's how I got to flat share with Hortense."

"That bastard."

"I'm sorry?"

"Please excuse my language. I just don't think too much of Max. Hortense stayed with him for a period before she moved to London."

"Max is the Uncle she stayed with?"

"The very one."

"I'm surprised that Uncle never mentioned that he knew Hortense."

"He got her the flat and everything." Mrs H looked disgusted.

"So he wasn't all bad then Mrs H. He got your daughter a flat."

Mrs H looked remorseful. "Well I suppose I am being a bit excessive. He was very kind to me when your father started ignoring me." She looked into the distance. Sofia tried to see what she was looking at. She was looking right through an Egyptian mural on the opposite wall. "They were good friends. But Max was the one who was the most grounded. He was kind and a good listener you know. But he was annoying with his high and mighty ways about being a man of the cloth. Man of the cloth my foot indeed. That cloth only came out when it suited him and he removed it whenever anything caught his eye..."

Sofia brought her memories to an abrupt halt. "Oh so he was a good listener? Well he could be Hortenses's dad then. Problem solved."

Mrs H clasped her hands together on the table. "I see you have your mother's temper."

"I really have to go now Mrs H." Sofia put money on the bill with a generous extra for Mrs H to have dessert and coffee."

"Sofia you are very kind."

"What's next for you Mrs H?"

"I'm here for another two weeks then back to Jamaica."

"Well have a safe trip. But I appreciate you coming." She walked out, looked down the road, thought a little and then came back.

Mrs H looked up wondering why she was back.

"Mrs H there's something that's still bugging me. You were so quick to tell me that you had an affair with my dad and yet I remember you from my dad's funeral. You came in and tried to pay your respects but my mother wasn't having it and wanted you to leave. I heard you tell her that there was nothing going on and that you and my dad were just friends. I remember that as clear as day and I think that you do too."

Mrs H looked embarrassed, like someone who had been unmasked. She put down the dessert menu. She could not bring herself to say anything.

"You see you messed around with her mind by telling her that nothing was going on and yet both of you betrayed her day after day. What I will never understand Mrs H is why people tell lies and then make the people who are trying to tell the truth seem crazy. It's all just a game and I don't know if you can get any meaner than that. Another damning thing Mrs H is that you told me point blank that you didn't know my parents. There is no way that you would forget Kingston and Nouara Blackwell is there? I'm sorry Mrs H but I'm really struggling to believe you."

"Sofia," is what Mrs H finally managed to say.

"Goodbye Mrs H." Sofia left the cafe and walked back to the office wiping tears that she couldn't help but cry.

CHAPTER 43

Sofia stood outside number 107 Harrow Street, a few yards away from the newsagent owned by Mr Raj. As soon as she rang the bell the door opened.

"Sofia is that you?"

"It's me Uncle Max."

"What brings you to Dorset? Come in dear."

"Oh I thought I'd come and see mum and dad and I wanted to check on you."

"Good to see you my dear." He gave her a soft hug and she kissed him on the cheek.

During tea and Mcvitie's chocolate biscuits they enjoyed a few episodes of Desmond's. This was Uncle Max's past time since retirement.

"So how are you?" he asked.

"I'm ok Uncle. I just get a bit tired sometimes."

"You need a holiday. Book a couple of weeks in Jamaica. It will do you good. Plus it's about time you go and meet some of your dad's family."

"I know Uncle. It's well overdue."

"Family is everything you know."

Sofia nodded. "You're right Uncle."

"You heard from your brother?"

"No not for years."

Uncle Max shook his head. "You two have got to end this. All you two have got is each other."

Sofia stood up and took the dirty cups and plates to the kitchen. She spent a bit of time washing up before returning and sitting next to Max.

"Uncle, do you know Hortense Ambrose?"

He hesitated. "There are two and I know them both. Why do you ask?"

"I didn't know you knew my flat mate."

"I did. I found that flat in London you know."

"Did she live with you first?"

"She did but that was the first mistake I ever made. I took her in as a favour to her mother but I was not about to have my house used as a meeting place for her boyfriends. Her mother was a friend to your parents so I was helping a sister you know. We were all very close back then so I couldn't say no to one of our own. But my house is God's house. I refused to be party to the works of the devil. So I kicked her out you know."

Sofia frowned. "You kicked her out? I thought you found her a flat.

He nodded. "But later I felt my Christian duty tugging. I couldn't just leave her in the cold you know. It wasn't right."

"But why didn't you tell me Uncle?"

Max barged on. "Out of the goodness of my heart I found that flat for her. But she complained sore about the rent. London is expensive you know. When you said you wanted to go to London and needed a place to stay I thought that I was doing you both a favour."

"But you made it like it was just a general advert for a flat. Why didn't you just introduce us?"

"Well she knew who you were so why didn't she tell you that both your parents knew each other? Listen, I washed my hands of her and I told her mother that I wouldn't be helping her daughter anymore. Her mother didn't like it but I have a reputation to uphold."

Sofia looked at him as he spoke. When he had finished she looked thoughtfully at the television. Hortense had literally accused him of being a pervert and he had accused Hortense of being a wild partying boyfriend lover. Sofia decided that it would be impossible to know who was telling the truth. She resolved that she was not going to be the tennis ball in the service of their lies. The truth in this matter was worthless to her so she let it go.

Half an hour later, Sofia said her goodbyes and made way down the street towards the cemetery. As she walked down the rocky pathway, along the blue picket fence she thought on what Max had told her.

Nouara and Kingston's graves were side by side. Both inscribed with words that were so far from the truth; 'loving wife' and 'loving husband'.

The tombstones had a mini rose garden each. The plants were flourishing. This surprised her as she had not been there for a long time. Both sites had been swept and the grass patches were kempt. Someone had been taking good care. Her first thought was Max as he lived close by and was their oldest friend but he had never taken this much care in the past so why now?

She sat on the bench in front of the stones and took in the air. She looked at her father and then at her mother. She remembered the pain and began to imagine how life would have been if only her family had loved one another.

"Sofia."

She was startled. She turned around. "Langton."

"You alright?" he said as he puffed out some smoke. He had aged. He looked scrawny. His clothes hung around his body, in bags. His shirt was not tucked in. It hung below his navy, Nike hoody. Tattoos of thorns ran up the back of his hand and Sofia assumed that the patterns may have continued up the rest of his arm. He wore rings over almost every finger and two heavy weight chains, which could pass for gold, around his neck.

"Yes," she said. "How are you?"

He sat down next to her as the smell of weed was transferred to her nose as he displaced the air on the bench he sat on.

"You've come to see mum and dad?" he asked.

"Yes." The back of her hand began to sting. "Did you do all

this?" She pointed at the rose garden.

"My partner is into that sort of thing." He puffed some smoke again. "Want a smoke?" He passed her the spliff, she declined. "Suit yourself, this is premium brand."

"Nah I've kicked the habit."

"So Sofia don't smoke weed no more?"

"No." She looked uncomfortable.

"You used to be a stoner."

"Not anymore."

"No need to knock yourself out anymore then?" he mocked.

"No need."

"You're a happy clapper now." He chuckled.

"If you're referring to Christianity, then yes."

"These two are dead now so who needs weed hey? These idiots messed us up."

"Then why are you still smoking?" asked Sofia.

"Because I like it," he answered.

She sighed. "So where do you live?" she asked.

"Across the road."

"You live across the road?" She looked at the line of brown brick terraced houses. "How long have you been here?

"I never left Dorset." He threw his cigarette butt on the ground and stamped it out. He picked it up again and placed it in a small lip balm type tin that he had fished from his pocket.

"So you see Uncle Max often then?" she asked.

"What business have I got with that old fart?"
Sofia did not dare to answer.

"Do you want a cuppa?" he asked.

"Yes please." She frowned as she saw him put the little tin back in his pocket. "You're reusing your roaches now?"

"You're not a stoner if you waste weed. Around here I'm known as a stone cold stoner. I have to keep my rep. Waste not want not hey?"

He led the way as she followed in silence.

121 Priory Lane was the greyest, brown bricked rundown

building that Sofia had ever seen. The front garden hosted everything from a broken toilet seat to several tied black bags with God knows what. The front door was a very dark blue. The paint was peeling off. To the side was a small stool. Underneath it were numerous cigarette butts.

Langton flicked the letter box two times. Shortly someone began to unlock about three internal bolts. A petite scrawny looking woman opened the door. She smiled and exposed a front missing tooth. Her hair was tied back in a dishevelled bun. She wore jeans and a fitting, short sleeved striped shirt. All up her arm were red blotches, some more red than the others. She pulled her hand with unkempt nails out so that she could flick the ash off her cigarette and prevent it from falling into the house. "You better not be smoking weed Linda." Langton barked, surprising Sofia. "I don't want this crap around my kid." Langton hurled a few profanities and Linda reciprocated as Sofia watched in embarrassment.

"Does this smell like weed to you?"

"Shut your mouth bitch or I'll shut it for you."

She noticed Sofia. "Who is this?" she asked Langton.

"My sister, get her some tea." Langton brushed past her.

Her countenance changed. "Oh how lovely you're family. "Come in please. I'm Linda."

"Oh thank you. I'm..." before Sofia could say her name she saw the cutest baby waddle towards her. She was a ball of chubbiness. She had adorable curly, black hair, brown, glassy eyes and cafe latte skin. Sofia was smitten.

"And who do we have here?" Sofia asked as she walked into the living room of the two up, two down very humble scantily furnished home.

"This is your niece love. Her name is Sofia."

"Her name is Sofia?"

She turned around and looked at Langton who had slouched on the blue couch which matched the blue stained carpet. Their eyes met. Hers were tears glassy.

"I named her after Grandma," he said.

"Oh," she said and breathed out deeply and spoke in a painful quiver. "Well it's a beautiful name and she's a beautiful baby." She touched the side of her head which had a slight ache.

For most of the hour that Sofia spent in her brothers home she felt much like when she was 18 and at the mercy of all of his insults and put downs. He had not changed. However, even though he was using the same old weapons they had less of an impact. Langton's opinions were not important to her anymore.

The best thing about her time was the hot cup of milky tea that had been passed to her in a white china mug. It was the best cuppa she had ever had. And of course her play time with little Sofia.

After leaving a much needed £20 note for groceries and a card with her phone number, home and work address she left with the memory of Langton's smirk which he produced each time he dished out the back handed hidden insults. It was no surprise that upon arriving home she curled up in a ball on her bed and cried herself to sleep.

#

Several weeks later Sofia was back to her work routine of late nights and early mornings. Langton had called her a few times. She had responded by visiting his home, bringing groceries and leaving the money that Langton had asked for. She enjoyed coming to see little Sofia who had grown to love her aunty. A bond was also growing with Linda. When Langton went out for a spliff they had the opportunity to discuss the new bruises that seemed to surface on Linda's body every time she visited. Linda's explanation was always a fall or bumping into something.

Sofia struggled with her decision not to confront Langton. It was clear that he was beating Linda but she feared that any attempt would cause him to push her completely out of their lives. If she kept quiet it would allow her to keep checking on little Sofia and Linda.

However, things seemed to have escalated when Linda called Sofia in a panic. Sofia had been working late at the office. She was alone and Jacob had urged her not to stay too long.

"Slow down Linda. What's happened?" asked Sofia who was trying to pacify Linda who was in a tight ball of stress.

"Langton is pissed and he's been talking about coming down to yours. I've been trying to get hold of you."

"Pissed about what?"

"I told him that you know that he beats me. He thinks you're meddling in his family so he said he would come and kick off at your workplace. Show you what's what he said."

"What?"

"I had to warn you."

"Where is he now Linda?"

"I haven't seen him for a couple of days."

"Don't worry. I will talk to him."

"He was pissed Sofia. I don't think you can..."

"I can handle him. How are you and little Sofia?"

"We're ok. I've left him."

"What?"

"I know he's your brother and everything but I'm scared. I can't do this anymore."

"So where are you staying?"

"I'm with a friend. Look I've got to go. Please be careful."

"Thanks Linda I will. You take care too. I will ring you tomorrow and if you hear from Langton let me know"

Sofia hung up the phone. She stood up and looked out the window. It was dark with just the street light providing a dim light. She closed the office blinds and started packing up by placing all her files in her bag then shutting down the two laptops she had been working on. She put on her jacket, grabbed her bag and switched the light off before walking out of the office.

A crash outside of the window made her jump. She walked to the window and pulled down one of the blades of the blind for a peak. She sighed. One of the blue recycling bins had fallen down and plastic bottles were rolling down the lane. She spotted Sam the security officer trying to run after them. He succeeded with a few but let the rest get away. She smiled.

Once outside she walked past the security officer shelter. "Good night Sam."

"See you tomorrow beautiful," he said as he watched her walk down the lane. Sam was a little sweet on Sofia but he drew the line and decided she was out of his league.

As she walked down the road she thought about Langton and what he was thinking. Linda had sounded very alarmed and this made Sofia nervous. She walked past Amakele cafe and headed down the narrow path towards the station. It was dark and damp, the only light coming from the flickering street lamp. She pulled her jacket closer around her and began to pick up speed. She had done this journey several times in the same conditions but this time she felt a little on edge.

She went round one of the two corners in the path. This was the corner next to the Coca cola billboard that was ruined by the words '*Happy 50th Jacki*' in white graffiti. Sofia had always wondered why the graffiti artist had not finished spelling the name 'Jackie'. She was convinced that the name should have ended with an '*e*'. She had debated whether the artist had been caught in the act before he or she could spray on the 'e' or whether the artist could not spell. Then on other occasions she would wonder whether the Jackie in question was a frequent traveller on this route. If not then why would a birthday wish be plastered in a place that she or he was unlikely to see?

The light flickered on the graffiti sign. Sofia looked at it for comfort and tried to pick up speed but her body crashed into someone.

The impact was overwhelming, bringing her heart down into her stomach. She assumed he was a man. He wore a hoody; in a colour she did not pay attention to. He grabbed both her elbows.

"Look where you're going babe," he said.
The smell of weed hit her nose, or at least she thought it was

weed. "I'm really sorry," she said. Her bladder began to ache. She felt the sweat erupt in her armpits. He let her go and walked on. She grabbed her chest and took in a breath.

After collecting herself and without looking back she took on a slight gallop but again she was stopped by something, maybe a rock that made her lose her footing. Her body crashed to the ground, arms outstretched. Her ankle took a twist and her elbow took the weight and the grazing. Her bag went flying.

Before she could get up, two strong hands raised her from behind her armpits. That strong sense of weed was present again. One of his arms clasped tight around her arms and chest. She wriggled to get free but he held her tight. Her heart was pounding. "Langton, stop please," she cried.

His very strong hand covered her mouth. She was overwhelmed by the distinct smell of Garnier Cucumber moisturising hand cream. She managed to free one arm and began to elbow him and kick. She pulled and twisted. He covered her and held tighter from behind. Tears began to flood down her cheeks. Her emotions were a mixture of terror and anger. She continued to kick, pull and twist but was beginning to tire. His hand was now firmly clasped over her mouth. He began to drag her. She pulled and pushed and gave as good a fight that she could give. One heel fell off. The pain of the grazing was excruciating.

He too appeared to tire. He had dragged her as far as the bushes but then dropped her. Through her dishevelled hair she saw that his hood had come off. She felt a sharp prick in her arm. She tried to get a look at him through the hair, leaves and tears but then what followed was darkness.

Sofia lay there limp. He threw the needle he had used, to prick her, into the thicket. Then he dragged her further like a black refuse bag.

CHAPTER 44

Sofia woke up with a splitting headache. She sat up. It was not her bed. It was not her linen. She pulled the covers off her. She was still wearing the clothes she remembered wearing at work. She tried to move off the bed but her wrist was moved backward in a sudden jolt. The pain in her wrist was sharp. She tugged again but found that her wrist was chained to the head board. She tugged and tugged but it was secure.

"Can somebody help me?" she shouted.

"Hello. Please. Help."

She banged the metal wrist cuff on the bed frame over and over hoping that it would bring someone to attention. But there was still silence.

She felt herself starting to panic. She didn't know where she was or how she got into the room. The pain in her grazed knee then became apparent. The scraped skin and dry blood stung bringing tears to the corners of her eyes. Her tears were a mixture of the excruciating body pain and the thought of whether she was ever going to be freed from this place. She looked ahead and that's when she saw them.

All were floor to ceiling and rectangular in shape. Every inch of the walls was covered except for the whitewashed wooden door which was directly in front of the bed. When she turned, behind her, they were there. When she looked above they were there.

Their presence began to scare her. She wondered why they

were there. Who would want every inch of their room covered by them? Who would want to stare at themselves all day and every day? Her eyes began to cry but then she shut them tight because she did not want to take another look in those mirrors.

She screamed again, "Help." She remembered the struggle with the hooded man. "Langton," she cried. Why had he brought her here? She thought. "Langton, please. Why are you doing this?" She hung her head down, avoiding the mirrors. "Langton, please. I'm scared." No one answered. There was a deadness of silence. After a few more futile attempts at calling her brother she curled up into a ball and pulled the duvet on the bed closer to keep out the chill that was beginning to surface. Defeated she laid her head against the headboard and sobbed.

After what seemed like hours she heard a lock being loosened from behind the white door. She froze and pulled her arms in but her wrist was jolted back to the bed frame. Her heart was pounding.

The door creaked open to reveal the figure that was dressed in a silver suit, a crisp white shirt and a shiny black tie. The shoes were polished to perfection. They reflected the light from the side lamps.

"Omalicha nwa (beautiful one)," he said.

She could not believe her eyes. "Uche?"

He let out the most evil laugh she had ever heard him laugh. "Nwanyioma (beautiful girl), Tomato jos (attractive girl). Where have you been?" He stopped in front of a mirror and surveyed himself.

"Uche what are you doing?"

"If the mountain won't come to Mohammed then Mohammed must go and fetch the mountain." He laughed. This wounded her. "But actually you're not a mountain anymore. You look good. My influence I guess."

"Please let me go," she pleaded.

"But you've just arrived. And I had to go and change out of that hoody. You know that's not my style."

"Why am I here Uche? Just let me go. I have a restraining

order. You can't do this."

"I too have a restraining order. You are restrained to my bed." He giggled and turned to the mirror. He and began to rub some cream from a tube he had pulled from his pocket into his cheeks. He rubbed and rubbed. The distinct smell of weed surfaced again. He saw her watching him from behind. "It's new research. CBD oil has been found to make the skin look younger. I decided to use the real thing. I grow my own weed and I mash it into Shea butter. You see I did admire something about you after all. The gardening I mean." He chuckled and continued to rub. "It's a miracle. I will rub it on you tonight. You have some lines all in the wrong places." He laughed a belly laugh.

She felt sick. "Let me go Uche."

"You wanted to deny me of my rights. God hates divorce so he will back me in this. I'm doing what I should have done a long time ago. I'm taking you back as my wife."

"What for? You got what you wanted. You never loved me. You wanted what I had but I was too stupid to see that."

He laughed and clapped his hands. "Here we go again. I married you for papers? Idiot. You are just rehearsing what your fiends were telling you. And where are they today? I heard that Skye is married, baby on the way. And where are you? I told you they were all jealous of you and were waiting for when they would surpass you."

He pushed her buttons. "I never ever said that you married me for those papers but I came to my senses because of the way you treated me. You treated me like dirt Uche. If not for papers, then why Uche? Why?"

He didn't answer her. He was transfixed. "Umm..." he said. He took a step back and began to rub further. He smoothed over his eyebrows and caressed his hair that had been smoothed over by a thick gel. He adjusted his tie "Wow," he said. Then he began to adjust and caress every inch that he could access whilst releasing disturbing moans. "Umm you look good," he said to himself.

Sofia watched in horror. It was him but he was different in

a very disturbing way. He had lost it somehow. "Let me go," she pleaded. "Please I need the toilet." He ignored her. "I'm going to wet myself...on your new white sheets," she added.

She snatched his attention. "Idiot." he bellowed. This made her jump. "Piss on my own sheets? Me? Uche Chidinma Onyeme? God forbid." He raised his thumb and index finger then clicked them.

"I need the toilet now."

His eyes bulged. "Hold it. Hold it. You wan (want to) do piss on my sheet and bring smell here? God forbid." He moved with haste like a mad man. He pulled what looked like a fish hook from his pocket. He moved closer to her and grabbed her wrist. He pushed the fish hook in the hole on the band that was on her wrist. After a few clumsy twists the band opened and loosened her wrist. She rubbed it. He grabbed her forearm and dragged her. She pulled away and tried to break free. She kicked him. The kick infuriated him. She had loosened the silver stitching on the pocket of the shiny suit. In an instant she saw a man possessed. Like a spider his body covered hers and hurled her to the bed. His right hand grabbed her right breast and began to squeeze. She screamed as he squeezed harder. She felt as if he was going to rip it from her chest. He violently let go. She grabbed her chest and curled into a ball. The tears were gushing from both eyes.

"If you try it again I will finish the job. If you think Im joking then try it. TRY IT," he shouted.

"I'm sorry," she carried on sobbing. "Please let me go."

"Shut up," he said. "Shut up jo (shut up please)."

"Uche I will do anything. Just let me go home please."

"You will not go home until we are married again. How dare you divorce me?"

She turned around. "You signed the papers Uche. Just let me go. Is this what all this is about?"

"Me, sign the papers? God forbid. You forged my signature."

"You signed them Uche."

"Me? Uche Chidinma Onyeme, agree to divorce? You dirty liar. I'm a married man I don't do divorce. You want to deny me access to what is rightfully mine? I made you."

Sofia sat up and moved away from the patch of urine that had gathered underneath her. In the scuffle her bladder had let her down.

Uche noticed it. He grabbed his head with both hands. "Chineke (My God). My beauty has been destroyed. Hey. My life is now stinking."

She froze. She was embarrassed.

He was in his element. "Dirty woman. A woman of your age cannot use the toilet. We give you toilet but you choose your pants. Hey God forbid. I tried to give you everything but this is how you repay me. Look at your life now. Wee in your pant because you divorced me. You are cursed because of your wickedness towards me. I am a good man but look at your life."

She looked at him but did not respond. She held everything within her to try and stop herself from going on the defensive. But his words gnawed into her. She tried to focus on the pain in her chest instead.

"I chose you because I saw how weak you were. You couldn't resist me could you?" He laughed loud. "You see I wanted to help you. I mean let's be honest here. How could a shabby woman like you grab a man like me? I mean come on."

She mustered the courage. "You're right. I was weak."

He was startled. But he tried to save face. "On that we agree."

"And you helped me to see just how weak I was." She grabbed her aching chest which had started to quiver. Perhaps she was cold.

"I paid for everything. If it were not for me…"

"You're right Uche. You did everything because I never believed that I could." Her breathing was laboured but she persevered. "You helped me to realise that I was selling myself short by being with you." Her confidence caused his piercing exterior to begin to soften. "And yes I was shabby because I didn't know how to value myself. You showed me that I needed to look in that mirror and see me. That person in the mirror is valuable."

"You see," he said but he was unsure whether she agreed with him in the way he wanted her to.

Her breathing was laboured but she rode on the inner strength that was mounting up. "I thought I was nobody and so I married you because you agreed with me. You saw me as a weak nobody whose blood you could suck. But I don't blame you because I was sucking my own blood. I was bleeding myself dry. I was attracted to you because I knew you would help to finish me off."

He was undone. His eyes were like that of a child. "Me, Uche Chidinma Onyeme suck blood? This is idiotic. You're crazy."

"Maybe I am Uche. But all I can say is I know who I am now. That knowledge helped me to leave you. I valued myself enough to know that I didn't deserve you. I deserved better.

He smirked. "Is that why that gardener left you? You think I don't know what's going on with you? I own you so I know everything."

"No Uche. I left him for me. I deserve better. I deserve to be valued.

"So that's why you had no man when I met you and will never keep a good man."

"Good men don't belittle you. Good men don't overstep your boundaries or control you."

"I am a good man," he snapped. She jumped and knocked the flesh in her chest. She winced as the pain was excruciating.

Someone moved the door knob. Uche became nervous.

Sofia looked on in hope. The door shot open. Peter came in.

"Ah my guy I've been looking for you everywhere. I thought to look down here. What is this room for anyway? I have always seen it locked."

Sofia looked at Uche. Her eyes were bloodshot, her nose full of snot and her hair in a hot mess. Uche took two steps back. He looked around as if looking for a hole to climb into. Peter looked at Sofia in surprise.

"Ah. Ogene(what is going on here)?" Peter asked.

Uche looked as if he was calculating an answer. He smirked then stopped as if he realised that no explanation would work this time. Without a word he shot out the room, pushing past Peter.

"Uche," he shouted. "Uche," he turned to Sofia. "What happened here?"

She stood up and limped towards the door. The pain was excruciating. He tried to grab her arm to help her. "Let go of me," she said with sharpness.

"Sofia you're bleeding."

She looked down at her chest and saw the growing pool of blood on her clothes. She looked at him then the light turned to darkness. She collapsed in his arms.

CHAPTER 45

Three months had passed since her ordeal with Uche. The room with the mirrors had been the height of his abuse. But it was all over and he would never bother her again. He was arrested and charged with grievous bodily harm and kidnapping. The last she heard from her Lawyer was that he had been repatriated back to Nigeria whilst kicking, screaming and shouting the words, "Me, Uche Chidinma Onyeme back to Nigeria? God forbid."

The chest drain had been removed and she was now free to walk around without tubes sticking out of her body. The surgery was successful, save a slight twitch of pain in her chest every time she breathed. The countries best plastic surgeons had worked with her and no one without telling them could have guessed that one breast was a silicone implant.

It took her a while before she could speak about what had happened to her. For days she sat by her hospital bed looking out the window. It was as if this was the end. The last of what she had was taken. There was nothing left to abuse.

They had brought in counsellors to speak to her but no one could convince her that it was time to live again.

On one particular day whilst still looking out the window and hugging her purple fluffy morning gown she decided that she was going to give up. She did this by crying for hours, refusing to eat and sleeping in her chair all night causing her feet to swell.

When she woke up she perceived it was the next day. The chill in the room was sharp. She reached out to the blanket on the hospital bed and pulled it. She wrapped it around herself.

"Sofia."

She was startled. She turned to see who had called her.

"I'm sorry I didn't mean to startle you," he said.

A halo of warmth surrounded her. "Michael."

He pulled the armchair that was on the other side of the room and placed it opposite her.

"It's so good to see you."

"How are you feeling?" He sat down.

"I'm ok," she said.

"It's me Sofia. How are you really feeling?"

She crumbled. "I'm tired," she said.

"Let's get you into bed." He held her under her elbow to take her weight as she waddled into bed. His touch and his help made her feel like home. He tucked her in. He saw her tears. "Why are you crying?" he asked.

"You're so kind to me."

He smiled and raised his hand to wipe the tears away from her cheek but then he disappeared.

Sofia woke up and found herself in bed. A nurse had come in with her breakfast and was opening the blinds.

"Morning Sofia," she said. "Fancy some breakfast?"

"Nurse, how did I get into bed?"

"Oh you gave us a scare last night young lady. One of the night nurses found you on the floor, so we hoisted you back in."

"I'd fallen out of bed?"

"Yes my dear. Thank goodness no broken bones."

"Oh. So no one came to see me?"

"Well you didn't have anyone yesterday. Why do you ask?"

"No reason."

"Maybe someone will come in today? But you need to get your strength up. Dr says you could be going home tomorrow."

"That soon?"

"Well my dear you've really picked up in the last couple of days. A few miracles have been happening for you my dear. Right, now have a cup of tea at least."

#

Applause erupted around the room as Zane West came on the platform again. Sofia sat in the audience on the front row looking on in awe at him.

"Well I want to thank all of you for attending this conference. It has been phenomenal. I want to thank you because each of you had the courage to say 'I matter'. You took the time to discover 'you'." He pointed at several people in the audience until his finger finally landed on Sofia. "You are the hero and I am incredibly honoured to have shared these last couple of days. Thank you for trusting me." The room roared as everyone stood up and applauded him. Zane was overcome with emotion. "Thank you everyone. On that note it gives me great pleasure to present to you the icing on the cake. This guy was not on the list of speakers. I had begged him to come but he couldn't cancel an engagement. But just this morning the appointment cancelled on him and so he called me up asking if it was ok to come and hang out with me. I was like 'are you insane?' Of course I said. Then I told him that 'bro you have to come and say a few words. This is an absolute treat guys. Here to be interviewed by yours truly, everybody give it up for America's Therapist Dr Mike Marshall." Sounds of shock filled the room then the audience erupted again with claps, whistles and what sounded like drum rolls as Michael walked onto the platform. He came on with the brightest smile and waving as he walked towards Zane. Sofia could not believe her eyes. He walked closer to the front where Zane was standing, then he saw her. He stopped for a moment. Looked at her and gave a slow wave, which she reciprocated. April who had been sitting in the front row on the other side of the room pushed her head forward to see who Michael had waved at. She spotted Sofia.

April barely listened to the interview because all she could think of was the way that Michael had looked at Sofia. It was a look that she had not seen in a very long time.

After the conference was over everyone gathered at the meet and greet luncheon. When it was Sofia's turn to meet Zane she was so excited. He was very polite and kind looking. He thanked her for attending the conference and said that he hoped to see her at his next few events. She thanked him and was about to leave when he said. "Please come and meet Dr Mike. Mike."

"Oh no that's ok. You don't need to disturb..."

"Mike, come and meet this lovely lady. She's attended most of my conferences in London."

Michael's heart began to pound as he saw Sofia walking towards him. April spotted them walking over to Michael and took on a slight sprint until she stood very close to him. Sofia saw the manoeuvre but kept her composure.

"Sofia. How are you?" He held out his hand for a shake.

"I'm well Michael."

"You know each other?" asked Zane.

"Oh? How do you know each other?" April thrust her arm out, which pushed Michael back. Michael saw April's arm then looked at Sofia in embarrassment. "I'm April, Michael's girl-friend." she said.

"Pleased to meet you April. I'm Sofia." Sofia shook her hand.

"So where do you know Michael from?"
Sofia and Michael looked at each other. They hesitated.

"Old friends from London," she said.
Michael smiled with relief. "Yes."

For the rest of the afternoon Sofia mingled trying as much as possible to avoid bumping into April who was trying at every moment to ascertain the real connection between her and her boyfriend. She managed to dodge April by creating fake toilet breaks every time they met. All the while she didn't notice that Michael's eyes at any given moment were following her around.

When he caught Sofia alone he grabbed the opportunity

and walked over to her. He grabbed two glasses of elderflower water from a waiter who was passing by and went to sit next to her on the wicker settee surrounded by orchids.

"I got you a drink," he said.

"Oh I'm not drinking alcohol at the moment."

"It's elderflower water."

She smiled. "Thanks,"

Michael took a sip of his. "I was surprised to see you in the audience."

"I was just as surprised as you. I hear you're quite a sensation. I got a chance to look at some of your videos earlier and I think it's really impressive."

He blushed. "Oh I just love what I do."

"It seems like you're helping loads of people."

"It seems so."

She put her glass down. "Well I'm one of your followers on Facebook now." She smiled at him.

He laughed. "I'm honoured." There was a brief silence in which he fought to find what to say. "So how are you?"

"I've been ok."

"Sofia, it's me. How are you?" Their eyes met. They sat without speaking. He, looking at her and she at him. It was an unspoken, agonising love.

Her exterior melted. "Thanks for your care Michael. Honestly I am ok." She winced.

"Are you ok?"

"Just a bit of chest pain, that's all. Probably ate too much kiwi fruit."

"Can I get you anything?"

"No I think I need a rest. I should get back to my hotel room.

"Where are you staying?"

"At the Waldorf."

"I could drive you," he said.

"No I've booked a car but thanks for offering."

"Look if you don't mind, write down your number here."

He gave her a card. She looked at him and nervously wrote down her number. She handed him the card. He then gave her another card with his number. "How long are you in New York for?"

"I've got a week. I thought I would have a bit of a holiday."

"Great. I could show you around. We could catch up, if that's ok with you."

"Thank you that would be lovely."

"Perfect, so I'll ring tomorrow?"

"That sounds good." Sofia picked up her purse and left. April came and stood by Michael. "Are you going to tell me what that was all about?"

"I just gave her my number. She's a friend."

"How long is she here for?"

"She leaves in two days."

"Perfect, the day after me. I wouldn't want you to get up to any mischief while I'm in Europe." As April walked away Michael gulped down the last of his elderflower water.

Two days later Michael was waiting for Sofia to come down to the lobby at the Waldorf Astoria.

They had a great day with a boat ride on the Hudson and long refreshing walks in Central park. They got to know each other on a different level just as Sofia and Michael. They ended up in a cafe and talked over enormous burgers and fries. The laughter was infectious and the food was divine.

Sofia put her glass of chocolate milkshake down. "I've had a great time.

"Me too. We should do this again."

"I would love that. Forgive me for asking but was April ok with this today?"

He wiped his mouth with his napkin and looked down at his plate. "I didn't tell her."

"You didn't tell her? Why?"

He sighed. "It's a bit complicated. It's just best that she doesn't know. She's in Europe right now and thinks that you're in London."

Her countenance fell. "You lied to her?"

"Only because I didn't want to cause an argument and I really wanted to spend time with you. It was wrong of me and I'm sorry that I've put you in the middle of this. I'll call her and tell her." He waited for her acknowledgement. Look, I really enjoyed your company today and I hope I haven't spoilt it for you."

"Thanks for being honest. I really enjoyed today and no, you didn't spoil it for me."

"I'm not your therapist anymore but I would love to be a friend."

"Friends, yes God knows I need more of those. Thank you Michael."

They carried on eating and both cleaned their plates before ordering ice cream then coffee.

Sofia reached for her coffee but overstretched her chest. She winced.

Michael put his cup down. "Are you ok?"

"I'm ok. Really."

"I don't mean to pry but it looks like you've been in pain for a while. Forgive me I'm a doctor."

She breathed in deeply "I've had this pain ever since the surgery."

"Surgery?"

Her eyes were beginning to fill up. "I had a mastectomy."

A frown line appeared on his brow. He could not articulate the fear, shock and dread he was feeling. They looked at each other for what seemed like a while. She was trying hard not to cry because this would exacerbate the pain. He just didn't know what to say. Instead he took her hand in between both of his and held her.

"Thank you," she said and pulled away from him in a way that made him understand that she was not trying to get away from his touch.

He mustered up courage. "Did they get all of it?"

"Well they said I'm in the all clear."

He heaved a sigh of relief. "Thank the living God."

"If Uche hadn't attacked me I wouldn't have found out…"

"Wait, Uche attacked you?"

"He attacked me and then kidnapped me." He held her hand again. "It was crazy and he was crazy. He ripped part of my chest off."

"What? So that's why you had the mastectomy."

"No he just tore off a big chunk of skin but when the doctors were examining the wound they found the lump. It was malignant and right there and then I went through a mastectomy and implant surgery."

"Oh God. What you've been though. I can't even begin to imagine how you're feeling."

"I'm ok, honestly. I'm just glad that it's over. If Uche hadn't attacked me I might never have found out that I had cancer. And I might not be here today. I heard this saying once; we always have to look for the blessing that the storm left behind. Uche tried to harm me but funny enough his intentions catapulted me into a new lease on life. It's like a second chance."

"You're such a strong woman."

"Nah, I really believe that God kept me through all of it. Left to me, I would have given up long time ago."

He nodded. "So what happened to Uche?"

"His friend found us and I don't remember much else after that. But I heard that he was arrested then deported. Not just because of his attack on me but some other reasons that I'm not quite clear about.

"Well I'm glad he's far away. My goodness Sofia." The tear he was fighting so hard with escaped and shot down his face.

"Don't cry Michael or you will set me off."
He smiled. "Sorry." He let go of her hand then wiped his cheek with a napkin.

"Oh Michael you've been a friend. Thank you for listening to me."

"I love listening to you Sofia. If you ever need anything, I mean anything at all I'm just at the end of a phone line. I mean it. I won't be too busy to listen. Friends?"

"Friends... I could really do with some water," she said.

"You need some water? I'll get you some." He beckoned a waiter to come to their table. "Would you prefer elderflower water?"

"Oh God no, please."

Michael frowned. When the waiter arrived he spoke, "Could we have a glass of water for the lady please?" The waiter left. "I always assumed that elderflower water was your favourite drink."

"No I hate the stuff. I drink it out of habit but I hate it. And I think this is first time I've ever discussed my disgust for elderflower water."

He released a small smile. "Then why do you drink it?"

"Several years ago I guess I was trying to fit in or be polite so I drank the stuff so as not to offend. Then in a weird way I made myself keep up the lie. But no more lies for me Michael. We're friends right?"

"Of course," he said.

"Well this friend of yours hates elderflower water." The waiter arrived and set down the glass of water in front of her. She rolled her eyes and gulped down the water.

She made him laugh. His laugh set her off but this pulled on her chest but made her wince.

"Oh Sorry," he said. But she laughed some more and so did he.

He took her back to the Waldorf and before leaving gave her a long hug and a promise to keep in touch. He loved her but he was with April and was not willing to break April's heart.

CHAPTER 46

Sofia had returned to England to a totally new life routine. She had spoken to Michael only once or twice but lost contact after he left New York to live in Paris with April who had opened a new branch of her gourmet chocolate chain. Sofia knew that Michael had decided to give his relationship with April a chance and for that she was happy for him and ready to move on and see what life had in store for her.

Life had taken a turn. The hours that she used to spend in the horticultural lab were transformed into hours where she would write. She enjoyed taking her laptop to her local cafe, finding a cool spot with her favourite coffee then writing for her new column in the *Guardian* or blogging for the *Culture Magazine*. If she wasn't writing she was attending the latest motivational seminar or rolling in the grass at the park with Skye and her son Ocean.

There were also the frequent visits to the garden centre to have her chats with Stan.

"Great to see you Sofia," said Stan as he carried the tray full of marigolds and put them on the shelf at the Garden Centre.

"Hi Stan I really missed you." She walked over to him and gave him a hug.

"Good holiday?"

"Yes the best. I caught up with an old friend in New York."

"Lovely," he said. He shifted the tray on the shelf whilst he thought for a little. "So how is your health?" He turned around to look at her.

Her smile was the painful kind. "I'm on the mend Stan. I almost lost my life but now I'm determined to live it to the fullest. Thanks for asking."

"Well if you need any help love you only need to give a shout. You know that don't you?"

"I know that Stan, and thank you."

He heaved a sigh. "Well, now that we've got that out of the way, what can I do for you?"

"I heard you have some tea plants," she said with interest and looking to see if she could spot them.

"Yes they came in just last week. The boss has just come back from his trip to Africa and he brought these from the Eastern part of Zimbabwe, from erm..." He went to fetch his note book in which he jotted several notes about the plants. He went to the middle of the book, shifted the book mark out the way and scrolled down the page with his finger. "Ah yes, that's right. It's called *The Tanganda tea company*."

She raised her eyebrows. "The Tanganda tea company? Never heard of it." She spotted the plants on the floor at the far end of the centre. "They look really healthy."

"And the scent love, is gorgeous."

"How much are they?"

"£10.99 a pot, love."

"I'll take two," she said. Her eyes caught the end of a carpet of colours.

A vast number of potted flowers were arranged in layers of blues, pinks, lilacs and white. Instead of following Stan to the tea plants she went to drink in the beauty of them. She stood and looked at the beauty of each petal and how intricately they were designed. The flowers were the evidence of the existence of a master designer whose canvas was the world.

Stan was still talking as he picked up the tea plants. It is when he received no reply to his question that he realised that Sofia was not behind him. He scanned around the centre and found her, in the distance, gazing at the blooms. He understood the look on her face. He sighed and smiled and walked towards the counter where he laid the tea plants down. He called across to her. "Something caught your fancy?"

She took in the numerous scents then breathed out. "Yes Stan. Something definitely has."

Two weeks later she was at the bottom of her garden dressed in dirty, dark green overalls and brown gardener's boots. The ground had already been prepared with a shape scored out with perfect precision. The viola's, blue sails, lavender, clemantis, dalia's, antirrhinium perennials, several other flowers and various shrubs were all lined up in rows and set free from their pots ready to be transplanted into the earth. She walked over to the wooden garden table upon which what looked like a map had been pinned to it. It was the map of her garden and a replica of the shape that had been scored out of the ground was on it with numbers and a colour code to the side. She picked up her fork and began to dig by number. She started with number one digging out 30cm squares. She was methodical at digging out square by square, number by number and colour by colour. She was not aware of how much time had passed. She was engrossed in her project which slowly but surely was taking shape.

She pushed the last batch of pretty in pink flowers in the last square. She brushed the sweat from her brow as she stood back in awe. She walked over to the wooden garden table and unpinned the map from it. She looked at it then looked at her masterpiece on the ground. She checked every line and ensured that every colour matched her original intention. It was an accomplishment. What was in front of her was the most stunning butterfly carved out in flowers. This labour of love signified that the real Sofia had come home and the butterfly was a prophecy to herself that a new life had begun.

From this day, further time passed. But her life showed that she was living for her as she took each moment to appreciate the life that she almost lost.

Her relationship with her brother had remained exactly

the same way as it had always been. It turned out that he didn't remember the day that he supposedly threatened to attack Sofia. He brushed it off and stated that he was most probably stoned. Linda had left him and he was converted into the brotherhood of dads that visit their kids because they couldn't make it work with their kids mum. But he was faithful to the visiting up until he was put in prison for a coke deal gone wrong. Sofia remained faithful to visiting her brother once a month at Belmarsh prison. The visits were awkward each on either side of the table never looking at each other and trying to eavesdrop on other's peoples conversations because they had barely anything to say to each other. One of the barely anything conversations was about Sofia being faithful to visiting little Sofia Grace. Her delight in making conversations about his daughter was met with nonchalance. She brushed it off but was proud of the fact that she had done her duty to watch over her niece one day of every week.

#

It was summer again and time for the Chelsea Flower show.

Sofia put on her best frock and sandals and donned her Italian celebrity sunglasses. This year was particularly special as she had been commissioned, with lucrative cheques, for articles about the show. She took her camera which she had borrowed from Jacob with a promise that it was fail proof, meaning every photo taken had a perfection guarantee attached to it. Jacob's claims were slightly suspect but it was her best and only option under the circumstances.

With confidence Sofia snapped away, taking snaps of the gorgeous gardens. But when she came to the olive tree her life took a turn.

In the past the olive tree had been her personal space to sit down and mope about her lonely life but this time was different. The olive tree had opened a doorway of hope.

She came closer and zoomed in. She thought the focus

wasn't good enough so looked at the lens, rubbed it then zoomed in again. She had seen right the first time. It was him. Her heart skipped a beat.

She walked right up to the bench. He had his back to her but she knew it was him.

"I used to love this spot," she said.

She startled him. He turned to look. His eyes met hers then his sad countenance lifted. His face was a picture of relief. "Used to?" he asked.

Sofia moved closer and put her hand on the bench. "Yes used to. I've found a different spot."

"So what's changed?"

"Old memories. Letting go of the past I suppose."

He nodded. "New waters?"

"Yes."

He smiled. "But it's still beautiful here."

She smiled back. "I have a new kind of beautiful now."

He breathed out and nodded as he watched her move to come and sit on the bench. She laid down her bag that had a bunch of wrapped Dalia's in it.

"So what brings you to England?" She put her camera down.

"The Chelsea Flower Show of course."

She was disappointed that his response was not 'I've come to see you.' "Oh I see," was her quick reply.

He seemed nervous. "I've always loved it."

She plunged in. "Where's April?"

"April decided that she wasn't ready for a serious relationship."

"Oh... I'm sorry to hear that. Really I am."

"It's ok. She wanted to focus on her business and we agreed it was for the best." He looked to catch her eye. "And you?"

"No I'm not seeing anyone at the moment. I'm..."

"Me neither," was his very quick reply.

"Oh."

He cleared his throat. "I don't suppose you'd care to join me on a stroll in the gardens?"

"Stroll? That sounds like a line out of a Jane Austen book." He chuckled. "Jane Austen?"

She nodded. "Yes kind gentleman I would love to join you on a stroll."

His cheeks pinked up and fought with his caramel brown complexion. "By the way my name is Michael," he said.

She laughed a little laugh and stretched out her hand. "I'm Sofia."

They shook hands then walked together down the garden path with elbows interlocked. It was the most natural and peaceful thing.

EPILOGUE

2021... Hertfordshire

C lunk, clunk, crunch was the sound of the wheels of the double buggy as it was pushed through the snow. It was the 23rd of December, two days before Christmas and excitement was at an all time high in Michaels home.

He decided that the excitement had reached its boiling point so the plan was changed to a special lunch at their local cafe and a cooling off period with the children in the snow.

Earlier Michael and Sofia had been playing a game of chess. As Sofia reached for one of her pawns Michael grabbed hold of her hand.

"What?" she asked.

"You're my best friend."

She smiled softly. "Oh, I thought I'd made a wrong move."

"No you're playing fine."

She moved her pawn with her other hand. "Well you're mine too."

"I need you to trust me Sofia."

She frowned. "I trust you. Is everything ok?"

"I love your children like they were my own."

"I know you do."

"Do you trust me?" he asks again.

She held his hand firmer. "Michael I trust you. Now what is it?"

"Ok. I love you." His words were arrows that shot straight to the core of her heart. "I always have and I always will." Their eyes met. He wiped the tear that had rolled down her left cheek. "You have to trust that I won't abuse whatever you tell me."

She held up his hand to her mouth and kissed it. "Do you trust me?"

There was a slight hesitation as he fought to stop himself from bubbling into overwhelming emotions. In a quiet tone he spoke. "I trust you with everything in me."

"I have loved you for longer than I can comprehend. You're so kind, you're amazing with the kids. You've shown me time and time again that you love me. I don't have to guess with you."

As she looked into his eyes and rambled on about how amazing he was and about how grateful she was to have him in her life she hadn't realised that he had a sparkling diamond ring waiting in the palm of his hand. "Marry me?" he asked.

"What?"

He got down on one knee. "Will you marry me?" His eyes searched hers in desperation.

Both her hands covered her mouth in an expression of shock. Then in one clean lunge she hurled herself onto him and hugged him. "Yes I will," was her reply. He gently took her hand and slid the ring on her finger. She was so happy. He pulled her in for an embrace. Before he could kiss her one of the children came rushing into the room and yelled "Uncle I'm hungry." They let go of their embrace.

"Ok it's time to go out. Let's all get our coats."

The kids yelled for joy as Sofia and Michael dressed them in their hat, coat and gloves then strapped them into the buggy. The children had no idea that the two people they loved dearly had finally come to the most natural progression in their relationship.

Outside the streets were quiet. The air was crisp and fresh. Sofia held onto Michael as tightly as she always did and he made sure that his fiancé could feel the grip of his elbow as he pushed the buggy.

They decided to turn into Garfield Street to avoid the barriers that had been left there for weeks by road workers.

Halfway down a man was hurriedly pushing black bin bags into the boot of a taxi. He rushed to the front door of the house and picked up the last bag. As he got to the boot a shirt fell out.

Sofia looked up and at the upstairs window, of the house where the bin bags were, stood a woman looking out. She was looking at the man as he bent down to pick up the shirt.

The woman looked tired and sad. Sofia stared hard at her and recognised the pain that the woman was feeling. The man was leaving her and it was as if he had taken every bit of strength that she had left and had shoved it in the bin bags he was pushing into the taxi. Sofia's eyes met with hers. The woman stared at Sofia until Michael asked Sofia to cross the road and continue out of view.

As they crossed the road the man who had stood up straight with his shirt in his hand flashed an angry look at Sofia. She could not believe her eyes as the man was Uche. The pain in her chest which travelled along the scar line pricked her like a needle with such force. She grabbed her chest. "Ouch," she said.

Michael stopped. "What is it? Are you ok?" He held her waist.

Sofia looked back at Uche whose face had morphed into that of another man unknown to her. "Nothing she said. It's just my chest playing up again."

Michael rubbed it for her. "After Christmas we are having this reviewed because something has to be done about it."

Michael turned around at the sound of the taxi boot being slammed shut. The man muttered a few words, "Freedom, at last. Now I can breathe." Then he jumped in the taxi and shut the door.

Sofia and Michael continued walking to their cafe.

#

"Ladies and gentleman welcome to today's show. I'm your host Mackina Shaw and what a line up we have for you today." *'Applause and cheers'* "Our first guest tonight is a friend to the show Dr Mike Marshall well known as America's Therapist. Millions view his show called Monday's with Dr Mike and there are countless testimonials of how he has helped to change people's lives with his words of encouragement. Dr Mike welcome to the show."

The camera zoomed onto Michael and applause and cheers erupted. "Thank you for having me on the show," he said.

"Dr Mike it's a pleasure and we love having you here. But today's show is a little different from the last time we saw you. You've brought someone special."

"Yes I certainly have."

"Tonight's special guest is someone that Dr Mike describes as his confidant, sidekick and love of his life co-host Sofia Blackwell Marshall. Come on out Sofia."

Michael and Mackina stood up as Sofia walked onto the set amidst the applause and cheers. Mackina held out her arms for a hug as Sofia landed in between them. She turned round hugged Michael and gave him a small kiss. "You look beautiful," he told her.

"Thanks love." She sat down beside him on the couch.

"You look amazing Sofia. Doesn't she look stunning everyone? My goodness that shoe is to die for."
She chuckled. "Thank you so much." Sofia wore a white and red triangle mosaic body con dress with red Jimmy Choo stilettos detailed with gold and diamond studded heels.

Michael grabbed her hand and they relaxed back with interlocked fingers.

"So it's great to have you both. Let's talk about your show. One of your videos has hit 27 million views as of Monday. You're Facebooks' most popular motivational speakers." There was a round of applause. "This is absolutely phenomenal. Congratulations."

The camera zoomed to Michael. "Thanks Mackina. We're just so overwhelmed by the response and humbled that so many people testify that our programme really helps them. Those testimonials are the icing on the cake for us." Michael looked at Sofia for acknowledgement and she nodded.

"And now we hear that there are talks of a daytime TV show."

"Yes that's another opportunity we're really excited about."

Mackina shifted in her seat. "And when can we expect the show to hit our screens?"

"Our first show airs in April on ABC and ITV in the UK."

"Well we can't wait to see your show and we are all incredibly proud of you both."

Sofia and Michael expressed their gratitude.

Mackina turned to Sofia and the camera's shifted into her direction. "Sofia I've been dying to have a chat with the woman who broke the heart of practically every single woman in America by marrying their heartthrob."

Sofia laughed. "I am so sorry but you can hardly blame me? I mean look at him, he's gorgeous." She looked at Michael who was blushing."

"We certainly don't blame you. I was just kidding you are a beautiful couple. So ya'll have been married for how long?"

"It's been three months." Sofia looked at Michael.

"And how is married life treating you?"

"It's good. Really good," Sofia said.

"For me, it's the best thing that could have ever happened. I have the best girl." Michael pulled Sofia's hand to his lips, kissed it and looked at Sofia with an appreciation.

"That is so sweet and your love is beautiful to see. It's quite evident that y'all have a good relationship. And that chemistry shows on your Monday Motivation show. Why did you decide to do it together?"

Sofia looked at Michael who acknowledged that she could answer the question.

"Well as you all know Michael is the Therapist so I'm literally just the gatecrasher."

Mackina reassured her. "You are so not a gatecrasher. You are amazing on that show. Right everybody?" There was a round of applause. Michael was clapping too.

"Thank you. I really appreciate it." She absorbed the applause before it began to die down. "Well just like everybody I've been through challenges and have had the opportunity to come out on the other side. It was a natural progression for me to want to encourage others and watch them bloom. I guess that's the horticulturist in me. But just as a side story um... just after we got engaged we took a walk and on our way we saw a woman and a man and it looked like the man was leaving her because he was angrily packing bags of his clothes into the back of a taxi. Anyway the woman was watching him from the window. I stared at her and she looked so tired and beat down and she reminded me of how my life used to be. She looked so lost and broken. I guess it was at that point that I realised that I have so much within me to help women that were in the same position as that woman at the window. I want to see beaten down women rise up. And if I could just add this one last thing, I would say that before you get into any relationship you have to know who you are, know your purpose and love yourself. " There was a round of applause.

Mackina was nodding. "I'm a firm believer of that too. Knowing your purpose and loving yourself. That's amazing. But could you tell our viewers why that is so important because I am sure that we have people who are watching and seeking advice on a new relationships or those that are seriously reviewing the relationships that they are currently in."

"Of course. Well Mackina if you don't know your purpose and you don't love yourself it's very difficult to be happy. And when you join yourself to someone when you are not happy or content with yourself you may end up frustrating them or vice versa and that for many people has become a living hell. I firmly believe that a lack of purpose in one's life can make you a magnet for people who may try to destroy your life."

Michael joined the audience in clapping.

"Absolutely wise words Sofia. I hear you have a book coming out."

"Yes it's called the *Woman at the Window* and of course I was inspired by the woman that I saw that day. It's a fictional account that takes you through the struggles of a woman abused by her husband and the risks she takes to leave the relationship and rebuild her life."

"Fantastic. That's my kind of story. When should we expect it?"

"In September."

A picture of Sofia's book cover appeared on the screen.

"Well I can't wait and I'm sure everyone in here is excited about it. We will be sure to get our copies. Anyway for a truth you have risen up Sofia. You touched a little bit on the challenges you have been through. In the next segment we hope to talk more about the ordeal that you went through at the hands of your ex-husband." Sofia nodded and a line of pain swept across her face. "But for now let's talk on the lighter subject of how ya'll met?" The audience clapped.

Sofia smiled at Michael who cleared his throat. "Well that's one of my favourite subjects," he said.

Mackina teased him, "Tell us the long version Dr Mike."

He laughed. "That's exactly what I plan to do. This is a true story. Anyway, our paths crossed at the Chelsea Flower show in London. I clocked her and I thought, you know..."

Mackina interjected. "You thought stunning, love at first sight?"

"Totally," he said.

Mackina looked at Sofia. "So did you check him out too?"

Sofia was shaking her head. "No. I didn't get to see his face or I didn't remember him."

Mackina frowned and looked at Michael. "You didn't talk to her?

Michael laughed again. "Nope. I hesitated and walked away. But when I plucked up the courage I went back with the intention of talking to her but I couldn't find her. Then our paths crossed again at the mall and then at a garden centre and each time people got in the way and I missed my chance to talk to her. But I had this strong feeling that she was a part of my destiny."

"What? So how did you finally get to meet her?"

"I was floored when this beautiful woman walked into one of my counselling sessions."

"She was your client. So Dr Mike how did you flip that one?"

Sofia laughed and Michael held her hand again. "I didn't flip it at all even though it was quite hard for me not to. I tried to keep it professional but I fell in love with her."

"Aww... that is so beautiful," Mackina sighed. "Sofia how was it for you."

"I fell in love too. But it was difficult because he was my Therapist. I didn't know if I was infatuated because he was kind to me and I wasn't sure if the signals I was getting from him were even like let alone love. So I started a relationship with someone else and stopped my counselling sessions with him because it was getting too intense. But when we met again in New York our feelings were so clear to me. I was in love with him pure and simple."

"Sofia and Mike that is truly beautiful but after the break we're going to talk about the ordeal that Sofia suffered at the hands of her ex-husband and how it was a miracle that she came out alive. Join us after the break."

They took a recess during the commercial break. The makeup artists rushed to the set and began to powder their faces.

"You guys are doing great," whispered Mackina before the producer came and distracted her.

Fifteen minutes later, "5, 4,3,2,1 you're on." The camera moved to Mackina "Welcome back to the show. Before the break we were talking to Monday Motivational couple Dr Michael and Sofia Marshall. Now Michael and Sofia I'm aware that there is a lot about this situation that you can't discuss because of legal reasons. And my Producer has just informed me that we really can't hash out this story as we normally do. But Uche Onyeme, who is your ex husband abducted you and held you hostage. He took you to a basement and there we heard that he assaulted you and ripped off one of your breasts." There were several sounds of shock from the audience. "Is there anything that you can add to that?"

"We really can't discuss anything further because of investigations that are ongoing," said Michael as he squeezed Sofia's hand.

"Well Sofia we're just glad that you came out and lived to tell the tale. And we really wish the both of you the best of luck." They both thanked her. "Well on a lighter note you have brought along two very special people that I hear are very cute."

Two little girls appeared on the screen. The little girls dressed in cute frocks and hair buns were playing with some very bright coloured soft toys.

"Sofia and Mike your babies are as sweet as little puddings. They are so cute. Are they twins?"

Sofia decided to speak. "No, Sofia Grace is a little small for her age. She is my niece but I adopted her at the request of her parents. Tulip is my biological daughter."

"Well they are beautiful. Tulip looks like you Dr Mike."

Michael looked a bit uncomfortable as did Sofia. "Um I'm not Tulip's father."
Mackina looked shocked. "Oh, well I assumed. Ok so..."

"I don't know who her father is and..." Sofia looked lost and embarrassed.

Michael stepped in to help her. He was trying to fight tears and anger. "Sofia found out she was pregnant right after her ordeal with her ex husband. So all one has to do is connect the dots."

There was silence in the studio. After a short while Mackina took courage to break it. "We know that your ex-husband was deported to Nigeria without any trial. But we understand now that the deportation has been overturned. That means that the deportation shouldn't have happened.?

"That's right," said Sofia.

"So where is he now? Is he in jail in Nigeria?"

Michael jumped in. "We have no idea. So many mistakes were made in handling this case. He should never have been deported before a trial."

Mackina was nodding. "This is absolutely shocking. So as it stands we have a criminal walking free and we have no idea who will bring him to justice. I know this is a sensitive question but is there a possibility that your ex-husband could return to the United Kingdom because as it stands it looks to us that he raped you... allegedly."

Michael looked at Sofia then at Mackina. "At this stage umm..." Michael looked down then resolved to answer the question. "Yes there is a possibility."

Mackina asked him. "Is it a possibility about the alleged rape or him returning to the United Kingdom?"

"I would say yes to both."

Sounds of shock resounded throughout the room. Sofia looked broken. Michael tried to reassure her with his hand in hers.

Mackina took in a deep breath and looked around the audience. "It's not every day that I am lost for words. We can only imagine what you have been through. I wished we didn't but we've run out of time. But I hope we can have you back to talk more about what's going. All I can say is Mike and Sofia you are friends of the show. We love and support you and sincerely hope that one day justice will come.

Mackina stood up and opened her long arms wide and cradled them in her embrace.

A Note from the Author!

Hey there this is Saru and I am so thrilled that you have decided to read this book. This is a very special story to me. If anything resonated to you in this book or you would like to give an honest review please contact me through the following arenas as I would love to hear from you.

*Send me a tweet **@saruauthor on Twitter** or **search Sarudzai Mubvakure Twitter.**

*Send me a message on my **Facebook page** under this name – **Saru Mubvakure**

*Follow me on **Instagram** at **inspired_by_saru**

If you feel so inclined I would really appreciate an honest review on the platform where you purchased this book. Take care and keep believing in yourself!

Other titles by Sarudzai Mubvakure

A Disappointing Truth

The life of two black girls, in 1960s Colonial Zimbabwe, changes when they catch the eye of two English migrants who are in the country for the 'good life'. When the girls become embroiled in betrayal, love and rape their only hope for justice lies in what was seen by a 10 year old boy who has been terrorised into silence. Years later, Sarah Witt, a British business woman struggling with internal complexities goes on a soul searching trip to Zimbabwe for answers about the mysterious past of her deceased parents. As an unexpected shock connection between Sarah and the two girls slowly unravels she has no idea that her efforts are being thwarted by an organized crime syndicate 'The English Boys Club'. In this story with the cinematic backdrop of Zimbabwe's history, can the truth lead to healing?

Amelia's Inheritance

On the day she is born, Alana Pennyfarthing is left at the doorstep of an orphanage with a written note:

"This child is no longer wanted."

Years later her daughter Amelia Gruber, an underachieving recluse, finds herself struggling to navigate the dilemma's of being a 'poor White' in 20th Century Rhodesia and befriending a middle class black Lawyer Peter Mudondo. In the confusion of coming of age, finding her feet and trying to empathise with Peters mission to have land unlawfully taken from black people returned, Amelia discovers a family secret that is the missing piece to the puzzle of her family's existence. What she discovers may be too hard to bear.

Sarudzai's first non –fiction book

Let Me Be Your Carrot

In today's world of high speed technology, high standards and unrealistic expectations we can often find ourselves overwhelmed, tired and needing that 'motivational quote' to encourage us to go round the treadmill one more mile. The time comes when we must guard our mental health and set aside time for mindfulness. Let Me Be Your Carrot seeks to provide inspiration that will lift you and sustain you through the challenges of life and ultimately bring you out as the winner.

Printed in Poland
by Amazon Fulfillment
Poland Sp. z o.o., Wrocław